D0379559

Latifah Salom

The Cake House

Latifah Salom was born in Hollywood, California, to parents of Peruvian and Mexican descent. She attended the Los Angeles County High School for the Arts, where she learned the building blocks of artistry and imagery that eventually led her to her love of writing. She holds degrees from Emerson College, Hunter College, and the University of Southern California Master of Professional Writing program. She currently lives in Los Angeles. *The Cake House* is her first novel.

www.latifahsalom.com

NO LONGER PROPERTY
OF ANYTHINK
RANGEVIEW LIBRARY
DISTRICT

The Cake House

· A NOVEL ·

Latifah Salom

VINTAGE BOOKS
A Division of Random House LLC
New York

A VINTAGE ORIGINAL, MARCH 2015

Copyright © 2015 by Latifah Salom

All rights reserved. Published in the United States by
Vintage Books, a division of Random House LLC, New York,
and in Canada by Random House of Canada Limited, Toronto,
Penguin Random House companies.

Vintage and colophon are registered trademarks of
Random House LLC.

This is a work of fiction. Names, characters, places, and incidents
either are the product of the author's imagination or are used
fictitiously, and any resemblance to actual persons, living or dead,
events, or locales is entirely coincidental.

The Library of Congress Cataloging-in-Publication Data
Salom, Latifah.
The cake house : a novel / Latifah Salom.
pages cm. — (A Vintage Contemporaries original)
I. Title.
PS3619.A4389C35 2015   813'.6—dc23   2014028492

Vintage Trade Paperback ISBN: 978-0-345-80651-2
eBook ISBN: 978-0-345-80652-9

Book design by Jaclyn Whalen

www.vintagebooks.com

Printed in the United States of America
10 9 8 7 6 5 4 3 2 1

For Rohanna
For Nirmala
And for Julio, with love

The
Cake
House

CHAPTER ONE

I met Claude and Alex the day my father died.

The stranger whose name was Claude held my mother by her arms while she screamed. He stood with blood splattered across his face and over his clothing, and she slid through his hands like a child who didn't want to go to bed, didn't want to take her medicine.

My father lay twisted, a gun at his feet. One side of his head spilled red onto the sodden carpet, his blood spreading inch by inch in a widening circle. I fell to my knees and crawled toward him.

Claude shouted, "Get her out of here," and a pair of hands grabbed my waist and hauled me from the room, dragging me to the other end of the house, where sliding glass doors led to a garden with the silhouette of a fountain. I screamed, screamed until I started choking. Someone shook me, hard: the tall teenager with pale hair, paler than I had ever seen. In my neighborhood he would have been called *güerito* for that hair.

I'd only just met him. He was Claude's son and had been instructed to wait with me by the car when my mother went inside with Claude to talk. He had been silent and moody. Unnerved, I stared at the house until my father's car tore up the hill, coming to a jerky stop inches from the old Honda that my mother drove.

I tried to grab my father's arm, but he pushed me aside, banging on the front door until it opened enough for him to shove his way in. When I tried to follow, the boy caught me and wouldn't let go, not until the gunshot rang out.

Now he held me again, my back against his chest, his breath in my ear, chanting over and over, "I swear I didn't know he would do that. I swear it. I didn't know."

"Alex," Claude yelled. "Get over here."

The boy turned but still held me close. His voice vibrated against my back. "I don't think I should leave her."

Alex. His name was Alex, and that was something concrete to hold on to. I concentrated on the beating of his heart. In the distance, sirens wailed.

Claude scrambled into my view, blood sprayed across half his face like a bad sunburn. "The police are going to be here any second. I need your help," he said to Alex. "How is she?"

I started to scream again. Claude covered his ears until Alex clamped his hand over my mouth and sat me down on the couch. The sirens hurtled closer.

"Dahlia," called Claude.

My mother had wrapped a blanket over her shoulders to hide the blood staining her left sleeve and down the front of her ruffled sundress. Her hair, usually sprayed into buoyant waves, hung limp. She tried to light a cigarette, but her hand shook. Claude lit one for her.

"Rosaura," she said, her voice raspy. She wiped at the

blood on her cheek, leaving a smudge of orange rust. "Some men are coming here to talk to us, about what happened."

"What happened?" My throat hurt from screaming.

"Yes. They shouldn't need to speak with you. But if they do—"

"What happened?" I repeated.

She blinked. The sirens blared, and Claude said there was no time. My mother squeezed my face between her two hands, the cigarette hot near my cheek. "Listen to me."

"He did it," I said. "He did it."

My mother shook her head. "There's no time for this. Do you hear me? If the police talk to you, you have to tell them you don't know anything."

I scrunched my eyes closed, tried to push her away. The sirens died. There was a knock on the door and loud voices.

"Promise me." She grabbed my shoulders, shook me hard. "Say it. You don't know what happened. You didn't see. Rosaura, you do as I say, tell them you don't know anything. Tell them, or else—or I don't know what will happen. Do you understand?"

She was crying now, chest heaving. The cigarette smoke stung my eyes, and I couldn't breathe. I didn't understand, but I couldn't bear to see her cry. I could never bear to see her cry. When I was younger and she cried, I always begged her to stop.

"I don't know what happened," I said, and she relaxed her grip, falling onto the couch next to me, rocking back and forth. My promise not to say anything hadn't helped.

There was noise and commotion at the front of the house. Two officers in tan uniforms entered with Claude and Alex close behind. "She's been through a lot," said Claude. "We'd appreciate it if you kept her out of this."

I didn't move from my spot on the edge of the couch. Outside, the day grew dark, and then it was night. I stared through the sliding doors. The wind tossed the trees around, bending their tops this way and that. But if I refocused my eyes, the garden disappeared and I saw the rest of the room's reflection in the glass, could see my mother sitting in one of the dining room chairs, pale-faced and wrapped in her blanket as she spoke with one of the officers and described how my father had the gun hidden in his sweatshirt front pocket, how he'd pointed the gun at her and at Claude before pointing it at himself.

A man knelt in front of me, changing the focus once again.

"My name's Deputy Mike Nuñez," said the officer. "Are you all right?"

Deputy Mike Nuñez had dark eyes and skin a shade of brown that reminded me of my father's favorite sweatshirt, the ragged one that he always liked to wear.

"I wasn't in the house. I didn't see anything," I whispered.

He tilted his head. "That's all right. Do you live here?"

It was the last day of school. I had been hanging out with José and Sofie on the steps to Sofie's apartment building, talking about what I wanted when I turned fourteen and what our plans were for the summer, when my mother's car screeched to a halt in front of us. She demanded I get in, that there wasn't any time to explain. Our clothes were in garbage bags, and boxes spilled over the backseat. It wasn't until we sped down the freeway that I understood: We were running away. But I knew my father would follow us. And he had, all the way to this house and into the front room, where his body lay.

"I wasn't in the house. I didn't see anything," I repeated.

"Can you tell me who does live here?"

Claude and my mother continued speaking to the officer who was jotting notes on the pad in his hand. The blanket around her shoulders slipped each time a camera flash lit up the front room.

I licked my lips. "His name is Claude," I said. "He lives here, with his son."

Alex was watching standing back from the activity, near the stairs leading up to the second floor.

"Are they friends of yours?" asked the officer.

"I've never met them before," I said, "but I remember—"

"Please leave her alone," said my mother, stepping between us. "She doesn't know anything."

Deputy Mike stood up. "I was just making sure she was okay."

As they talked, their faces came in and out of focus. Behind them, two men placed my father's sheet-covered body on a gurney. My mother stopped talking and watched the body being wheeled out, forcing Deputy Mike to look up from his pad. I watched as well through the reflection on the glass doors, like it was a scene from a television show. Once the front door was shut again, the spell broke and movement returned to the room. In the reflection, I saw my father step into focus, framed by the doorway, as if his body hadn't just left the house.

His eyes met mine across the chaos.

That was the first time I saw the ghost.

AFTER THE POLICE LEFT, MY mother said I should go upstairs, away from the scene in the front room, but I wouldn't move. I wouldn't move until she brought me a glass of water, gave me a pill, and had me lie down on the couch. I stared at the cluttered walls full of paintings and bookshelves and shadows until my eyes closed.

When I woke, Alex was shaking my shoulder. "Come with me," he said. "I'll show you to your room."

My room was miles away in our apartment. "Mom?" I called.

"She's sleeping," he said, and held out a hand.

Groggy, I let him lead me up the stairs to the second floor. He pushed in a door on the left, revealing a room that was empty except for a twin bed against the back wall. Compared to my room at home, which fit only a twin mattress and a set of dresser drawers, it was cavernous. But my room had pictures of Madonna and River Phoenix that I'd cut out of magazines, and my stickers of Garbage Pail Kids stuck to the baseboards. It was home. This new room wasn't home.

"There are sheets and stuff here," said Alex, pointing to a folded floral blanket and pillow that were neatly stacked on the bed.

Yellow curtains billowed in the breeze. It was still night outside. My father's reflection flashed in the windowpane, the open wound on the side of his face fleshy and red.

"I can't stay here," I said, moving for the door, but Alex blocked me. "I want my mom. Where's my mom?"

"I told you, she's sleeping. She's been up all night. We all have."

I twisted out of Alex's hold and ran to the only other door—a closet, wide and deep. I dragged the sliding door closed behind me and crouched in the corner, feeling safe in the dark.

Alex gave a muffled curse. "Come on," he said. "What are you doing in there? Come out. It's okay."

I didn't answer. Silence followed, and I wondered if Alex had gone but I didn't want to risk checking.

"Here," Alex finally said, nudging the door open and stuffing the bedding through. "At least take the pillow and blanket."

After he left, I struggled out of my shoes, out of my jeans, and lay on the pillow in just my shirt. Hours passed. The light that bled through the cracks around the closet doors changed from gray to a bright white that cut through the darkness and sliced across my limbs.

Two voices entered. "She's still in the closet," one said.

"Well, leave her there until Dahlia can talk to her."

I took a quick peek. Alex and Claude had brought the garbage bags full of stuff from my other life and left them in a pile in the center of the room.

Claude walked toward my hiding spot. "How are you doing?" he asked, and I shrank back into the corner. "Are you hungry?" He turned to Alex without waiting for an answer. "Maybe you should bring up some food."

Alex brought a tray of food and left it outside the closet, but I wasn't hungry. At one point, when it was dark again, I stumbled out to find a bathroom but returned as soon as I could to the safety of the closet, dragging one of the garbage bags in with me.

The heat made me drowsy, and I dreamt of our apartment. I dreamt of José and Sofie, of hanging out with them at the mall after school, where sometimes José would buy us each a scoop of ice cream. I closed my eyes and dreamt of my father coming home from work, banging the door open and kicking it closed because his hands and arms were full with his briefcase and folders and papers. *There's my girl,* he said, and placed a kiss on my forehead. I told him I was hungry, and we went out for a burger, just the two of us, before my mother came home from the temp job she had at a lawyer's office downtown.

I dreamt of my mother finding me and saying, *Okay, it's time. Let's go. Let's go home,* and we would leave and maybe things could go back to the way they used to be. Or, if we left, would the ghost come with us? Would that become our new normal, my mother, the ghost, and me, in our old apartment?

"Rosaura," called my mother, and I opened my eyes. She stood in the open door of the closet wearing an unfamiliar blue dress. From the smell of cigarette smoke on her breath, I knew she was real and not a dream.

"Is it time?" I asked. "Are we leaving?"

"Don't you think this has gone on long enough?" she asked. "You're not even dressed. When was the last time you took a shower?"

Claude appeared behind her and placed an arm around her shoulders. A diamond on her finger caught the light. It glittered as she brought her hand up to her lips, searching for a cigarette that wasn't there.

She caught me staring and hid her hand in the folds of her dress. "You have to understand," she said, her eyes shifting to Claude, then to anywhere but me. "I have to think of our future," she said in a monotone, almost as if reciting lines. "And after"—she compressed her lips—"after what happened, with your father . . ."

I started laughing. It was funny because I had thought we might be leaving, but now we could never leave. My laughter disturbed her. She didn't know what to do.

"Rosaura, please," she said.

Behind her, the ghost appeared, hovering between

Claude and my mother like a minister at church, his arms spread wide. I shut the door in their faces. My mother tried to speak to me through the wood, but Claude insisted that she leave.

The silent weight of the house pressed in from all sides. I ripped off my shirt and stripped down to my skin, burrowing like a rat into my nest of clothing, blankets, and the pillow. I remained in this nest, breathing in the stink of my own sweat, sleeping and waking and sleeping again until I lost all track of time, waking to pitch darkness with my heart racing.

My father's ghost sat at the other end of the closet, facing me. I could see his glinting eyes, and his hair that flopped over his forehead the same way it did in life. But the bullet wound hadn't existed in life. The black stain of blood running down his cheek, down into his collar, was new.

I didn't wait. I pushed my way out of the closet, and when I tripped and fell to my knees, I crawled until I could stumble out of the room, down the stairs, down to the first floor, and pushed the sliding glass doors open.

Outside, a boy's bike had been left to lean against the side of the house. Black and scuffed with mud, the bike was too big for me—my toes barely touched the ground; the seat dug into my naked crotch. But still I managed to ride away, gritting my teeth with each bump over the sidewalk until I learned to stand up on the pedals.

The night was vast and open. I reached the sidewalk. Then the street. With gathering speed, I rode down the hill. I couldn't fly, but I could feel the wind and I could breathe. The chill of night lingered, but it swept the horror of the ghost away, swept out the heat and stifled fright of the house. Giddy for the first time in days, I sped around a corner, hair tangling in my eyes.

NAKED AND CHILLED, I RODE the bike through the empty streets of Canyon Country. These streets were different from the ones in my old crowded neighborhood full of families and music thumping at all times, kids frolicking in apartment pools, and me and José sitting on the steps of our building, his arm around my shoulder, his other hand resting on my leg. I used to giggle at him; I used to laugh.

In Canyon Country, the streets were empty and the sidewalks had trees planted in each neat square patch of dirt. The houses I passed were painted in tasteful colors that I imagined had names like Baby Turtle Bottoms or Sunshine Sally's Toes. Some had boats or large trucks parked in their driveways.

I rode, not caring how naked I was, how bizarre it must seem, or in what direction I went. Commuters watched with creased foreheads and open mouths, but it just made me laugh more: A car braked to a sharp halt; a pedestrian pointed as I rode past. Up hills, down hills. I discovered a park full of early-morning joggers and people walking their dogs; a tai chi class, another kid on his bike delivering papers. They stopped and stared.

A police car coasted on my left side, then drove around to block my panting climb up a hill. One cop, backlit by the dawning sun. Tall, dressed in a tan shirt that blended with his skin and his eyes: all over light and dark brown, like a chocolate chip cookie. I remembered him: Deputy Mike Nuñez. His badge flashed.

I imagined what I must look like, my skin red from the

chill, my hair a wild, mangled mess. A naked girl on a boy's bike, panting, lost.

"Has someone hurt you?" he asked.

"No," I answered, even though sometimes everything hurt.

He stepped closer, and I wondered if I should be afraid. The older kids in my apartment complex had all hated cops. They called them *puerco* and said I could never trust them.

Deputy Mike went to his trunk and got out a puffy, collared jacket to put around my shoulders. It covered me down to the middle of my thighs. I pulled it closed and zipped it up.

"All right, get in." He opened the car door.

"My bike," I said, swallowing around my dry throat. I gripped the handlebars.

"It can come with us."

"I'm not sure I remember where I live," I said. It was the truth; in my mad dash from the house, I hadn't paid any attention to the street names; I didn't remember being told the telephone number; I wasn't even sure I knew Claude's last name, although I should. It must have been told to me at one point. He was my stepfather now, I realized, and the memory made me want to sink down to the ground and pull Deputy Mike's jacket over my head.

"I know where you live. But first, I have to take you in," he said, putting the bike in the backseat like a prisoner. He waited until I climbed into the passenger side, and then he shut the door behind me.

This excited me. Being arrested was better than returning to live with Claude.

Deputy Mike adjusted his rearview mirror and said, "Buckle up." He didn't smile, but he paused to stare at me with his brown gaze. Then he put the car in gear and we drove away.

DEPUTY MIKE HAD A BLACK-AND-WHITE photograph of himself taped to the corner of the glove compartment. In the photo he was much younger, with a small boy sitting on his lap. It was the kind of photograph one got from a booth. The little boy wasn't smiling.

He picked up his radio and said something in his strange cop language full of numbers and codes, and told the person on the other end to contact Claude Fisk and ask for Dahlia Douglas. He said Claude's name like he knew him.

Without making a sound, I rolled the name "Fisk" around in my mouth. Fisk. Fisk. Fisk.

"It's Dahlia Fisk now," I said, speaking more to the window than to Deputy Mike, but he heard me, glancing from the road, then back again. He finished with the radio and hung the receiver on its peg.

"Your mother married him?"

I chose not to answer, listening instead to the chatter of the police radio, the disembodied voice of a woman directing officers here and there. Twice Deputy Mike picked up the radio to answer. They were looking for a missing persons report. There wouldn't be one, and I told Deputy Mike that. There was no reason for anyone to have missed me.

The sheriff's station was a squat building, low to the ground and built with flat bricks the same color as Deputy Mike's shirt. Even the leaves on the trees outside were beige, dried out, crumpling dusty to the ground.

The reception area had a bulletin board covered in "Wanted" posters of men and women with hollowed eyes, sneers twisting their mouths. There was one of a woman with wild hair, a scar splitting one half of her face. Her name was Audra Rose. Did she steal? Did she commit murder? I imagined she was one half of me. I could be part Audra Rose, split myself down the middle.

Claude's picture should be up there. I should take a pen and draw him in, his flat blue eyes fitting next to all the dead expressions of the other criminals, as guilty as any murderer.

Deputy Mike led me through a set of doors into a bigger room with desks and chairs. There were fans blowing air along with the air conditioner. After the cloistered heat of the closet, the frigid room made it feel like the arctic. He pointed to a chair next to a desk. "Wait here," he said, and left me alone.

The seat was uncomfortable, so I wandered around the room, curious as to what kind of criminals Canyon Country might boast; were they like José's brothers with their tattoos and colored bandannas wrapped around their upper arms and foreheads? Uniformed men and women came and went. Someone got me a cup of hot coffee. It was bitter but I sipped it for warmth. The clock in the center of the wall clicked each second that passed, like a vicious, even-toned cricket. A calendar pinned to a board had been turned to July. I stared at it for a long time, confused, wondering what day it was, how many days I had been living in the closet.

Deputy Mike came back. He sat in a chair opposite mine and indicated I should do the same. "Do you want anything from the machines?"

"Am I under arrest?" The seat was cold against my naked thighs.

He half smiled, and I wondered if he ever smiled fully. "Not today," he said. "But there will be some consequences.

An investigation. What you did isn't normal, do you understand?"

I nodded. I regretted it now, even though the freedom,
the wind on my bare skin, had felt so delicious, so wonderful. To exist for even a short time outside the walls of that
house that felt like my prison.

"Your father died," he said. "It's okay to be a little
messed up."

I knew he said that to explain my aberrant behavior,
but it made me feel ashamed. I hadn't thought of my father
while I was on the bike. I thought only of the ghost and of
being free.

He shuffled papers on his desk until his phone rang. "All
right," he said into the phone before hanging up. "Your parents are here. They're waiting outside."

I was tied to the chair, not wanting to stay and not
wanting to go. Perhaps Deputy Mike sensed my hesitation,
because he leaned forward and started to raise his hand to
touch my face before dropping it. It felt intimate, sitting
across from him wearing nothing but his jacket, my bare
feet against the cold floor.

"Tell me," he said.

I wanted to tell him about my mother running away on
a hot summer afternoon. That we had driven fast but my
father was still able to follow and had arrived at Claude's
house just minutes after us. And now we lived with Claude
and his son, Alex. I tried to tell him that I could barely stand
to be in the same house as Claude and that was why I hid in
the closet. I wanted to tell him about my father's ghost and
the wound that took over one side of his face.

"Are you scared?" he asked.

It wasn't right to say his eyes were brown. They had

green flecks in them, and the outside of the irises had a ring of yellow. "He's not my father," I said. It was the simplest explanation I could think of.

He nodded. "Does he hurt you?"

I wanted to say yes, Claude had hurt me more than any person ever had, but it was like I had lost my voice, like my throat didn't work, and I couldn't.

"It'll be all right," he said. "Believe me."

I wanted to. I wanted to take his words and hold them like a prayer against my heart.

He led me from the room into the reception area. My mother was there with Claude next to her, tall and blustery with his too-wide smile like a salesman in a commercial: *Buy my car, just nine ninety-nine down.* But he wasn't smiling now. My mother rushed forward, carrying a shopping bag.

"What happened to her?" Claude's voice boomed as he rested a big hand on my head, examining me in a perfect likeness of a concerned parent.

"That's our question," said Deputy Mike, all his gentleness gone.

Claude puffed up like a sail in the wind, but Deputy Mike ignored him and placed paperwork on the counter with a pen on top. "Your daughter was found at six fifteen this morning, unclothed, riding her bicycle down Lone Mountain Drive."

Tense silence followed. My mother closed her eyes.

"She's not mine," said Claude. At Deputy Mike's continued stare, Claude tilted his head. "But you knew that already. We hadn't realized she was gone."

Deputy Mike didn't comment. He tapped the paperwork he'd laid out. "The minor's legal guardian will have to sign.

Then she's free to go. I should warn you, I've notified Child Services."

My mother wiped her face and walked over, taking the pen. With stained cheeks, she scribbled her name. "Thank you," she said, but wouldn't look at Deputy Mike, wouldn't look at me either.

"Put some clothes on," said Claude, back in command mode, handing me the shopping bag my mother carried. "And then wait in the car."

I crushed the bag in my hands, moving to the marked bathroom off to the side. My mother had brought my "I'm a Pepper" T-shirt and an old pair of shorts. They'd forgotten to bring shoes.

Outside, someone had taken the bike from Deputy Mike's car and left it leaning against the building. Barefoot, I rode circles around Claude's car.

WE DROVE HOME IN CLAUDE's big steel-gray Mercedes, the hushed radio filling in the gaps between my mother's tear-filled sighs. Claude had jammed the bike into the backseat with me. A wheel spun in my face and a pedal pressed into my lap.

That first night, Claude's house had seemed mysterious and dark and strange, but in the full force of daylight I could see that it was just a big, lumbering house on steroids, painted a color fashionable people would call "salmon" or "coral" but I called pink. It looked older than its neighbors, a little superior, like a queen bee, sitting in perfect confectionery stillness. The other houses seemed to inch away, like it was a giant, unwanted cake.

Claude's house was the biggest house on the block. It

might have been nice a few short years ago, but it had been built without thought or planning and with cheap materials. This was to be my prison, this monstrous pink dessert.

Alex waited on the steps with his head resting on one palm, looking a little bored. He stood when the rest of us exited the car. I had forgotten how tall he was.

Claude took the bike from the backseat and handed it to me. It felt heavy and unwieldy in my hands. I still wore Deputy Mike's jacket over my "I'm a Pepper" T-shirt.

"You must be tired," I heard Claude say to my mother.

She didn't answer but grabbed my arm, her fingers digging into my flesh. "You don't leave that closet for weeks and then you run away?"

Claude made her let go, placing his two hands on both her upper arms. She swerved away from his touch.

"Maybe I am tired," she said, pinching the bridge of her nose as I tried to interpret the blush on her face. I didn't think it was entirely anger at me.

Alex wrested the bike from my clinging grasp, the coldness in his pale eyes making me flinch. He kicked the kickstand back on the bike. I couldn't tell whom he was mad at, whether he was mad at all.

Claude turned as he walked my mother toward the front door, a look passing between father and son that I didn't understand except to see that Alex's mouth tightened.

"Come on," said Alex to me, wheeling the bike behind my mother and Claude. His voice was nothing like how he looked. Not cold or hard but warm, melted honey dripping off a spoon.

I took a couple of steps but then stopped and stared at the front door, the courage I had gained during my escape draining away. I did not want to walk into that front room where my father had died. The ghost would be in there. Alex waited, his previous annoyance gone and replaced with a quiet attention. He walked the bike back to my side, and I saw in his face that he understood my fear. With a tilt of his head, he indicated the side gate leading to the garden. "This way," he said.

I decided the garden should be safe and free of ghosts and followed Alex. The sun beat down on the top of my head. My bare feet slapped against the brick-lined path, past the peonies and the daylilies.

The back of the house was as pink as the front. Alex parked his bike against the side where I had found it. He picked up a rag and began cleaning the wheels and the frame.

"Thanks for the food," I said, but then wondered if I'd dreamt that he had brought a tray of food. Maybe it hadn't been real.

He squinted and shrugged, returning his attention to the bike. I played with the zipper on Deputy Mike's jacket, sweating because the day was warm, but I didn't want to take it off yet. The jacket reminded me of my bike ride, of that freedom, and of Deputy Mike himself, who had been so kind. Instead, I bunched up the sleeves as high as I could, the excess fabric making it difficult to put my arms down.

I wandered off to the fountain and placed my hands on the brick barrier, turning them so that my fingers pointed back and I could feel the strain on my wrists. I leaned over, my weight on my arms like a seesaw, getting as close as I could to the water without touching.

Alex came up beside me and took a handful of water and flicked it at my face. I screeched with a sharp inhale of breath, and there was a furious fight as I splashed him back, squinting my eyes shut and laughing, until he caught my arms and made me stop.

Under the sun, I was breathless—from the cool water, from his nearness. He let go and we subsided back into awkward silence. Besides that first night when he had held me against his chest, this was the longest we had been in each other's presence.

I sat down on the damp, mossy stone, and Alex brought his bike closer to the fountain, picked up the discarded rag, and started cleaning again. I thought it was weird that he was cleaning his bike. It had clearly never been cleaned before. Nervous in the awkward silence, I began to hum.

Alex looked up. "Do you like music?" he asked, wiping at the handlebars. "Can you sing?"

"Not really," I said, but regretted it when he fell silent. It was the first time he'd ever asked me a direct question. I tried again. "There's a song I know, that my mother used to sing for me."

He flashed a smile full of white teeth. "Let's hear it."

The fountain appeared bottomless, full of tangled water plants. "Are there fishes in there?" I searched for the gleam of fish scales. I dipped my fingers in the water, causing ripples. It felt silky.

"Yes, but after all our noise and splashing they'll never show themselves. They like to hide," he said, sitting next to me.

Smart fishes. I looked at him. "Do you like my mother?"

"Not particularly."

"And I don't like your father," I said, wanting to hear his voice again. "What do you think about them getting married?"

He shook his head. With his long fingers, he picked up a stick from the ground and stripped it clean of bark. He was older than me, maybe sixteen, I wasn't sure. Thin, narrow face, narrow shoulders, he was unlike his father. I could pick apart his features: those that came from Claude, and those that came from elsewhere, like his eyes with their cool distance. But when he smiled he resembled Claude: a kind of charm with easy confidence. When he smiled, I thought I would do anything he asked.

Then I sang for him. I sang my mother's favorite lullaby. A French song, about a little bird caught stealing. She said her mother used to sing it to her. She said it used to make her laugh.

"Qu'est-ce qu'elle a donc fait,
La petite hirondelle?"

My song changed the way he looked at me, more like the way José sometimes had, but with Alex it made me feel dizzy, like I could fall backward, arms spread wide, to splash into the fountain and willfully drown. "Sing it again," he asked.

I did, holding on to the edge of the fountain.

He made me nervous, so I stared at the puffy clouds in the dark-blue sky until I finished. He could be patient and kind, but then his gaze would shutter and I couldn't tell what he was thinking.

"Were you worried about me this morning?" I wanted to tease him, wanted to flirt. To do something with my useless hands, I mounted his bike again, riding around the fountain.

He studied me as I wobbled, and I wished I hadn't asked anything or spoken, feeling foolish and young and ugly. He shrugged, dismissive. "You want me to say yes. I think you like to cause trouble."

"Don't you?" I countered, balancing on my tiptoes until I nearly fell, holding on to his bike as if it was the same thing as holding on to him. "Where's your mom?"

As soon as I asked the question, Alex changed. It wasn't a big change. He didn't shout or get angry and say it wasn't any of my business. He did nothing except continue to watch my haphazard progress on his bike.

"I don't have one," he said. "And no, I don't like to cause trouble." He tossed the stick he'd stripped bare out over the garden. It twirled in the wind and disappeared into the tall grass. "It doesn't get you anywhere."

He walked away, aloof once again. I started after him, but my foot caught on one of the pedals, scraping my skin. The bike crashed to the ground, falling at my feet with the handlebars twisted. By the time I disentangled myself, Alex was already pushing the sliding glass doors open, pausing only long enough to toss the dirty rag onto a pile of other dirty rags by the doors.

The scratches on my shin stung. When I looked down to study them, a second pair of feet appeared next to mine.

The ghost stood in the bright sunshine. I had been wrong to think that he couldn't appear in daylight, wouldn't appear in the garden. He was pale, solid, yet removed. He wasn't like those ghosts shown in movies or TV shows, see-through and made of mist. I had nowhere to hide, nowhere to run. This close, I could see the left side of his face, its pale, freckled skin marred by the black circle of charred flesh. He was wearing the same clothes he died in, his favorite sweatshirt with the front pocket and paint stains, his jeans, and his loafers with the holes in them. It was as if he'd climbed out of the water of the fountain to surprise me.

"There's my girl," he said.

He stared down at the twisted bicycle, which lay before us like a corpse.

"I remember when you were born. You were such a strange baby. You didn't cry when you first came out of your mother. The nurses were freaked out by your silence. So quiet, not a peep, but you opened your eyes immediately and looked at me and at the faces of the doctors and nurses with your bright eyes that always made everyone nervous. You had eyes like two black holes, easy to get sucked into. They said there was no way you could see yet, but they were wrong. You could see everything. So quiet and only a few hours old, you knew everything in the world. It scared me."

I took a step back, nearly overcome by an instinct to run. But he was my father. And his words grabbed hold and kept me planted to the ground. When he lived, he had talked all the time, to my mother about his work, or they had argued about money, but he had never spoken like the ghost did, with such calm, quiet determination. He turned his head, as if to examine the dead bike from a different angle.

"I felt guilty," he continued, as if he weren't speaking to me. As if I were the one who didn't exist. "Frightened of my own kid. I mean, you fucking scared the shit out of me. Your mom was sick when you were born, so it was just me taking care of you, and I sometimes left you in your crib, let you lie there. I'd look down at your fists balled up and struggling, all of you wiggling and angry, and your eyes wide-open and black. And so goddamned *silent*. I didn't want to hold you."

My face felt warm, and it hurt to breathe. Of all the things I had expected the ghost to say, it wasn't that he feared me. My father loved me. I tried to remember what he had been like alive, but the ghost was all I could see.

"I thought maybe that was why you never cried, because you were mad at me. You didn't make a sound, not until your mom got better and was able to hold you. Maybe you were waiting for her. And then, God, you were loud. After all that silence, your crying was so goddamned loud. I thought you would shatter windows."

Even as a ghost he had blue eyes. Now they were tinged with blood. The ghost stretched out its hand, but I stepped back, swallowing a cry of fright.

"We were happy once," he said, oblivious to my fear. "Before Claude took everything from me. We were happy, your mom and me. She loved me. Didn't she?"

So uncertain, my heart broke.

"Dad," I said, forcing sound through my throat.

"Don't trust Claude. He lies," he said, in that too-familiar voice.

Then he was gone.

CHAPTER TWO

The first time I heard Claude's name was in the living room of our apartment. My mother had answered the phone when it rang, listened for a moment, then turned to my father. "It's a Claude Fisk for you."

My father had taken the phone and gone into their bedroom for privacy. He didn't come out for hours, but when he did, he went to my mother and took her into his arms, excited, laughing. From then on, my father began and ended his day with Claude's name. In the morning, he would say to my mother, "I'm going to meet Claude later." And then again, in the evening, "Claude said it was a good idea to start now. I think he's right."

Through most of this my mother's expression was one of pale worry and concern that occasionally gave way to a burst of fear. "But how do you know?" she asked. "How do you know this isn't a mistake?"

They argued over Claude. I went into my room and tried to read with a pillow over my head. Then later, he talked animatedly to my mother, following her around the apartment. "We can trust Claude for this," he said. "This is our chance."

The ghost said not to trust Claude; my father had said we could trust him. Proof, I thought, that they were opposite. But the ghost had my father's eyes. And he had my father's voice.

After the ghost vanished into empty air, I stayed standing in the middle of the garden until the sun burned the top of my head and my legs shook. I walked through the sliding glass doors, up the stairs, and into the room that would be my room.

The mess shocked me. I had forgotten the garbage bag left in the center, gutted and torn in my mad dash from the room, left like a dead animal with its side torn open, spilling innards of sleeves, shorts, and pant legs. The trail of books and magazines, shoes, old dolls, and stuffed animals exploded out of the closet. I hopped from one clear island of carpet to the next.

My father hated mess—he used to pretend he would come after me if I didn't clean my room, counting to ten until I squealed with terror. Maybe the ghost hated mess, too. Or maybe he loved mess, because he was the opposite of my father.

I started with the clothing, matching socks and balling them up into a pyramid. Without a dresser to put them in, I left stacks of T-shirts, jeans, and shorts along the floor.

With each folded article of clothing, I unfolded a memory.

I remembered my father in our apartment pacing while on the phone, back and forth in the living room, tangling the cord around his legs. He talked for hours, phone call after phone call. Sometimes he shouted; sometimes he slammed the receiver down in triumph or in anger. Or he sat in the growing dusk, staring into space. "Hey, Dad," I said, "watch TV with me. Let's go for food. Let's go for a drive." But he shook his head, no.

Next came shoes, laid out in matching pairs along one side. Underneath the garbage bag of clothes I found a shoebox filled with old birthday cards and photographs of Sofie and me together in her backyard, building a fort from blankets when we were twelve. It hurt to think I might never see Sofie again, and I wondered if I could call her, if there might be some way to visit. I looked around this big room with its layer of mess and wished for Sofie to help organize it. She loved to line things up by size. She loved to make lists, then alphabetize them: lists of boys, lists of movie stars, lists of places she wanted to visit.

Stack the books, stack the memories.

I dug out a worn school copy of *Shakespeare's Tragedies* mixed in with several magazines my mother purchased at supermarkets—*People* for herself, *Teen Beat* for me. I cut out the pictures from both types of magazines and taped them to the walls.

I placed everything in short stacks in the center of the room, my clothing ringed by books and magazines, dolls and stuffed animals propped against one another. But then I changed my mind, grouping everything into small islands, needing a map to find my way to my underwear or my T-shirts. This left things messier than before, and I was overcome with a desire to toss everything out the window, to grab fistfuls of socks like baseballs and throw.

But night had fallen, with the moon rising over the mountains. I hadn't realized how much time had passed—

the whole day gone. It must have been midnight or later. I took a deep breath before lining everything up against each of the walls and leaving the center of my room bare and free. Laid out end to end, there were enough things to make it all the way around. There was an order to it: first my favorite shirts and jeans and shorts, then my next favorite, then the things I never wore, followed by my favorite books, my photos of Sofie and José, schoolbooks, presents from my father.

In my closet, I hung one piece of clothing—Deputy Mike's jacket.

BY THE NEXT MORNING, PLASTIC covered every inch of carpet downstairs. It crackled beneath my feet as I followed the wet-clay smell of fresh paint wafting from the front room. Tinny pop music played at a low volume. A stranger in splattered overalls took a roller and sloshed it in a pan of white paint before he turned toward the far wall, moving from top to bottom. The furniture had been taken away, and someone had pulled up the carpet, stripping the room bare.

I stood at the edge, not wanting to go in. Behind me, Claude sat on the couch in the living room, elbow deep in papers and folders with his shirtsleeves rolled up and his beeper rattling on the coffee table. He had the phone from the hallway pressed against his ear with his shoulder.

"I'll tell you what the secret is: Keep your eye on the future," he was saying. "There's poor mentality and rich mentality. Most think you have to get lucky to get rich, or you have to be dishonest. But you see, the rich," he said, spinning a pen around and around with his fingers, catching it every time, "the rich know it's their God-given right to be rich. Not because they're special or any bullshit like that. But because they're not afraid to take it when it's offered. This is a bull market; it's ripe. I'm offering low risk, and a pretty goddamned steady yield. You let me worry about the details."

I moved into his line of vision and he turned to watch me as he continued speaking.

"Yeah, well, do me a favor and leave it for now? I promise, tomorrow I'm all yours, and we'll go over everything point by point. Right," he said, and hung up.

His beeper buzzed again, vibrating a little jig, but he ignored it.

"You erased him," I said.

A look of surprise crowded around Claude's eyes. It was the first time I'd spoken to him, and it was an accusation. I could tell he didn't know how to react.

"Wait here," he said. "There's something I want to discuss with you." He snapped his fingers in a jokey way and moved past me to where a desk was squeezed between two bookshelves in the corner of the living room. It was an elaborate thing, made of cherrywood. I could make out the faint stenciling along its side: the image of a woman with turn-of-the-century hair, a small smile on her lips. He unlocked it with a key. The desk unfolded like a flower— the front part rolled up; then two panels hinged out to the sides.

The desk was a trove of unasked questions. I tried to peer around Claude's body to see what was inside it, but he was very careful to block my view.

"What's in there?" I asked.

"Just office-type stuff," he answered, taking out a pen and a sheet of white paper before folding it up again and locking it. Sitting next to me on the couch, he wrote the house's address down on the piece of paper:

11509 Shangri-La Road, on the corner with Jupiter Lane.

Shangri-La, the magical sanctuary hidden away in the mountains. My father and I had watched the old black-and-white movie together. Would it take a hundred years to escape this place? And when I did leave, would I shrivel up into an old woman? But in some ways it fit: the big pink house hidden away in the mountains, collecting an odd assortment of individuals over the years. But this wasn't an idyllic land, and none of us were at peace.

As if I were a six-year-old child, Claude made me memorize the telephone number as well as the ones for his cell phone and beeper.

"This is stupid," I said, but with an annoyed sigh I recited the address back to him.

"Good girl," he said, and took both of my hands between his much bigger ones. "I want you to do something for me," he continued. "I want you to think of what you're going to say to the social worker when they visit. We don't know when they'll come, but you should prepare now. Do you understand? You don't want to cause any more trouble for your mother."

He wouldn't let my hands go, his cologne so pungent I could taste it. I saw where he'd missed a spot shaving, under his chin.

I knew then that it was the Child Services visit that had prompted the speed of the front room's transformation, when, before, he'd let it linger, and that was the reason why Claude was home on a weekday. My anger rose again, but I nodded, and he let my hands go.

"One more thing," he said, rising to push the sliding doors open. I hesitated, but mirrored surfaces no longer scared me. The ghost wasn't limited to a reflection. He could come and go as he pleased.

I followed Claude onto the back patio, and there, waiting, was a brand-new bike. He wheeled it over.

"For you," he said, and I took it. My own bike, a girls' bike, as pink as the house, with tassels and a basket and wide pedals for my feet. He pointed his finger in his over-the-top way, which I was beginning to realize was his normal way of talking. "Don't you dare run away."

I steadied the bike by its handlebars, the perfect height for me. A cruiser, with a wide, cushioned seat.

"What do you say, Rosaura?"

My mother had come down from the third floor and stood inside. She had a pale silk kimono robe wrapped around her, and while her hair was loose and uncombed, it shone golden in the morning light.

I didn't want to say it, and she knew I didn't want to. But I couldn't see how to get out of it. I had never owned a bike before. I'd learned to ride on Sofie's bike. It felt solid and real, like its weight belonged in my hands.

"Thank you," I said finally.

He smiled. "You're welcome." He patted my head before going in. When he squeezed past my mother, she held herself still, then offered a cheek. His face softened, and he bent his head to kiss her before leaving the two of us alone.

She stepped down onto the patio. "Are you going to ride away again?"

There was a bitter edge to her question, and I was uncertain if she was still angry or not. She must have agreed to the changes for the front room. I knew it was irrational to want to keep it stained and unusable, but I couldn't help it.

"Just around the block. If that's all right with you?" I answered, unable to keep the sarcasm out of my reply.

Her lips thinned. She seemed ready to yank me to her side again, but instead she lifted her hand and touched my hair, then dropped it to finger my T-shirt. Rings of lazy gray cigarette smoke floated around her head. She was holding a notebook in her other hand. I'd seen it before, in our apartment. On evenings when my father was late coming home, she used to sit in the kitchen with it and a pack of cigarettes. She liked to draw and write, stick pictures in it, but she never let me see, hiding it underneath newspapers or in a kitchen drawer or somewhere in her room, where my father would find it and laugh at her for always wanting to keep some old school notebook that was falling apart. When I was twelve, my mother caught me sneaking a look at the notebook and snatched it from my hands, hiding it someplace I could not find. It came from a time when my father had been alive and we had lived as a family.

She saw me notice it, and her hand gripped it tighter. "Don't go far," she said.

I STOLE HER NOTEBOOK.

It was the first time I had gone to the third floor, its bedroom larger than any other room in the house. There was a giant bed against the back wall, disordered with mounds of pillows and a fluffy comforter. I hated to think that she slept here with Claude.

The notebook was left open on the bed, half-buried under the comforter. As I stood in the center of the room, I could hear the shower going. She must have been looking at the notebook before deciding to take a shower.

The ghost had said, "We were happy once." Maybe the notebook would show me a glimpse of that happiness. I picked it up and ran from the room.

In the kitchen closet, behind the ironing board and the vacuum cleaner, I found a flashlight and then went out into the garden. The heat of the summer had browned it around the edges like an old photograph, and crickets sang beneath the buzz of cars from the nearby freeway.

I sought the large row of bushes that marked the border between the garden and the wilderness of the hill that rose behind it. They were overgrown and prickly, creating a haven with a roof of twisted branches and patches of sky. On my knees, I crawled to a space where the ground was dry.

It was the type of notebook you bought for ninety-nine cents at a drugstore: college ruled, one hundred sheets of paper. She had written her name in childish curlicued cursive: *Dahlia*, with a star over the *i*. I traced the indentation of the ballpoint pen, then looked inside.

She had cut out the bulldog logo from her high school yearbook and glued it to the first page, but it had come unstuck and the edges were bent and ragged. A spiky collar bulged around the bulldog's neck, with the words "Home of the Bulldogs" written in block letters underneath its toothy grin. The pages that followed were filled with more cutouts of strangers, posing or in candid shots, with old-fashioned hairstyles and clothing. These must have been her friends from long ago, although my mother never talked about having friends, never had them over for dinner or spoke to them on the phone. With an indrawn breath, I recognized my father: young, foolish, laughing. There were pages full of him, each revealing a secret: He wore bell-bottom jeans; he had a mustache; he was on the track team. Pictures of him running or standing with his teammates, and captions that read: *Robert Douglas hurdles toward another win.* He tended to have a permanent look of surprise, as if he was always caught off guard. I stared at one shot of him in mid-leap over a hurdle, graceful, determined, all his limbs working together in harmony. I wanted that picture to continue, to become unstuck in time and roll forward so I could see him land, run, and leap again.

She had made her own yearbook with just those pictures she wanted, manipulating the images to tell different stories from the ones in the real yearbook. In and around each picture cut and taped into the notebook, my mother had drawn illustrations, portraits of the photographed subjects. Sometimes there were words: *wednesday, february, history class. It's raining today. Water soaked my bed. I sleep on the floor again. Mama cries in her bed no longer rising she's going to cry forever she's dying. I will name my daughter Rosaura after her.*

The energy of her handwriting filled me with unease. She drew many vines around her sentences, constantly entangled.

The stars stole into my bed again. He makes love like an overgrown puppy.

She cries in Spanish she says his name over and over in a whisper so I can't hear.

Toward the end of the notebook, I found a picture of an older man and woman standing beside my father. They resembled him: the man was balding, with something familiar in his ink-spot eyes, in the way his mouth slashed across his face like an unhealed wound. The woman had a prim smile, and she clutched her purse tight to her side. My grandparents. They had names in the caption: Henry and Judith Douglas. My father had rarely spoken of them.

On the last page of the notebook was one picture of my mother. A candid shot of her sitting on the bottom step of a small rise of stairs, a window above streaming light over her head and shoulders. The picture was black-and-white, grainy, slightly out of focus. Her hair looked darker than it did now, before she started dyeing it the color of warm honey. It fell over one side of her face. She sat with a notebook—her notebook, the same one I held in my lap—and raised her hand with an uncapped pen between her fingers as if she'd been caught in mid-gesture. Beside her she had a box with other pens. Underneath, the caption read, *Artist Dahlia Reyes sits in the upper atrium stairway, creating another masterpiece.*

I propped the flashlight so that all the light fell on her tiny black-and-white face. I went back to the picture of my father leaping over hurdles, stared at his grim determination, the shine of sweat on his forehead. I flipped back and forth between the two pictures, first my mother, and then my father, until I could place myself there, until I could walk between the bleachers, under old sunshine, and hear my father's pounding feet along the track. Until I sat with my mother, close enough to understand her secrets.

I thought that the notebook might tell if my parents had been happy. But it couldn't do that. There wasn't even a picture of them together. The bushes rustled; the trees shook overhead. My skin prickled. Just the wind, I said to myself, blowing hard enough to make the trees bend and sway, but

I could feel my father's ghostly presence breathing nearby. Did he want to look at the notebook too? Did he want to remember?

Something brushed across my face.

"Is that you?" I asked out loud. "What do you want? Why are you here?"

Someone called my name. I looked through the branches, but it wasn't my father. Instead, I saw Alex's blond head. Relieved, I let out the breath I was holding.

He crawled all the way in beside me. My heart pounded; my hands were cold.

"Were you talking to someone?" he asked. "I thought I heard you."

"Just to myself," I said, my voice weak and confused. "What are you doing here?"

"Looking for you."

My heart soared. How long had he been looking for me? He followed my shaking hands as I tried to put the notebook back in order. Some of the pages had crumpled, and a few more had torn off.

"Let me," he said, and started gathering the sheets back in place. He handled them as if they didn't hold incalculable treasures and then wrapped the notebook up in its plastic bag before handing it back to me. "Come inside."

But that was the last thing I wanted. When I made no motion to leave, he sighed and sat beside me. I lay down and he did the same, our shoulders touching. I turned onto my side and, wondering if he'd stop me, put my hand over his chest. We lay together and I counted his heartbeats. At first he didn't move, but then he put his hand over mine, fingers pressing against the inside of my wrist. Maybe he could feel my rapid pulse, and he was counting my heartbeats too. Puffs of warm breath from his nose tickled my skin. I traced his eyebrows with my forefinger.

He jerked his head away, scooted a few inches back. "This'll only make things worse."

"Worse than what?" I asked, really wanting to know, but the sound of the sliding doors followed by Claude calling for us caused Alex to scramble to his feet.

"We're here," he answered, then said in a harsh whisper. "You better hide that notebook if you want to keep it."

I tucked it underneath a low bush and left it in the dirt. He had been so quick to let his father know where we were, and so quick to know I didn't want anyone taking the notebook. Was that why he had been looking for me in the first place? Because Claude had asked him to? I frowned as Alex pulled me to stand next to him.

"What are you two doing?" Claude asked, his face illuminated by the light of the house.

"Just talking," said Alex, at the same time that I said, "Having sex."

The breeze whistled a funny little note, filling the answering silence. The last of the sun slipped behind the mountains, leaving the sky a dark, bruised purple. Claude squinted at both of us. Alex brushed at his jeans and tried to move past his father, but Claude stopped him with a hand.

"I'll talk to you later," he said, then dismissed Alex with a nod toward the house.

After Alex disappeared, he held my gaze until I felt smashed and bent. I stepped back.

"From the first moment I saw you, I knew you'd be the

tough one," Claude said, in a way I knew he meant to be sincere, wanting to compliment, wanting to make me feel special.

"You're scared of me." He seemed surprised, as if no one would ever think of him as anything other than kind and jolly.

"Terrified," I replied with as much sarcasm as I could, but he was right: He scared me more than anything in the world. I tried to leave, but his big hands clamped around my upper arms.

"Wait a minute, this is serious. Alex means well, but it hasn't been easy for him since—" Claude bit off what he was going to say, then paused and searched for different words. "Promise me you'll be careful around him."

"We were just talking," I said. Hasn't been easy because of what? What was he going to say? My mind whirled with possibilities.

"Talking is fine. In the house. Or at school. But you stay away from him. Do you understand?"

The crickets chirped and the half-moon rose to the top of the sky. He struggled to say more but seemed unable to come up with the correct words. "Go on," he said. "It's late."

He stepped aside and let me pass.

THE NEXT DAY, AS I sat at the dining table pretending to read a magazine, there was a loud knock on the front door followed by the *ding* of the doorbell.

A hush followed, a collective holding of breath. Claude was in the living room, the phone once again pressed to his ear. My mother emerged from the kitchen, very pale apart from the twin spots of color on each cheek. Claude waved at her, indicating she should answer the door. She didn't move. He waved at her again, continuing to listen to whoever was on the other end of the phone. It took her a moment, but she went to the front door and opened it. It was a man in a service uniform. The house heaved a sigh; no damning visit from Child Services yet.

He said he had a delivery for Claude Fisk. "Oh," said my mother, slow to recover. The man waited with a blank expression until she said, "Yes, of course, come in."

It was new furniture for the front room. My mother stood in the middle, pointing to one area with a cigarette in hand. "This way," she said, and the men set the furniture down in an L pattern. "No, actually," she said, "that won't work," and the men changed the configuration again at her bidding. And again. There were only so many ways a love seat and two armchairs could be arranged, but she could not be satisfied. From my vantage point, I watched the weary deliverymen as they moved the furniture yet again. They didn't understand that no matter where the new furniture stood or how fresh the paint smelled, how pristine and neat and clean the room seemed to be, my mother could not hide the memories of what had happened.

In the middle of another rearrangement, Claude finished his phone call and came in to rescue the men from a further repetition. My mother puffed on her cigarette, the stains on her cheeks fading while Claude tipped the men in cash and sent them on their way. The furniture lay where the men had set it down, the love seat off to one side, the two armchairs awkwardly grouped.

"Sorry, that was an important call," said Claude. He still

hadn't returned to work since my nighttime ride, saying he didn't want to leave my mother alone when things were so uncertain. Instead, his papers and files spread like a fungus over every surface in the living room while he spoke on the phone to nameless individuals, taking up so much space that not even three floors and a garden was enough to escape his overreaching presence.

"Aren't they all important?" she said.

"What's that supposed to mean?"

"I'm going upstairs."

"That's your answer for everything," said Claude. "Go upstairs, lie down. Look at that notebook, over and over again."

Silence.

"Did you take it?" she asked Claude, her voice low and rough.

"I don't know what you're talking about," said Claude, sounding frustrated and tired. "It's been weeks. I thought . . ." He paused, and maybe he took her hand, or reached for her, held her by the shoulders. When he spoke again, his tone changed. "Your daughter needs you. I found her alone with Alex last night, in the garden. I'm sure it was innocent, but she needs her mother right now."

"Don't you dare use Rosaura to manipulate me," she said, nostrils flaring. "Did you take it?" she asked again. "I can't find it."

"Take what? That old notebook?" More silence. My mother was outside my range of vision, but I could see Claude's profile, his searching, thoughtful expression. "I wish you'd let me buy you a real sketchbook. Throw that one away."

"No," she said. "No, no. I have to find it." She moved

into the dining area, where our eyes clashed before she went upstairs. I hid behind the magazine's glossy pages. Claude returned to his files and folders, picking up the phone to make another call.

Later, when everyone was asleep, I slipped out to the garden. The wind pushed at my back as I crawled through the bushes to retrieve the notebook. I ran back to the house as if wolves nipped at my heels, hugging it to my chest.

I went to Claude's dark cherry desk. I tugged at the top, but it was locked. Getting down on my knees, I flattened the notebook as much as I could and slipped it underneath the drawers. If I hid the notebook there and my mother found it, she would blame Claude instead of me.

Relieved to have it hidden again, I headed for the stairs, but the bright white of the front room caught my eye. It looked different in the moonlight, and there was a hum coming from inside. Heart pounding, I stepped closer to look and then relaxed. My mother or Claude had left a couple of fans plugged in and running, probably to air out the smell of fresh paint that clung to everything.

Closing my eyes, I took a deep breath and stepped all the way in.

As soon as I did, I heard a car screech to a halt, followed by a banging on the front door. My father's ghost stood in the entryway as if he'd just come in.

"I stood here," he said. He wasn't looking at me but at the floor and the door and the walls and the window as if trying to remember. "This is where I stood. And then I moved over there." He pointed, walking across the room. "And she stood over there, and he was there too. And we were all here."

He put his hands in his hair, looking wild, until he

stopped and straightened, and I realized something was different from the last time I had seen him. No wound, no blood. Behind him, the freshly painted white wall was a blank canvas.

Then there was a loud bang. Dark red sprayed across the white wall. I screamed. My father's ghost staggered but did not fall. Instead, he turned toward me; a fresh, gaping bullet hole blossomed on the side of his face, and he said, "I was here."

I screamed again. Stampeding feet. A sudden bright light, and then there was no blood, no ghost, nothing except the stricken face of my mother, grabbing my shoulders. She wore her silk kimono, and that was familiar, that was calming, until I saw Claude behind her, with his hair as wild as my father's ghost's had been, looking comical in his hastily wrapped robe. Claude reached for my mother and for me; he stood where the ghost had been.

My father was dead, and the man responsible held my mother in his arms.

"Get her out of here," I heard Claude say, preoccupied with my mother, who was very pale, her face ragged in the unforgiving lamplight. He was going to take me away from my mother, and I cried again, protesting, holding on to her until someone hauled me from the room.

Alex. He brought me up the stairs and into my bedroom. I fell silent, concentrating on the hard plane of his chest against my back, the beating of his heart. He had held me like this before, but this time his legs and feet were bare against mine. This time, he started singing the French lullaby I had taught him. His voice was a low rumble, warm against my back, and every molecule in my body relaxed, my head resting against his collarbone. His singing was a release, and I let it drag me down into semiconsciousness.

CHAPTER THREE

When I woke, Claude's and my mother's voices penetrated through the walls. They were wondering what they should do with me. Send me away. Put me in an institution for crazy people. Stick me in the attic; keep me quiet. Did this Cake House have an attic? I stared at the ceiling of my bedroom, listening to my mother's high-toned confusion followed by Claude's assurances.

We were all figurines on the different tiers of the Cake House, with painted-on expressions and fixed, plastic smiles: my mother and Claude standing with their arms linked, a gross parody of a happily married bride and groom. Alex and I on the middle tier, his pale yellow likeness next to my dark figure. My father would have the bottom tier to himself, to hold all the blood he'd shed.

The shadows in my bedroom pushed and pulled. They collected together, into arms and legs, but it was too dark and I couldn't see. A cold bath of fear woke me up, and I wished Alex had left the light on before leaving me alone.

Light might not stop the ghost, but it would make me feel better to see into the corners. I strained my eyes and could make out a smudge on the wall opposite. It might be the light switch, or it might be the ghost's face. If I stared at it long enough, maybe the light would magically flip on, but it remained off.

Just when I'd convinced myself to make a break for the light switch, the doorknob clicked and a shaft of light from the hallway sliced across the room. My mother entered. Her solid weight dipped the bed, and I felt her touch my forehead. The right side of her glowed, bathed in the wedge of light from the open door, but the rest of her melted back into shadow.

She was real; she was my mother. I breathed in the ashy scent of her skin, familiar and reassuring.

"What did you see?" she asked, her voice stripped and bare. She brushed my hair away, fingers dry and cool.

Instead of answering, I caught her left hand in both of mine. The diamond ring on her finger sparkled in the light from the hallway. With my forefinger and thumb, I turned the ring around to hide the diamond against her palm. Then I turned it back around the proper way. I turned it around again. And again. The ring loosened.

My mouth opened and the words to tell her were right there, waiting to be spoken: My father's ghost lived in this house, he was still here, and he wanted something. It should have been easy to say, but I remembered how she had looked the day my father died: white, bloodless, and ravaged.

"Nothing," I said, turning away so she would leave, while at the same time not wanting her to go. I wanted her to sit with me until I fell asleep, but I didn't want to have to say it.

"Do you hate me?" she asked, the same way she might ask if I had done my homework or if I could help her cook dinner. "I hope you don't hate me. It's not right, to hate your mother."

My throat closed. Sometimes I hated her more than I hated anything else. For bringing me here. For leaving my father. For letting Claude put that ring on her finger.

"Although maybe you should hate me," she said. Her eyes glittered like diamonds. "Sometimes I hated my mother. Never marry, she said. It's a mistake. Don't have children. They'll only hurt you. I should have listened."

My father, with his hesitant laughs, his nervous energy, the way he used to twirl her around, never stopping until she pried herself free: He was her mistake. But perhaps I was the bigger mistake.

Behind her, a shadow broke away from the rest. The shadow spread. It came up behind her with arms outstretched. Ready to swallow us in his embrace.

I gripped her hand, too afraid to move, to do anything but hold on.

"What is it?" she asked. She started to turn around to look, but I jerked her hand in mine and shook my head, unable to speak.

"Dahlia," called Claude. His silhouette loomed in the doorway.

"Here," she said to him, but she was still watching me with concern and confusion.

"Come to bed." Claude opened the door wider, causing all the shadows to scatter and revealing nothing unusual except for the ring of my possessions lining each wall.

She nodded and started to stand. "Pick up your things from the floor, Rosaura," she said, then turned to leave.

"Wait," I said, frantic to keep her with me, grasping at her hands. If she chose Claude, I might lose her forever.

My fingernails scraped her skin as she pulled away. She cried out and cradled her wrist. I could see the scrape my nails had caused along her skin.

"You're bleeding," Claude said.

"It's fine," she said, letting him take her away.

I said that I was sorry, but she was already in the hallway. Claude shut my door, leaving me in the imperfect darkness with silence pushing in from all sides. There wasn't even a ghost to keep me company.

THE NEXT MORNING I RAN downstairs to be first in the kitchen, but Claude was there scrambling eggs in a frying pan and wearing a frilly apron over his clothing. He beamed at me. "I was about to call you," he said. "Breakfast is served."

Conflicting desires battled within me: I wanted to ignore him, reinforce how much I hated him, but I was also hungry. He didn't notice, busy serving eggs and toast onto a plate and pouring a glass of orange juice. He sat at the table and studied me with his bright, expectant blue eyes until I gave in and sat down opposite him.

I picked up the fork and stabbed a piece of egg. "What?"

"Your mother and I have something to do today, but just for a couple of hours," he said, as if wanting to reassure me.

I managed an indifferent shrug, but it hurt to think that my mother would leave me in this house where my father's ghost lived to go with Claude, even for two hours. He watched as I ate. I knew he was thinking of the previous night and how I had freaked out. I was trying to figure out a way to say there was nothing wrong when my mother walked in. I looked behind her, but there was no Alex. I wished I had been smart enough to stay in my bedroom too.

Claude stood up when she entered. "Well," he said, holding out his seat for her, and then placing another plate with eggs and toast on the table. She hesitated a moment before taking the offered seat.

"Thank you," she said. "This looks great. You shouldn't have."

He leaned over and gave her a kiss on her cheek. "The luncheon starts at noon, if you could be ready by eleven-thirty. Wear the new dress, and those earrings." He spoke with an easy mixture of request and command before leaving the kitchen.

My mother and I remained silent. She looked at the eggs with a revulsion that I shared, and then she scraped the rest into the trash. I could see the red scratch along her left arm where my fingernail had marked her.

"Where are you going?" I couldn't hide my resentment that she was leaving. But maybe she had left often during that time I was in the closet and I hadn't even known. "Can't I go too?"

She shook her head, as if to clear it, then focused her attention on me. "Will you help me get ready?"

I used to love to watch her dress, watch her put her makeup on. She knew this. Maybe this was her way of apologizing. As we passed the second floor, I strained to hear anything from Alex's room, but there was nothing.

Her new dress hung on the open closet door, tasteful in a pastel blue. As she took a shower and dried her hair, I organized her makeup: lipsticks lined up, brushes arranged tallest to smallest.

She sat at the new vanity Claude had bought and put on makeup like it was war paint: a little too much blush, lips painted a too-dark red. It was her normal way of putting on makeup, but it seemed more out of place in this strange bedroom than before. She smacked her lips together, smoothing out the color. Then came the dress, sliding over her shoulders, swinging down around her hips.

All she had to do was put her shoes on to complete the outfit, but as she lifted her gaze to the mirror she froze. I looked, too, and saw confusion and disgust cross her face. Without warning, she swept her makeup off the vanity, scattering it across the carpet.

Then she took a deep breath and grabbed a tissue with a quick jerk of her wrist. She rubbed at her lips.

"Wet a towel for me?" I went into their bathroom to get a washcloth. When I returned, she'd picked up all of the makeup. I handed her the washcloth and she scrubbed her face clean, starting over again, this time with neutral colors, a soft, clean foundation and light rosy beige on her lips.

"What do you think?" she asked.

She looked like a character from a television show where families lived in the suburbs and mothers wore sweaters draped over their shoulders. Together, we looked at her image again, her hair brushed to shining gold, diamond drops in her ears; she was perfect, and different from before. Something had changed in the hour it had taken for her to dress, some indefinable metamorphosis that took her even further away from the mother I knew.

I went with her downstairs and was surprised to see Alex sitting at the dining table, dressed in ironed khaki trousers and a light yellow polo shirt that matched his hair.

It hit me that Alex was meant to go with Claude and

Latifah Salom

my mother to this luncheon, all of them together, and that I wasn't going with them. They were going to leave me alone, without even Alex as company. It felt like a betrayal, a deliberate insult meant to say I was not wanted, not cared for, not needed.

Claude whistled as he entered the living room with a smile. "All ready?" he asked. "Good. I'll be just a minute."

"You're all going? Without me?" I said, outraged with disbelief I couldn't control.

"That's right," he said, not reacting to my anger.

I hadn't expected him to admit it. "You don't want me with you. Keep the crazy kid at home, right?"

Claude pursed his lips. Beside him, my mother and Alex stood mute, apparently unwilling to come to my defense. Maybe they didn't want me to go either. "After last night, I think you should stay here and rest."

"But what about Child Services?" I asked, trying to hold on to my panic, feeling sick to my stomach. "What if I call the police and tell them you left me alone?"

Anger snapped in Claude's eyes, and he took a step in my direction. "You're going to stay home, and you're going to rest, and you're not going to cause any trouble," he said in a measured tone.

I didn't understand. If he was so worried, why didn't he keep Alex home with me, at least? Or better yet, take me with them? Whatever this "luncheon" was, it was important to Claude, important enough that despite the imminent visit from Child Services, he would risk leaving his crazy step-daughter at home alone rather than bring her with him. And he needed the appearance of a family, together. Looking at my mother, the way she was dressed, she fit in with Claude and Alex more than with me, and I could see in her face

· 50 ·

that she couldn't or wouldn't encourage Claude to bring me with them.

THEY LEFT AND I REMAINED standing in the living room, uncertain what to do next. I faced the front room, darkened and full of shadows because the curtains were drawn. Alone in the house for the first time, it was like I could feel the different layers settling with the weight of all that was unsaid. Before the ghost could return, to say those unsaid things, I made my escape to the garden, where at least I could pretend to be free.

Faded petals littered the flower beds, fallen from flowers that lacked the strength to hold their heads up. I dug my fingers and hands into the dirt, the top layer warmed by the sun, and busied myself collecting the corpses of poppies and daisies and dahlia flowers. The Mercedes returned and I heard the car doors slam shut, but I didn't get up from my work in the garden. The flowers had all died and they needed to be buried.

The side garden gate creaked open and shut. I didn't turn around, but I could hear someone crossing through the tall grass. A moment later, a pair of neat leather shoes stepped close, and Alex knelt down beside me. The sun made my eyes water, but I was happy to think that he'd come straight back to the garden to see me. I pushed my hands farther into the dirt.

"They've all died," I said with a sigh.

"It's the heat." He watched me dig a fresh grave and lay a dandelion to rest next to a sister daisy. "The heat killed them."

I took a fistful of dirt in my hand, raised it perpendicular before me, and then let it go. The dirt fanned out as the wind picked up. "I think they died of sadness."

"That's dumb," Alex said, and, careless of his still-immaculate khakis, he dug a hole next to all the others, an unmarked mass grave, and laid a dead flower to rest. "But it's obviously important to you."

He wiped his dirt-covered hands on his khakis. Did he also think I was crazy? He wouldn't quite meet my eyes when I leaned closer.

"Did you have a good time at this stupid luncheon?" I asked.

"No," he said, and even though his face hardly changed, I thought he might be amused by my resentment.

"Why couldn't I go?"

"Hey, you have a bike now," he said. "Let's try it out."

He led me to where our bikes stood. Instead of taking his, he took mine instead.

"What are you doing? That one's mine."

"I like yours better," he said. "It's newer."

I followed him through the side gate to the front drive-way and street. He helped me sit on the handlebars, but I still fell halfway into the basket, screeching in fright, but he was careful as we sailed together. Downhill, with the wind blowing my hair all over the place. On sidewalks and off, until we hit a curb and I almost fell but he grabbed me around the waist. His hand was warm against the skin of my stomach.

"Now it's my turn," he said. Despite how much taller and heavier he was, he hopped onto the handlebars, but I wasn't strong enough to hold him up and we toppled over in a heap onto the lawn of a neighboring house.

He dusted himself off and pushed the bike away. There was a long, streaky grass stain across his chest and shoulder, ruining his polo shirt. I touched the stain. He looked at it and made a face that was a cross between "oops" and "who cares?" that made me smile. For some reason, his willingness to ruin his clothing felt like a gift. I kept my hand on his shoulder. "Why couldn't I go with you today?" I asked a second time.

Alex inspected his knees, which were also stained. After our yelling earlier while we rode my bike, his silence was unnerving. The skin at his neck glistened with sweat, flushed pink from the heat and brightness of the day.

"Ask me anything else," he said.

There were so many secrets, and I didn't know where to look for answers. My mother didn't speak at all. The ghost told me not to trust Claude. And Claude said to be careful with Alex, that he hadn't been the same since . . . something, long ago.

"Did your mother ever live here with you?" I asked.

Alex turned his face away. A car honked, and a lemon-yellow Volkswagen Bug drove up with a couple of girls in the front seats. I couldn't see the driver, but the girl in the passenger side stuck her head out the window. Pretty face, with dark hair pulled back in a half ponytail framing freckles and a small, upturned nose. She waved and called his name.

I pushed at the tangled mess of my hair, wild and rough around my face. The girl got out of the car and smiled when Alex walked over to her. They looked like a matched pair, even with the stains on Alex's pants and polo shirt. She should have been the one to go with Alex to a country club lunch.

"Just thought you might like to go see a movie," I heard her say with a touch of uncertainty.

Alex hesitated, but then the other girl, whom I still couldn't see, yelled from inside the car, "Come on, Alex, we're bored. Get your butt in here."

Did he prefer the sweet request or the demand? I wondered.

"Do you know how to get back?" he asked me, and I realized he was planning to go with them. "Straight up the street. You got it?"

"Yeah," I said, and there was a moment when I thought he might change his mind, say to the girls in the VW Bug that he was already busy and he didn't want to go to the movies with them. He wavered, but then the girl in the driver's seat honked, and Alex looked back at the car.

"Tell my dad I'll be back later," Alex said, and with a wave in my direction, he got into the car and drove away.

CLAUDE CAME HOME IN HIS suit with his jacket draped over his arm, his briefcase in one hand, and questioned me with a glare and an annoyed tug of his tie. "Did he say where he was going? Or when he'd be back?"

"The movies, I think," I said, and shrugged, wondering if it was a betrayal of Alex to tell Claude this.

Claude stared as if he wasn't sure to believe me, or as if maybe what I had said held another meaning or there was a hidden truth.

"All right," he said, then headed for the stairs.

Later, after we had all eaten, without Alex, and my mother went upstairs, I didn't want to go to my room or go to bed yet, so I waited for Alex to come home. I went into the kitchen where I could watch the front driveway through the window.

There was banging and movement from the living room, and I froze, heart hammering in my chest for fear of the ghost until I recognized the sound of Claude's footsteps. I inched toward the door of the kitchen and spied Claude crouching by the cherrywood rolltop desk. My heart lurched; I was certain he had found the notebook. But he had no reason to search for it; it wasn't worth anything, except to my mother and me.

He hadn't seen me, too engrossed in whatever he was doing to notice that the kitchen light was still on. I tried to make out the shape of him, his arms resting on the desk. He was muttering to himself and pressing his forehead down onto the wood.

His hands were folded as if in prayer, and he took in a big lungful of air. I wondered if he might start crying—he didn't seem like himself—and I turned away, uncomfortable to see him vulnerable.

The front door creaked open, then shut with a dull thud. A moment later, Alex walked in and turned on a lamp, transforming the living room from a wonderland of mysteries to the dull world of carpets, tables, and walls. I stepped back into the kitchen so they wouldn't see me.

"It's past your curfew," Claude said, with steel and a quiet scolding that didn't fit the man I'd just seen.

"You playing the concerned parent?" asked Alex, somewhere between annoyed and disbelieving, but he didn't deny his tardiness. Silence followed, filled with the busy noises of distant traffic and a dog barking a couple of houses over.

"Things are a little thin, son. You'll have to do better this year. The same sort. Understand?"

There was a pause, and then I heard Alex run up the stairs.

I peeked around the kitchen door and saw Claude as he stood with his hands at his sides, rubbing his fingers together as if he had touched something sticky and was trying to wipe them clean. He turned to face the desk again. "Damn," he said under his breath, so low I had to strain to hear him.

CHAPTER FOUR

Claude cooked breakfast again and called everyone down to eat together at the kitchen table. I watched both Alex and Claude for hints that might help me understand their conversation from the night before, but they didn't speak to each other at all. Alex ate his food in silence, and Claude spoke only to my mother. To escape from the tension, I went out to the garden and got my bike, deciding to ride up and down the street.

After a sweaty couple of hours of trying to bike up the hill, I saw Claude's big gray Mercedes drive away. I went back to the house and dumped my bike next to Alex's before pushing the sliding doors open. The dark gloom of the living room felt heavy with the caged heat of the day.

I stopped when I heard his voice in the hallway.

"Did you tell her it was Alex calling? Did you say my name?" Pause. "I'll hold." Then a longer pause.

Alex was on the phone. I had not seen anyone other than

Claude ever use it, but that wasn't what stopped me; it was how his voice sounded: rough, strung out, strangled.

He played with the phone cord, wrapping it around his hand, then letting it go, then wrapping it around his hand again, whipping the cord against the wall, in circles, like a jump rope. With each whip against the wall, the cord made a *thwapping* sound.

"When will she be free?" Alex's voice regained some of its normal timbre. I wondered if he was calling the VW Bug girl from the other day. "No message," he said, now sounding haughty. Without saying goodbye he ended the call, staring at the receiver for several seconds after he placed it back in its cradle.

I must have made a noise, because he turned and our eyes met.

"Who were you trying to call?"

"Where've you been?" he asked, studying my face, my body.

I passed my hand through my tangled and damp hair. "I went for a ride."

"That it?"

"Yeah, why? Should I get naked again and head for the hills?"

Unimpressed, he leaned against the wall and watched until I couldn't stand it anymore.

"Sorry," I said.

"It's all right." He started up the stairs, then looked over his shoulder. "Come up to my room?" he asked. He glided away. "Or don't come. Either way."

ALEX LIVED LIKE A GUEST in someone else's house. His bed was made, the pillow in the exact center. No posters, nothing on the walls, no clothing on the floor or shoes left in the middle of the room, no sign of life except for the disordered stack of vinyl albums leaning against his stereo.

In a competition of weird rooms, I wondered which one of us would win. At least mine looked lived-in.

He went straight for the stereo and switched it on, plopping the needle down on the record that was already there. I was grateful for the swelling guitar and drums that helped hide my growing awkwardness. Uncertain where to sit that wouldn't disrupt the obsessive order, I lingered in the center. Alex wasn't paying attention, going through his records, taking some out, tucking others back in. I inched toward his desk, daring to sit on the chair.

His desk was pristine—not a pencil out of place, papers stacked, and a dictionary and thesaurus ready and available. Not a speck of dust on the desk surface, with his desk calendar, stapler, and scissors all at right angles.

I took the tape dispenser and pulled and ripped off a long strip, then taped my mouth shut, adding a second strip. The adhesive tickled my nose, but I kept adding more until the moisture from my mouth made a bubble. With my mouth sealed shut I went behind him and tapped his shoulder. When he turned around I raised my hands like claws and mumbled as threateningly as I could before I started laughing, ruining the effect.

"Very funny," he said, reaching to rip the tape from my face, but I sidestepped.

On one corner of the desk stood a framed photograph of a woman who shared Alex's distant, chilled expression.

Not beautiful, or at least not the way my mother was beautiful. But perhaps she might have been pretty in the way that novels liked to call "striking" or "handsome." She aimed her stare at the camera, daring it to take her picture and trap her in a plain metal frame.

I picked it up.

"That's my mother," said Alex.

Stunned that he volunteered this information, I peeled away the tape across my mouth. "Where is she?"

"New York. Paris. London. I don't know. Somewhere else."

"Do you talk to her?"

"She calls sometimes," he said, speaking almost before I finished asking my question, and then he took the frame and stuffed it into a drawer in his desk. He crouched by the stereo and changed records, choosing a violin concerto instead of rock music, haunting and vicious and beautiful. He was like a yo-yo, landing in my hand for one second but then gone again in the next. It kept me wanting more. I couldn't keep up. And now, as before, a subtle change occurred after he mentioned his mother—he couldn't sit still.

"Sing that song." He licked his lips, twirling an album cover in his hands so that I couldn't see what the picture was, and started humming my mother's lullaby despite its clashing with the violin. Above our heads, reflected light from the red plastic stereo cover danced on the ceiling, not quite on beat but almost: a second too late, a beat off. It made me dizzy.

Did he ask all the girls to sing for him? My voice picked up where his had faltered, at first humming, but then I sang the words. The violin hit a high note and drowned out my voice.

"What does it mean?" he asked.

"It's French," I said. "About a little swallow that steals three sacks of wheat and then gets hit three times with a stick."

We lapsed into silence, not entirely comfortable. He flicked through his records. I thought of my friends from before, Sofie and José, wondered if they wondered where I had gone. I hadn't found the courage to call Sofie yet. Even though it had been only a few weeks, already I felt like I had been gone from my old life for years. I didn't know what I would say to her. José had probably moved on to another girl, maybe even Sofie; she had bigger breasts, she was tall, with long curly hair. They seemed like specks of dust to me, my memories of them, my life in that apartment, all that came before. I had moved so far past I didn't know my way back. My father's death had pushed me out of reach.

I slid like Jell-O onto the floor, plopping onto my back. "Are you popular?"

He lay next to me on the floor. "Define popular."

I rested my head on my hand. "Who was that girl, from yesterday?"

There was a trace of amusement in his eyes, as if he had expected me to ask that question, and I wished that I could take it back. "No one," he said.

I didn't believe him. Was she his girlfriend? Did he have other friends? I didn't want to think of Alex with other people yet. For now, he was mine.

"Play this one," I demanded, picking up an album at random.

"You like the Dead Kennedys?" he asked with a smirk.

I nodded, although I had never heard of the Dead Kennedys. He went along with it and put the record on. We sat on his floor and listened to his records. He showed me album covers of bands that he liked: Judas Priest, Red Hot Chili Peppers. He played the Violent Femmes. He preferred vinyl to compact discs, rambling on about analog versus digital. I liked the girl singers the best, like Liz Phair singing, *"Fuck and run, Fuck and run."*

I caught him staring, backlit by the light coming in from his open window, and I remembered that he had held me a few nights ago. And it hadn't been the first time. No, the first time had been the day my father died. Arms locked around my chest. I had kicked; I had screamed. The memories caused blood to rush in my ears, making it difficult to listen while he spoke about a group called fIREHOSE and another called Minutemen, like I'd gone deaf but that was all right. In my internal silence, I rose onto my knees.

His lips stopped moving. His eyes were that deep gray again, dirty ice. I took his hand and made him stand with me; then I leaned against his chest. We didn't move until I heard my mother call my name. I let go and stepped away.

I left Alex's bedroom and almost ran into my mother coming down the stairs from the third floor.

"Help me search," she said, taking my arm and making me follow her to their bedroom. She headed straight for the walk-in closet. "It has to be in here somewhere."

I knew what she wanted, where it was hidden, and it wasn't in this room. "What are you looking for?"

"The notebook. I know you know what I'm talking about. I know you've seen it." She pulled out suitcases, opening and emptying drawers. "Help me find it," she demanded, shrill and desperate.

Not knowing what else to do, I dragged the vanity chair over so I could stand on it to search through the handbags and hat boxes and winter clothing stored on the top shelf of the closet.

She tossed shoes over her head, searching through the drawers again even though she had emptied them a moment ago. Struggling, she pulled the integrated closet unit out.

"Why would he take it? Why would he do that? It has to be here somewhere," she said.

My throat closed as if a fist squeezed it shut. I wanted to get back to Alex and his records. Couldn't he hear what was going on? With blurred vision, I searched through Claude's sweaters, the secret of the notebook feeling like lead in my belly.

"There's nothing here. I don't know what I'm looking for," I said. "Mom?"

Her crying had ceased; she didn't move, absolutely still while looking at something deep in the closet. She scrambled back, returning the drawer unit into place and standing up.

"What is it?" I asked.

"Nothing. It's fine." Her entire demeanor changed. The sudden quiet was in direct contrast to the hysterics from a moment ago. "It's not here. You can go."

I fled from the room as if the carpet were on fire. Once on the stairs, I slowed down, taking each step with a full heartbeat in between, confused and afraid for her. For the first time since I stole the notebook, I regretted taking it.

On the second-floor landing, I heard laughter. Girlish laughter. Sunlight streamed in through the window at the end of the hallway, splashing over the wall and over Alex's door, which I had left open. Alex stood with his back to the door, but over his shoulder I saw the dark hair and upturned nose of the VW Bug girl. She sat on the windowsill, leaning backward.

I'd left Alex for twenty minutes. No one ever visited, but here she was in Alex's room, like she could teleport herself there. I was surprised and hurt. She must be his girlfriend. I couldn't think of any other reason. His perfectly made bed showed twin indentations where they had sat together, but his desk was untouched, the photograph of his mother still inside. That was something, at least. He hadn't shared *that* with the VW Bug girl. But there was no music playing. He had turned his music off. He hadn't shared that with her either; I was sure of it. That would be too much of a betrayal; he wouldn't have done that.

Then Alex shifted to one side and revealed a third person in the room: a boy, shorter than Alex, with a buzz cut and an oversize jean jacket, out of place in the heat of the day.

The boy moved and tried to grab her, but she stuck out her leg to block him. "Tina, what the fuck do you think you're doing? Get down from there," said the new boy.

"I want to know if Alex would catch me. Will you?" she asked, speaking to Alex. "If I let go?"

"Stop playing," said Alex.

"Come on, get down," said the other boy.

"Why should I? I want to jump. I bet I could jump from here." She twisted on the windowsill and bent her leg to swing it over, wobbling as she lost her balance, squealing. "Whoa," she said, then did it again. "Come on, be my hero."

Alex grabbed her around the waist and pulled her into the room, while the boy stood with his arms held close to his body, as if he was afraid to touch anything.

"Jesus Christ, what are you trying to prove?" asked Alex.

She was breathless and bright-eyed. "See, I knew you'd save me."

"Are you high?" Alex disengaged her arms from around his neck, clearly not amused.

She swallowed, still breathing hard, and tried to touch his chest again. "No. Not really. I know you don't like that."

"A little help here?" Alex said, speaking over her head.

"What do you want me to do?" the boy asked, but he went to her other side. "Here," he said, reaching deep into his front jeans pocket and taking out a wrapped plastic bag. He withdrew a rolled-up joint and lit it with a lighter, taking a quick puff before holding it out for the girl, who closed her eyes and inhaled.

"That's your solution?" asked Alex, stepping back from the girl. "By the window," he said, waving his hand in the air to dispel the smoke.

"Man, what do you want from me?" asked the boy, but he guided the girl to the window, making sure to block her so she wouldn't get it into her head to climb out a second time. Compared to Alex, he was gentle and patient with her.

"Like that's going to help. Why'd you bring her?"

"It'll take the edge off. And she didn't give me a choice. Sorry."

"Both of you have got to get out of here," Alex said, and sighed. "If my dad sees you, he'll flip."

"You're the one that asked for my help." The boy offered Alex the joint, but Alex shook his head.

"My parents don't know that I'm here, if that's what you're worried about," the girl added.

Alex didn't answer.

"I'd never tell them. They call him every day, you know. They leave messages." Her eyes had dulled but then brightened as she reached for him. "I wanted to see you." Her voice was rough from the smoke. She lifted her head, then saw me standing in the doorway to his room. "Who are you?"

The two boys turned around. With sudden force, I slammed Alex's door hard against the inside wall, cringing at the unexpected loud *crack* it made.

"Do you need something?" Alex didn't swear or yell, but he spoke with a chill in his voice.

I lifted my chin, angry that these strangers were here with him in his room but not knowing what to say. Then the phone rang.

The ringing echoed through the entire house. Alex and I stiffened, and he shook his head slightly to let me know not to answer. Alex and I were not supposed to answer the phone when Claude wasn't home. For some reason, Claude distrusted answering machines. "Wait," said Alex as the phone kept ringing and ringing. "It isn't Dad."

How did he know? Did Claude call by code? Two rings, then nothing, then three more rings equals safe to answer. The phone rang and rang with no one to answer it.

It couldn't be the girl Tina since she was there. Was it some other girl? I remembered that desperate, awkward phone call he had made. Was that person calling him back? He was wondering the same thing—I could see it, the way he creased his eyebrows briefly, squashing down the instinct to answer the phone.

"Should someone get that?" Tina asked.

Ringing, ringing, someone answer the ringing.

As if he could read my mind, Alex sprinted at the same time I did, elbowing me down the stairs to be the first to pick it up. My hand closed around the telephone receiver. Gasping, out of breath, I said, "Hello."

"May I speak to Claude Fisk?" asked a woman's voice.

Of course it was for Claude. "He's not here," I said, disappointed. I wrapped my hand around the cord like Alex had.

"Is this Rosaura?" The woman pronounced my name differently. Most people said "Rose-zara." But this woman said "Ro-sow-ra." I went still and looked at Alex. Glad for the excuse, I leaned in close to him so he could hear as well. "Fetch your mother, my dear. Tell her it is Mrs. Wilson from Child Services."

The dreaded call, the one that had my mother wringing her hands and Claude coaching me on what to say. Hearing Mrs. Wilson's voice over the phone brought a curious calm, a release of an unseen fear that had been knotting my belly.

Without looking at Alex, I set the receiver down on the table and ran back up the stairs, past Tina and the boy, who had come out into the second-floor hallway to watch.

"Mom," I said. "There's a Mrs. Wilson—" I stopped, surprised to see that the room was put back together, the closet neat enough to put Alex's room to shame, and that my mother was lying down, curled on her side. "There's a Mrs. Wilson from Child Services on the phone," I finished.

My mother shook her head. "I'm not here. Tell her I'm asleep."

"That'll only make it worse."

"Do it," she hissed, but I tugged her arm until she rose and together we went downstairs. "I can't talk to her. Tell her I'm not here. Tell her I left the house."

We got to the phone, my mother as white as the furniture in the front room. Like a child refusing food, she shook her head with quick, sharp jerks. I heard the tinny voice of

Mrs. Wilson saying over and over again, "Hello? Mrs. Fisk? Hello? Can you hear me?"

My mother begged with her eyes.

"I'm sorry, Mrs. Wilson," I said into the receiver. "She can't come to the phone right now."

Mrs. Wilson was quiet on the other end for so long I thought she had disappeared or had hung up, but then she spoke. "Tell her, and your stepfather, that I'll be by for a visit tomorrow morning, Thursday, at nine A.M."

From the look on my mother's face I could tell she heard. I said goodbye and hung up.

I thought she would call Claude, go running to him for comfort. Instead, once the dread of the phone call had passed, she blossomed with anger. "I suppose you'd be happy to be taken away."

"From here? You're joking, right?"

"This isn't funny."

"Then you should have talked to her. She knew you were right here."

"Being angry with me won't change anything, won't—" She closed her eyes. "It won't fix this."

She and I stood by the phone until my mother let out a breath and stepped away.

"If she calls again, I'm not home," she said, pausing when she met Alex coming down the stairs with Tina and the unnamed boy in tow. She stopped and looked at the two strangers and then at him. "They shouldn't be here," she said, light and amused, and then continued on her way up to the third floor.

Alex walked his guests to the front door. Tina's pretty eyebrows were creased in confusion.

At least the phone call had one good result: It got rid of her.

CHAPTER FIVE

My mother came into my room early in the morning carrying a shopping bag. She shook me awake and dragged the blankets from my body. "Get up," she said.

My first thought was that we were running away again, but my mother rattled the shopping bag and took out a long green dress.

"Put this on," she said. "Come on."

"It's too early."

"That woman could come at any moment." My mother sounded scared, and as I became more awake I noticed the wild light in her eyes, the pale cast of her skin. "It's a pretty dress," she said, as if that were reason enough to wear such a ridiculous thing before eight in the morning. "Come here. Put it on. I bought it for you."

I held the dress out to look at it. Embroidered flowers lined the hem. Sleeveless and gathered in the front, made from a flowing fabric like silk. It was something out of a teen catalog, modeled by girls with perfect hair caught in mid-laugh and surrounded by friends having the kind of fun I never could have.

The dress still had its tags; it had cost one hundred and ninety-five dollars. I'd never worn anything so expensive before.

"When did you buy this?"

"Oh," she said, jerking the tag off. "The other day, at the country club. There was a sale. Turn around." She reached to pull off the T-shirt I'd slept in, then tugged the dress over my head. Her hands were blood warm on my arms. I stood in front of her while she tied the sash around the back. "It goes well with your eyes," she said, smiling. "Do you like it?"

She said she'd bought it, but she'd bought it with Claude's money. I thought of those old novels where people had to dress for dinner and went to parties every night. I almost laughed thinking of Claude requiring Alex to dress in a suit. But it fit now—we would all be dressed like dolls standing lopsided on the icing of the Cake House. "This is what you want me to wear?"

"It's almost eight now. We don't know when she's coming. We have to be ready," she said, turning to make my bed and forcing me to move. "What else do you have to wear?"

Nothing else like this, and she knew it. She started snapping the shopping bag until she could fold it, her movements sharp and choppy.

She looked around my room, as though realizing for the first time what I had done with all my things.

"Are you going to leave your room like this?"

"What's wrong with it?"

She took a deep breath through her nose, then reached into a pocket for a pack of cigarettes and a lighter. Taking a fresh cigarette from the pack, she let it dangle from her bottom lip. Her lighter sparked but produced no flame. She swore. "Do your mother a favor and go light it for me," she said. "You can use the stove."

Many of the kids from my old apartment building smoked, but I never had. My mother smoked too much. It had frightened me, to breathe smoke like a dragon.

"Why can't you do it?" I said.

"Oh, don't fight me, Rosaura. Not today. It's not difficult."

I hesitated, suspicious that once I left the room she'd take that opportunity to shove my clothing and books and everything else I had so carefully ordered into the closet. I prepared myself for a fight, but then she deflated and the frantic energy she had come in with bled out of her. She sat down on my bed, reaching to pick up one of my shoes that I'd left in the middle of the floor.

"I like the room the way it is," I said.

She nodded. "Just go. I won't touch anything. I'll just tidy."

I knew she was mad at me for answering Mrs. Wilson's call, but I didn't want her to be worried; I didn't want her to be afraid or to cry. I went down to the first floor, noticing how the armholes of the green dress pulled with uncomfortable tightness and how the bodice itched and scratched.

Standing in front of the stove, I held the cigarette, watching the flame on the burner dance. The cigarette was still damp from my mother's mouth.

Before I could lower my head to the fire, Alex walked in. He noticed my dress, then the cigarette between my lips.

"Where did you get that?" Alex snatched the cigarette from my mouth. "Your mother?"

"Give it back." I reached for it, but he put his arm against my chest, his eyes so frosty they were better than air-conditioning. "Yes, it's hers," I said. "Give it back."

"She asked you to light it for her?"

"Yeah, so what? I can do it." I reached for the cigarette again, but he blocked me a second time.

Taking the cigarette between his lips, he bent over the flame, put the tip in the fire, and inhaled. His cheeks sank in for a moment; then smoke trailed from his nose and mouth. I was tempted to steal a pack of my mother's cigarettes and ask Alex to light each one for me.

He ran up the stairs, taking several steps at a time, and I followed right behind as he marched over to my mother. I was afraid he was going to throw the cigarette, but he handed it to her, lit end facing away.

"That's pretty lazy, even for you," he said. "Here's your fucking cigarette."

"She wasn't going to smoke it."

"Do that again, and I'll tell my dad." Alex turned away, heading for the stairs.

Her mouth in an ugly twist, my mother took the shoe that she was still holding and threw it hard. It smacked against the wall by his head.

White-faced, he turned. She had the other shoe in her hand, ready to throw it.

A loud, booming voice made us all jump. Claude stood behind me like a giant.

"What are you doing?"

My mother let the shoe fall to the floor with a dull thump. She turned away and with a shaking hand took a drag. "I'm tired," she said to no one.

"Dahlia," said Claude, "that woman will be here any minute."

"I know. I'm just going to lie down. For a moment."

"No, you're not," he said.

Alex also turned to leave, trying to slip past his father, but Claude blocked him.

"Both of you, you'll wait downstairs."

My mother didn't move, waiting until Alex went past first. She followed a moment later.

Claude sighed, then looked at me. "That's a nice dress, very pretty. But can I trust you?"

"To do what?"

"Behave yourself," said Claude, more amused than not.

"I'll behave if you behave," I said. Light streamed in through the window, illuminating the lines that crowded around his eyes and creased his forehead. He started to speak, but the sound of a car pulling up to the driveway interrupted and he snapped his mouth shut. There were footsteps and a knock on the door.

We stared at each other, the moment suspended like before glass breaking or a gun firing. I went down the stairs first.

MRS. WILSON'S GLASSES ECLIPSED HALF her face. Behind the lenses her eyes were as round as quarters.

"There she is. Hello, dear," she said with a broad smile, sticking her hand straight out. Her neat, strong fingers squeezed mine before she marched over to Claude and gave his hand one hard shake.

My mother lingered behind us both, her hair down and

framing her face. She took Mrs. Wilson's hand but said, "I'm not sure why you're here. I tried to tell them not to waste your time."

"We take our job seriously," Mrs. Wilson replied. "As it is, you had plenty of notice for my visit." She turned to where Alex loitered by the stairs. She offered her hand again.

Claude ruffled Alex's hair. "This is my son, Alex."

When we moved into the living room, Mrs. Wilson became distracted by the artwork Claude had on display. She loved the paintings. She admired the cluttered shelves of collectables.

"Are these originals?" she asked, and Claude gave each piece's history.

"Art can be a good investment," said Claude, adjusting a Chinese vase he claimed was a lucky find from an estate sale.

"Oh, I agree," she said, gazing at a framed, one-of-a-kind piece of modern art from the late 1960s that to me looked like a bunch of pale, squiggly lines.

Confused, I watched Mrs. Wilson. She was here to speak with me. How could she stand there like this was a normal house and react to Claude like he was any other gracious host, proud of his ugly home and his stupid art collection?

Alex put a hand on my shoulder, as though he realized my distress. Since Tina's visit, he had avoided me, or maybe I had avoided him, but now he pressed his hand down and shook his head, telling me to keep my mouth shut.

Mrs. Wilson finished peering at a framed news clipping headlined "Local Businessman Donates Time and Money to Charity" accompanied by a blurry photograph of Claude with a bunch of men in suits. She adjusted her glasses and took a good look at me. "That's a very pretty dress," she said, in that way that adults sometimes speak to children, as if wearing the dress was something to be proud of.

I realized that this person, who until that moment I had not even dared to hope would be some kind of savior, would be of no help whatsoever. She could not look at me and at my mother, at Claude and Alex, and know of the cancer that ate away at all of us. I blamed the dress my mother made me wear, as if it covered hidden bruises and cuts beneath my skin.

Mrs. Wilson said, "Why don't the kids run along and I'll speak first with the parents?"

Alex steered me from the room—pushed me, pulled me—through the sliding glass doors.

Once outside and away from the adults, I started yanking at the collar of my dress. It was a stupid dress. I wanted it in rags. I wanted it torn, pulling hard on the sash around my waist. The dress cut into my neck, choking me. I gritted my teeth.

Alex stood by the fountain, arms crossed, leaning against the low brick wall. I had come to know the subtle differences in his collection of cool, detached expressions. This one—a furrow between his eyebrows, the slightest flush to his cheeks—meant he was nervous, even though all he did was watch.

"What do you think?" I asked. "Maybe I should rip the whole thing off?" My fingers itched for a pair of scissors to cut the dress to ribbons. Instead, I grabbed hold of a bunch of fabric and yanked until the buttons flew like bullets, disappearing into the tall grass.

"It won't work," said Alex.

Through the sliding doors, I could see Claude and Mrs. Wilson in the living room. If I'd had the strength, I would have picked up the big stone vase that passed for decoration in the garden and thrown it through the glass. Instead, I kicked my bike and watched it crash against Alex's, knocking both onto the cement patio.

Hearing the crash, the adults looked out to the garden, but Alex moved and blocked my view.

"This won't work," he repeated. "She'll think you're a brat; that's all. Pissed off at her stepfather, like a million other kids out there. Pretending you're crazy for attention and running away. You think that woman doesn't know a hundred kids like you? She's already written you off; otherwise, she wouldn't have called before showing up, not if she thought you were in any real danger. You think she won't see through your act? Because that's what it is. An act."

"I could tell her the truth," I said, but I felt cold. He was right. I knew he was right.

"And what truth is that?"

"I could tell her the truth about my father."

Alex looked at me for a long moment. "You don't get it. They won't blame *him*."

The glass door slid open. My mother called for me, but my name died on her lips when she saw the state of my dress.

"Is she okay? Is she hurt?" asked Mrs. Wilson.

Alex stepped in front of me. "She's fine. She fell off her bike, but she's fine."

I forced myself to look beyond Alex at Mrs. Wilson and my mother, and at Claude standing like a great big towering bear over both of them.

"She tore her dress; that's all," Alex said.

Mrs. Wilson seemed concerned, fussed over me, lamented the dress. "Well, if you're feeling all right, why don't you and I have our chat now?"

Over her head, I caught Claude's hard, knowing stare. My mother protested.

"It's not right. I should be with her," she said.

"Technically, I don't have to ask. But it's just a chat. There's nothing to worry about," said Mrs. Wilson. "We'll use your room, I think. Rosaura, can you lead the way?"

Claude whispered something in my mother's ear. Her hand fluttered to her lips; she had come to the end of her cigarette and wanted another one. With one last look at her and Claude, I led Mrs. Wilson to my bedroom.

She waited outside while I changed into shorts and a T-shirt. I sat on my bed and called for her to enter. Mrs. Wilson stopped when she noticed my clothing and belongings lined up along the walls. I had forgotten that it might seem weird to strangers.

"No dresser?" she asked.

I shrugged. "I like it this way. I know exactly what I have."

She took a moment to consider this, but I could tell she wasn't convinced. Light streamed in across the room and she walked toward the open window, careful not to knock over the stacked T-shirts and jeans. For that simple consideration, she didn't seem as useless as I first thought.

"Look at that view of the garden. Your stepfather could use a gardener," she added, amused by her own observation.

For the first time, I noticed her handbag. It looked handmade, decorated with printed photographs patched onto purple fabric, like the kind you get at a mall or a shopping center. Bring in your precious family photos and print them on T-shirts, bags, mugs, and more, great holiday gifts! The bag was littered with faces: Mrs. Wilson surrounded by children, all shapes and sizes. Mrs. Wilson stood behind, or in front of, or beside a child or a teenager, beaming into the camera, a hand on a shoulder, sometimes two. All smiles. All happy, gleeful faces.

Noticing my attention, she held her bag up for me to see. "My kids," she said, flattening the folds of the fabric. "This is Jimmy." She pointed to a large kid with a round face. He seemed twice as wide as she was tall. "He was my last. And Marcela"—pointing to another—"she was before him." She flipped the bag over: Mrs. Wilson posing with three pimpled teenagers. Mrs. Wilson holding a toddler in her arms. Mrs. Wilson at a birthday party, hovering over the gap-toothed grin of the birthday boy.

Could I end up on her bag? If there was no space left, I could go on the bottom. I wondered if she had many of these handmade collages.

"So," she said, putting aside her collection of troubled children, looking around for a chair to sit on. I made space for her on the bed. Perched slantwise to face me, she took out her clipboard and flicked through her paperwork. "It's your birthday at the end of the summer. Are you going to have a party?"

I said nothing. My parents had always struggled with throwing birthday parties. Too hard to organize, too time-consuming, never enough money. There had been one party with José and Sofie. We had cake and a piñata and pin the tail on the donkey. I remembered my father's hands on my shoulders as he spun me around until I was dizzy, the world tilting sideways as I swung the bat and tried to hit the papier-mâché lion. José beat the piñata into submission, swinging and swinging the baseball bat until he gouged the great beast's side and made it rain candy.

"Do you like living here?"

Any answer I might give seemed stupid. She thought the garden was great, the house big and roomy. I wondered how much she knew. I had thought she would ask why I had run away.

"No," I said.

She tilted her head to one side. "I understand your mother recently remarried?" She flipped a page, read, flipped another. "And that your father passed away." She crossed her hands over her clipboard. "That must be very difficult."

Passed away. I had not thought of him as "passed away," only dead.

"Is that what it says?"

"It says he committed suicide." She said it gently, but it felt like taking a baseball bat to a papier-mâché animal. So simple, so easy to wrap up and discard an ugly word like "suicide." It put the blame on my father; it made the rest of us victims. I dug my fingers into the bedsheets.

Mrs. Wilson returned to her clipboard. "You can tell me anything, you know," she said.

Anything. There were many things I could tell her. I thought of my mother waiting downstairs, no doubt smoking a forbidden cigarette. She never used to smoke so much before. My father had disliked the smell of it on her breath, and she used to brush her teeth over and over again before he came home, spraying the room with air freshener, spritzing perfume on her clothes, her wrists, her neck. Is that what she meant by "anything"?

Mrs. Wilson kept her gaze down on her clipboard.

I thought of my father, who I felt certain would have hated this woman, because she invaded our space, because she wore purple and purple reminded him of that bitch lady from work who also wore purple. In private, he would curse her name but then smile to her face, becoming meek and polite and desperate to please. She had the upper hand. She had the power.

A tree swayed in the garden, visible through the window. The ghost appeared behind Mrs. Wilson as if stepping out from behind a curtain. My thoughts of my father must have conjured the ghost. His eyes landed on me in the same expectant way they had in life when I hadn't cleaned my room, when I hadn't eaten my dinner. "Do I have to do everything? Don't make me come over there."

And I knew, this was it. The ghost was here, and he was telling me it was time to make things right. This was why he was here. This was why he haunted me. After I did what he wanted, then maybe he could leave and be free and haunt me no more.

I snapped my eyes back onto Mrs. Wilson, my heartbeat pounding in my ears.

Mrs. Wilson looked up, saw my face. "*Is* there something you want to tell me?"

"Claude killed him," I said, lightheaded that I had managed to speak out loud. I was certain that this was what the ghost wanted me to say.

Mrs. Wilson became still; she seemed to inhale without breathing.

"Whatever the police said, it's not true," I continued. "It was Claude's fault."

My father's ghost flashed in the edges of my vision, like a piece of glass reflecting light. Over and over, insistent, *look at me, look at me.* But I couldn't look at him and look at Mrs. Wilson at the same time.

"If he didn't pull the trigger, he might as well have."

Mrs. Wilson hadn't moved. "That's very serious, Rosaura."

"It's true," I said, my voice low.

Her manner changed. She had seemed a joke to me, someone who, like Alex had said, would see me as another dumb kid like all the others. I was a chore to be finished and marked as completed. But now I wasn't sure: She was listening to me, her gaze calculating, penetrating.

"Is that why you ran away? Why didn't you have any clothes on?"

It was gently asked, but I heard the criticism. My behavior cast doubt. Alex had been right. I couldn't tell her how the cool air felt sweet on my body, or that I ran from the house because my father's ghost had appeared in the closet beside me.

"It was hot and I couldn't breathe. I wanted to go outside, and then I just . . . kept going."

Don't look. Don't look at the ghost. My eyes watered from the effort of not looking. But I had to see him. The ghost had come forward. He stood behind Mrs. Wilson, but instead of the relief and peace I expected to find, the ghost's face contorted with fury. He reached for Mrs. Wilson, a hand hovering over her mouth.

Cold dread splashed over me, and I jumped up. "That's all I want to say."

Mrs. Wilson's forehead creased when she saw my expression, and she glanced behind her. But there was nothing there.

"Just a little longer, Rosaura, I promise," she said in a reasoning tone. She must have thought I wanted to go out. She thought I was looking toward the garden and wishing for freedom. She didn't know about the ghost.

I moved to the window so Mrs. Wilson had to turn. Somehow, I had gotten it wrong, all wrong. Instead of relief at telling the truth, instead of showing happiness, the ghost was angry. He had tried to silence her. Or maybe his hand over her mouth meant I should try to shut her up—but she wouldn't stop asking questions.

"Have you seen your stepfather with unusual amounts of money?" she asked.

"He always has money," I said, keeping my eyes fixed on Mrs. Wilson. Flicker, flashing in the sunlight. My father wasn't finished yet. "Why?"

"Nothing, just something Deputy Nuñez mentioned."

"Deputy Mike?" My heart leapt at the mention of Deputy Mike's name.

She smiled. "You made quite the impression. How long has your mother known Mr. Fisk?"

I couldn't remember. It seemed like I had been held hostage for years, waiting for rescue. Rapunzel, left in her tower chamber.

"A few months," I said. "Dad knew Claude from before."

My father had said Claude was running a game—a game he could beat. I opened my mouth to tell Mrs. Wilson this, but the ghost crossed the room, solid for a moment, and I snapped it shut.

He disappeared.

"Does Mr. Fisk buy your mother a lot of gifts?"

"Yes," I said, and only that. If I didn't speak, the ghost vanished. If I tried to tell the truth, he reappeared. I didn't want to answer any more questions, knowing now that I had made a mistake in speaking at all.

Mrs. Wilson persevered. "Have you seen where your stepfather works?"

"No."

I could see her thinking. She took her time, her eyes fixed and unmoving, ponderous and large. "Tell me truthfully," she said, putting aside her clipboard. She held her hands out, and I left the window to sit next to her on the bed again. "How has it been?"

She had square, clean-cut nails. Not a hangnail to be seen, not a spot of nail polish. I had to take shallow breaths to stop myself from crying. But I couldn't cry. If I cried, that would be telling the truth, and the ghost would come back.

"It's not supposed to be like this," I said at last.

"Your father and mother, did they get along?"

Movement caught my eye; the ghost appeared, maybe wanting to sit on my bed too. Intruding, insistent, and I closed my eyes, willing him to go away. I didn't know the answer to that question anyway. What did he want me to say? They were happy. They loved each other. My mother used to cry when my father wasn't home. She'd cry in her room, and when I went to her, she'd push me away and tell me to leave her alone.

Mrs. Wilson understood, even though I hadn't spoken. She took my hand again. "All right," she said, "All right. I know it's hard; I know it isn't fair. I want you to be strong. No more running away; no more fighting your stepfather. You be good, and I'll see you again. I'll come back and we'll work this out together, okay? I'm here now," she said.

For some reason I believed her. I needed to believe her. She was real, and she was strong and held my hands in hers.

In that moment, I loved her more than I loved my mother, more than I had loved my father. Mrs. Wilson would make it right. Mrs. Wilson would save the day. She would heal this great big wound in the center of my life. Faith filled me with hope and love. In that moment, I wanted nothing more than to be one of her kids, to find my way onto her hand-made bag, right in the center, so she could proudly point to my smiling face and say, "That's Rosaura; she was my last. She's doing real good now."

Mrs. Wilson stood up to go, but I wanted her to stay.

"You'll come back?"

"Oh yes."

"Will you come for my birthday?"

She smiled. "Certainly, if you want me to."

I walked with her into the hallway, nearly vibrating with suppressed energy. The ghost disappeared again. Maybe that meant he was done; maybe he realized telling Mrs. Wilson the truth wouldn't hurt him and that I would keep him a secret and it was going to be okay.

"Well, Rosaura, I want to thank you. You're a very pleasant young lady," she said, turning to face me. "And call me Polly." She handed me a card. "All my kids call me Polly. You can reach me at that number. Anytime."

Her name was printed in block letters: POLLY S. WIL-SON. The points of the card dug into the pads of my fingers. When I looked up, my father's ghost stood behind her, his expression hard and unforgiving. His hand reached for Mrs. Wilson's shoulder.

I caught my breath, and with a question in her eyes, Mrs. Wilson turned to follow my gaze.

It happened like on a television show: Everything fast reduced to slow motion. Her foot slipped on the first step. She cried out, one piercing shriek. Her arms went up and she knocked me back as she fell, tumbling from step to step, scraping the wall, reaching for the railing, catching one of the framed photographs that lined the staircase instead:

a picture of a six-year-old Alex riding a pony. Another scream, maybe from me. She thumped all the way down.

At the bottom of the stairs Claude appeared. He ran to catch her, but she was already on the floor. Bent at an odd angle, twisted like how the bike had been when it had fallen at my feet, her glasses askew on her face. Her handbag lay at her side, her kids' faces looking up, smiling.

CHAPTER SIX

For the second time that summer the house crawled with policemen, firemen, EMTs. We couldn't move Mrs. Wilson, couldn't even sit her up or give her a glass of water for fear that she had broken her back or her neck and might be paralyzed. She groaned on the floor.

Outside, unknown neighbors stood on the lawns of their houses. Kids rode up and down the street on their bikes, slowing to a crawl while they gawked and tried to see what was going on, watching as the EMTs put Mrs. Wilson on a gurney and removed her through the front door, one wheel squeaking with each rotation.

I went outside to the garden. I walked around and around the fountain, wanting to drown, wanting to hide, wanting to go away and never speak again. The grass cut my bare legs and stuck burrs to my socks, but I kept walking. I wanted the tape from Alex's room to tape my mouth shut forever. My fault, all my fault. I misunderstood what the ghost wanted and he had almost killed Mrs. Wilson. But he had used me to do it, my words, my voice.

Clouds littered the sky, although here and there a shaft of light fell to strike the earth. I remembered my second-grade teacher, Mrs. Tadakian. She took my class on a field trip to a park on a wet day. Too wet, she complained, but the sun broke through the clouds as if through a prism, scattered and fractured. Mrs. Tadakian looked up and said, "Oh, it's God's light."

In the backyard, the sky had God's light, straight out of a photograph on a thank-you card sold at a drugstore or a supermarket with a line or two of Scripture: "For the Best Dad."

But was he the best dad?

A long-legged stride broke through the tall grass. Deputy Mike took a seat next to me. I had wanted him to come, and here he was, except it was for the wrong reason. He held his hat in his hand, twirled it once, then laid it down on the grass, where it sat crooked, jaunty, to one side.

"You want to tell me what happened?"

What it must look like, that this happened so soon after my father's death. Maybe he thought death hung around wherever I was, lurking in the shadows and waiting for unsuspecting victims to happen by, like one of those carnivorous plants lying in wait. In this case, death looked like my father.

Alex worried that I kept acting crazy when I wasn't, but I was crazy. Only crazy people see things that aren't there; it's the guilty ones who see ghosts. If I closed my eyes I saw Mrs. Wilson at the top of the stairs, the ghost reaching for her.

Deputy Mike waited for me to speak. I tried to pick my

way through the truth. "We were talking in my room. She'd asked about my dad, about Claude. She mentioned you."

"I spoke with her," he said.

I yanked a long blade of grass, peeled it in two, yanked another one and did the same thing, tying the pieces together into a bow. "I told her . . . I told her—"

A breeze blew. It rushed through the tree branches. Leaves fell like rain. The ghost stood in the middle of the bushes, one side of his face oozing blood. He put his finger to his lips and shook his head. A warning: *Don't do it again.*

"Take your time," Deputy Mike said, and I began to panic because I knew he thought I was preparing to reveal a secret. But I was trying to breathe, trying to figure out what I could say.

"I told her what it was like living here. And how I hated it, how I hated Claude sometimes." My voice dropped to a whisper, afraid that even this was too much.

"Then—then, she was leaving, and—

"She slipped," I said, looking at Deputy Mike until the ghost faded. "It was the way she fell; she couldn't help it."

"Did you talk about anything else?" asked Deputy Mike.

I shook my head, no. I refused to say that I thought Claude was responsible for my father's death, for fear that something would happen to Deputy Mike. And I couldn't say the ghost caused her accident because I disappointed him.

Deputy Mike didn't say anything, rising when the other officer called his name.

"I'm sorry," I said, wanting to say more, but my throat closed and the words stuck and wouldn't become unstuck no matter how hard I tried.

"It was an accident. It wasn't your fault." His warm hands covered mine, brown skin over light, and then he left.

Dead leaves flew across the grass, the trees shivered, and the sun took cover behind a cloud, draping the garden in shadow. The ghost came to take Deputy Mike's empty seat beside me.

"What do you want?" I asked, and folded my arms over my head.

"Remember the bluebell earrings?" He spoke in a voice the texture of sandpaper. "I bought them for her. They cost a fortune. Remember how pretty she looked?"

I didn't care about any earrings. "Just tell me what you want or go away."

"She said they hurt her ears, but she would put them on when I asked her to, because I liked to see the blue against her skin. She lost one of the pair and tore apart the apartment looking for it. 'Don't worry,' I said. 'No, no, it's all right.' But I think she lost it on purpose so she didn't have to wear them anymore. Nothing I gave her was ever good enough."

I tried to be as still as possible, gazing toward the house. My mother sat with her head bowed and her hair pulled back with one hand.

"Look at her," he said. "Look at your mother," he repeated.

I had thought that the ghost wanted revenge on Claude, but now I wasn't so sure. Maybe he wanted in death what he had wanted in life: to be close to my mother, to love her and touch her. He couldn't let her go. He wanted to haunt us all.

As if my mother sensed that I was watching, she turned to face us. Bluebell earrings dangled from both of her ears.

When I turned to see if my father's ghost noticed, he was gone.

DEPUTY MIKE WAS TALKING TO Claude when I had gathered myself enough to come inside.

Claude flicked his head toward the stairs. "Go up to your room, Rosie."

"But I want to stay. I'll be quiet." I wanted to know what Claude was going to say. I didn't want to be alone.

"Alex is upstairs," Claude said, knowing that was usually enough incentive.

I crossed to the foot of the stairs. Alex was sitting on the top step, his guitar across his lap. Claude and Deputy Mike couldn't see him. He made space for me, and I leaned against the banister, trying not to think that Mrs. Wilson had stood in the same spot.

"Where were you when Mrs. Wilson fell?" I heard Deputy Mike ask.

"We were both here, in the living room," Claude answered. "She asked to speak to Rosie alone, so what could we do?"

"I wanted to go with them," my mother said. "She's my daughter; I should have been there."

"Were you upset about the visit?" asked Deputy Mike, asking a question he knew the answer to.

"Of course we were upset. Wouldn't you be?" Claude's tone hinted at laughter.

Sounds of paper against paper. Deputy Mike read, "You said, 'I heard her say goodbye and then she was screaming, next thing I knew she was on the floor.' Did something scare her?"

"I imagine falling down the stairs would do the trick."

Next to me, Alex huffed a short laugh. It was the first time I saw him show anything close to admiration for his father.

"That's convenient, isn't it?" Deputy Mike's voice was as calm and as gentle as ever.

"Excuse me?"

"She could have broken her neck. Problem solved."

Even without the benefit of seeing their expressions, I felt the tension in the cross fire between them. I slid down to the next step on the stairs, and then again, until I reached a point where I could see both men standing face-to-face, locked in a silent battle.

Claude took a step back, facial and body muscles relaxing. He made a gesture with his hands. "Rosaura was the only one who witnessed the accident, and that's exactly what it was, an accident. You want more details, you'll have to talk to her."

I couldn't tell if Claude believed what he said or if he was lying. Maybe he thought I was guilty; maybe he was trying to protect himself.

But then something inside Claude shifted, and his face contracted with worry. "Look, you saw Rosaura; she's making herself sick over this."

A soft twang of a guitar string caught my attention, and I looked back to see Alex shaking his head. He was always shaking his head at me now. Was he saying, *Don't say anything*? Or was he saying, *No, it wasn't your fault*? Or maybe it was a general, *No*. No to everything.

In the living room, Deputy Mike considered Claude and then put his hat on his head. "Thank you for your time." His tone had changed, suddenly sounding as if this was a normal social visit, a friendly neighborhood how-de-do. "This is a really nice house."

"I've worked hard on it." Claude went along with the act and walked Deputy Mike to the front door. I stayed where I was, not caring if they knew I had been listening.

"I'm curious about what you do for a living, Mr. Fisk."

Laughing, Claude waved a hand. "Hasn't that been asked and answered already? That's no mystery, Deputy. Financial advising. Investments. Wealth management."

"Oh, right. Of course. Good money in that?"

Claude swelled with a slow, measured breath. "Sometimes."

"Where did you say your office was again?"

"Burbank, but you knew that already," said Claude. "Are you going to come down sometime? I'd be happy to have you." He smiled, this time with his entire face, nothing but smoothness, open and inviting.

Deputy Mike gave an answering smile. "Maybe. But I'm afraid I'm an under-the-mattress kind of guy."

"I know. I can tell," said Claude. "But you'd be welcome anytime, Deputy."

I followed as they went into the front room. Claude opened the door.

"What happens now?" asked Claude.

Deputy Mike looked out to the street. The ambulance and the other officers had left already. There weren't any spectators left; everyone had gotten bored and gone home. "We have to get Mrs. Wilson's statement," he said. "But once we have that, that'll probably be the end of it. Of course, another Child Services caseworker will likely be assigned."

Claude relaxed and held out his hand for Deputy Mike to shake. "Of course."

Before Deputy Mike had turned away, I pushed past Claude. Deputy Mike looked down at me but then nodded at Claude before heading down the driveway to his car. I started after him.

Claude grabbed my arm. "Let him go, Rosie," he said.

I started to tug my arm free, but behind us I heard my mother say, "Oh God, oh God."

She was at the other end of the house, trying to pull open the sliding glass doors.

"I can't breathe," she said, fumbling with the latch.

She had been holding it together, but now that the officers were gone, she didn't need to pretend anymore.

"I have to get out."

Claude pushed me out of the way in an effort to reach her, but she was outside on the patio before he could make it.

"Come back inside," he said, calm, measured, his hands held out.

"No, I can't breathe in there." She pushed him away, half crawling, half walking to the edge of the cement. She went down to her knees. "We should never have come here. I didn't think things could be worse. I thought we might . . . But this is a nightmare."

Claude tried to lift her off the ground, gripping with a hand around each of her biceps, but she slipped through his hold like water. "Dahlia, enough," he said.

She shook her head, tried to say more, but every word came out malformed. To muffle her cries, she bit her hand.

"It's okay, it's okay," he said, trying again to hold her. "It was an accident; we'll get through this, please, please."

Every ragged strip of emotion she let fall made Claude wince. In the face of her pain, he seemed so unsure. This was something he couldn't fix, couldn't throw money at to make better.

She twisted her hand out of his grip. "I never should have left him. But you kept calling. And you were always there. Why? Why couldn't you let us go? You said it would be better. But it's not better. And now . . . We're bad luck. There are policemen in your house, again, because of us."

Claude ducked his head. I was fascinated by the way he opened and closed his hands. It was startling to realize he had something in common with my father. He thought he'd stolen her from him, but he was learning he couldn't hold her either.

"Come inside," he repeated.

"You don't understand," she cried. "I've even lost the notebook. I can't find it. I can't find it and I don't know what to do, and he's gone, and—"

She started to walk deeper into the garden, then stopped in the middle of the grass.

She sat down hard with her back to all of us. Claude went to her, but she shifted so she couldn't look at him. He tried again, and again she pushed him away until he clamped his arms around her.

I had to do something. Without looking at Alex, I went to the cherrywood desk and crouched down on my hands and knees. The notebook was still there. I flattened my hand and managed to grab hold of the plastic wrapping, pulling it out from its hiding place.

Hugging my precious bundle, I turned as Claude and my mother came inside. He had one arm around her shoulders, her face streaked with trails of sooty mascara, her hair wild and loose. But she stopped when she saw me. She said my name, but then her eyes fell on the plastic bag held at my chest. Her expression darkened with recognition.

"Where did you get that?"

"I found this and—" I realized I didn't have a good reason for why I had taken the notebook and was only now willing to give it back. "You were looking for this, but—"

Her sadness shifted smoothly into anger. She crossed the few steps to pinch my arm with her strong hand. "You had it all this time?"

"I just wanted to look at it." I held the notebook close, trying to twist out of her grasp. "I wanted to see what was inside; that's all. Let me go," I cried.

She tried to wrench it from beneath my arm. I wanted to give it back to her, as a gift, but she had to take it back, to tear it away, and that made me hold on as hard as I could.

"It's not yours anymore," I said. "You don't deserve it. You're the one that brought us here. You made him kill himself."

She slapped me and my head flew back. She slapped me again; her ring cut my cheek.

I screamed, thrusting the notebook at her with all my strength.

Claude yelled for us to stop and grabbed hold of me around my waist. He yanked me to the side. I knocked over a vase. It shattered when it hit the coffee table, jagged pieces of porcelain flying everywhere.

Stunned silence followed. There was blood on my hands and cuts on my arms and legs. I touched my cheek and felt wetness, my fingers coming away painted red.

When she saw the welling blood from the cut on my face, made by her diamond ring, my mother closed her eyes, reaching behind her to try to find the couch.

Claude went to her. She was shaking, trying to breathe. I took one step, but Claude said, "Enough."

His voice was like a hand against my forehead, and I stopped. I picked up the notebook from the floor and, despite Claude's order, set it on her lap. She curled one hand around it.

Claude's eyes passed over the shattered vase, rubbing at his jaw. "Christ," he said. "You would do this to your mother? After everything?"

"Don't," said my mother. "It's not her fault. Leave her be."

Claude shut his mouth. He stood up and helped her stand. She started on her own for the stairs, not waiting for Claude.

"Help Rosie clean this up," Claude said to Alex, watching my mother go. "And you—" He took a deep breath and turned to me. I braced myself for another hot bellow. Instead, he deflated to normal size. He put a finger under my chin and tilted my face up so he could see the cut on my cheek and the imprint of my mother's hand on my face. "I'm sorry," he said, and then turned and left.

CHAPTER SEVEN

Alex moved my limbs and guided me through the living room and up to the second-floor bathroom like I was a puppet. Pastel blue tiles, pastel blue walls. My breath wheezed. The chill that started downstairs disappeared, and I was left feeling sluggish and tired. My head drooped.

There was blood on my shirt. I was tired of blood and peeled the shirt off.

Alex wet a washcloth, turning to face me, but stopped when he saw me naked from the waist up. His pale cheeks flooded with color. He stood still. The air filled with the rasp of my breathing, with his. Then his eyes dropped.

Small lumps for breasts with dark nipples, and hips beginning to flare. My skin was peanut colored like my mother's, but I had little of her beauty and even less of my father's freckles or his long limbs.

I don't know why I did it. I wanted to make him uncomfortable. To shake him up and have him really look at me. I took his hand with the washcloth, passed it over my face, then down my neck, over my chest. His body tensed and he stepped back, grabbing a towel from the rack.

"Clothes," he said, throwing the towel around my shoulders, pulling me out of the bathroom and into my room. He searched through the piles of my clothing for underwear, for a shirt and a pair of jeans, remembering to fish out my shoes from the bathroom. He mixed up my carefully ordered stacks of clothing, putting the yellow skirt next to the green shorts and leaving my jeans in a heap. I would fix things later.

I pulled a T-shirt over my head. I thought he would turn away, but he didn't. Together, we went downstairs. In the back of the kitchen, he opened the utility closet and handed me a broom. We got to work cleaning, and the only sound between us came with the low tinkle of the porcelain as we swept up the pieces of the vase into a pile.

Alex bent over with the dustpan. "That vase was expensive."

"How expensive?" I asked, picking up one piece of porcelain that was larger than the rest. One side was white and the other had yellow and blue glaze, the suggestion of a pattern.

He shrugged. "Thousands," he said. "You probably like that."

"You're right," I said. "The more expensive the better."

He shook his head, but I could see him try to hide a smile.

THAT NIGHT, MY MOTHER CAME to visit me while I was in the bathroom. The tile felt cool against my knees. My mouth tasted sour; my hair stuck to my cheeks and neck, damp with sweat. I closed my eyes and lay flat on the floor, afraid to look anywhere for fear of seeing my father's ghost again. It felt like a betrayal of him, to dread. The cut on my cheek throbbed.

My mother appeared in the doorway to the bathroom, her robe billowing. "Can't sleep?" she asked, lifting me to a seated position. Her hands were cool, checking for temperature, a featherlight touch.

I wondered if I had lost my place with her. Could she forgive me for taking the notebook? She tilted my head to one side so that she could look at my left cheek. The wedding ring on her finger caught the light. As she traced the cut, her eyes searched mine, asking a question of her own: *Can you forgive me?*

"I'm sorry I took your notebook," I said. "I wanted to look at the pictures."

It was more than the pictures, though. To me, the notebook held the secret of who my father was, hidden somewhere in one of the photographs. I thought I knew who my father was, but I understood him less every day, when I should have understood him more.

She looked at her hands: slender with long fingers that tapered to points. I put mine next to hers, but our hands were not alike. Mine were darker, with hangnails and raw cuticles, scars from cuts and scratches acquired in the garden or from my bike, or even from before, when I played with José, always a little too rough.

"He took most of those photographs," she said. "That's why I kept them."

"For the yearbook?" I hadn't realized.

"Yes. Except for those that he was in. He used to love taking pictures."

"Why'd he stop?"

Her eyes grew unfocused. "He got bored with it. There were other things that he wanted to do more." She opened a drawer and found a brush, passing it through my hair. "You're so much like him," she said.

I was nothing like my father. Not in the way he looked, all freckled and blue-eyed. I'd asked him once where his family came from, but he said he didn't know. Something Scottish, he thought, maybe French, and for a while I dreamt there had been a mistake in heaven before I was born, that I was supposed to end up blond and blue-eyed but came out brown haired and forgettable.

My mother smiled at my disbelieving glare. "You're both stubborn."

Nighttime noises drifted in through the bathroom's open window: owls, crickets, a rustle of leaves and branches that betrayed a creeping cat or some other animal crawling in the garden.

"But you hated him," I said, no longer able to hold on to the ghost's insistence that my parents had been happy. I knew they had never been happy. I didn't want my mother to hate me too. I didn't want to be like my father, filled with bitterness even in death.

She pulled back, took my head between her hands, careful with the still-tender cut on my cheek.

"What makes you say that?" she asked.

"You ran away."

All this time, and I hadn't stopped to wonder why we had run away on that day. I knew my parents fought all the time, I knew there were problems between them, but all that had been there before. I didn't know what had changed. My mother had never said; I didn't know her side of the story.

Her eyes were dark. "Maybe sometimes I did hate him.

But it was the moments I loved him that hurt. If I had hated him, it would be easier."

She stood up. The doorway behind her was a dark, open maw. If my father's ghost lurked, he wasn't showing himself this time.

"I miss you, Mom."

She opened her arms, and I sighed as I fell against her.

"If we leave right now, Claude would never know," I said after several moments had passed. I didn't say that if we left right then, the ghost might not know either. That maybe we could escape both of them at the same time.

Her grip tightened, and I could hear her heart speed up. "And where would we go? With what?" She paused, and when she spoke again her voice had changed, becoming thin and frail. "You may love your father, Rosaura. You should love him, but there's so much you don't know."

Tell me! I wanted to say. *Tell me everything!* But instead I asked, "Do you love Claude?"

She sighed. I thought she meant to ignore my question and leave, but then she said, "Wait here."

The house creaked and shook. Wind spanked its sides. When she returned she carried a cardboard box. I sat on the toilet and she sat on the edge of the tub.

"This belonged to your father. I thought you might want it," she said, handing me the box.

It held an old camera, the kind with a lens that needed focusing. The back of it opened to reveal an empty slot ready for a fresh roll of film. I put the strap around my neck and lifted it up to see my mother through the viewer. I tried to focus on her face, but she sat too close and her nose and mouth and eyes all blurred together.

Part of the black plastic was chipped, and another part had

a crack that someone had tried to glue closed. Suddenly, the memory of my father's hands holding the camera unlocked in my mind. I remembered him taking my picture and taking my mother's picture, asking us to stand or sit close together while we smiled and looked at the camera and said "cheese."

The box also had a bag of film. She showed me how to thread it. I loved all the different manual parts, working together. I took my first picture of her sitting next to me, not caring that I couldn't get it all the way in focus and hadn't used a flash.

I took my mother's hand in mine. We sat together until she rose.

"You should go to bed," she said, and waited in the hallway until I stepped inside my bedroom. As she walked to the stairs, I took her picture.

IN THE DAYS THAT FOLLOWED, I took more pictures, thinking that perhaps I might make my own handmade bag covered in photographs. I took pictures of Claude and more of my mother despite having no way to develop them. Alex allowed for one picture, maybe two, before he would start refusing, and would not sit still or look at the camera or smile. He would not pose for me, so I had to catch him when he was least expecting it. I took pictures of him when he played his guitar, with his fingers pressing the strings against the frets.

When I ran out of film, Alex took the used film, developed it, and bought me more. I had been taking pictures anyway, clicking through shot after shot—without film I could take as many pictures as I wanted, over and over again, wondering how they would have turned out.

"Where did you get this?" I asked. I had planned on asking my mother if we could go buy more, but he beat me to it.

"Just take it. If you need more, tell me," he said, holding the camera-store bag.

I examined each photograph in the stack Alex returned to me, eager and curious to see what my camera and I had captured on film, but in every picture of my mother, she was wrapped in a shroud of smoke like ghostly arms, and I was afraid to look further.

A NEW CHILD SERVICES CASEWORKER came to the house to question us. This caseworker didn't have a special handbag. She didn't take my hand or promise to visit on my birthday.

During the interview, Claude and my mother and I sat together on the couch, presenting a unified front. Claude held my mother's hand, and I sat on her other side, with Alex standing behind. My mother let Claude do all the talking. If the caseworker asked her a direct question, she paused before answering, as if working hard to remember how the words might string together to make a sentence.

When the caseworker questioned me, I had nothing more to say. And although I saw no sign of the ghost, I was too afraid to speak for fear that the caseworker might get run over by a car, or some other horrible thing would happen to her.

"What about Mrs. Wilson?" I asked. I had my camera in my hand, wanting to take the caseworker's picture, but I was too shy to ask. Mrs. Wilson would have understood the need for a photograph. "When will she come and visit? Is she all right?"

But the caseworker didn't answer. Instead, she recommended therapy, maybe a family vacation. Her suggestions were met with smiles and nods from Claude before he showed her to the door with assurances that they would address the agency's concerns right away and that they looked forward to her next visit.

As soon as the caseworker left, my mother sagged with relief.

"You were great," said Claude, returning. "Everything is going to be okay. We're nearly out of it now."

"Are we?" she asked, giving him a piercing look. I thought she had sounded stiff and unwelcoming in front of the caseworker, but the woman hadn't seemed to care or take notice. Or maybe she had noticed and had written quiet observations on her clipboard to be filed in some office far away and forgotten. Her notes might say: *Stepfather smiles too much—keep an eye on that one. Mother a little slow, resentful. Unhappy? The son doesn't appear to speak. And the child in question is . . . fully dressed, at least.*

The next day, Claude bought my mother an etching. The artist was some long-dead person with the initials *CEF*. It wasn't very big. He hung it in the last remaining empty wall space, right over the cherrywood rolltop desk. It depicted a simple scene: a dilapidated wooden stairs, a dirty child sitting in mud, and the child's mother standing nearby, churning butter.

My mother's dark eyes were fixed on the lines of the etching, moving from top to bottom and then back up again, taking it in with arms crossed over her stomach and chest, hugging herself.

"It's an original," Claude said. "I thought, after everything that's happened recently, you deserved something special. Do you like it?"

It was like he had bought her a reward for running away from my father, for marrying him.

Studying the etching, she plucked a cigarette from an already-opened pack and lit it, taking a long inhale.

She opened her mouth to speak, to thank Claude, to say how much she loved it, to admire the artistry, the use of light, to say the things she was supposed to say. Instead, she began coughing and couldn't stop.

The etching was forgotten. When I glanced back at it, the glass reflected my father. I whipped my head around, but he was gone.

CHAPTER EIGHT

My birthday fell a couple of weeks before school started. "I'm older now," I said to Alex as he fixed bowls of cereal, one for himself, one for me. "Fourteen. An established teenager."

"What's that supposed to mean?" he asked around a mouthful of cornflakes.

What I wanted to say was that now he had to take me seriously. Now he could tell me things. Now we were alike, and I could be his friend instead of a weird stepsister. But I didn't know how to say that without sounding like a weird stepsister.

"You're still a kid," he said.

"So are you."

Claude entered the kitchen and saw the two of us sitting at the table. "The birthday girl," he said with a clap of his hands and a grin. "Ready for your big day? The birthday girl gets anything she wishes."

"We could go to the mall, I guess," I said.

Unperturbed by my apparent disinterest, Claude hollered for my mother to hurry up. In less than twenty minutes we were on our way.

The Mercedes purred like a sleek tomcat, ambling around street corners, creaking when it stopped at red lights. Claude drove at a sedate pace with the radio playing Top 40 hits. From the backseat, I could smell his cologne, which reached to all corners of the car and seemed to press me farther against the leather of my seat. It surprised me, how Claude managed to fit himself inside the car.

On the other side of the backseat, Alex retreated behind noise-canceling headphones, tapping the rhythm of the music out on his legs. I inched closer so I could put my hand next to his thigh, pretended to kick him by accident, but he ignored me as much as he ignored the rest of the world.

"Are you excited, Rosie?" asked Claude. He grinned through the rearview mirror. "New school, new friends. It all changes in high school, you know. That's where you get made. You'll be lining them up, sweetheart, and knocking them out."

Claude seemed oblivious to the cartoonish quality of his words. But maybe if we all playacted enough, the lies would disappear by some unnamed magic.

"Sure, can't wait. The more boys, the better."

"All right, make fun of me," said Claude. "But mark my words, you're going to have a great time in high school. I did."

His tone changed. My mother turned to look at him, her eyes hidden behind a new pair of diamond-studded sunglasses. Claude put his hand on her leg, squeezing. She turned back to the passing scenery. Alex kept nodding to his music.

The Mercedes lurched to a stop in the mall parking lot. Waves of heat rose from the black asphalt, radiating upward, making me squint. I was the first one out of the car, followed by Alex, whom Claude quickly pulled aside. He whispered something, and in the next moment Alex mumbled, "Yes, sir," with a nod. The headphones came off and were left on the backseat.

My mother was the last one out.

Before anyone could react, I grabbed Alex and started marching toward the mall entrance.

He tugged at my hand. "What's got into you?"

"It's my birthday," I answered. I couldn't tell if he was annoyed, but he hadn't let go, so I swung our hands back and forth. "They want me to be happy. I'm trying to be happy."

"Is it working?"

Behind us, Claude and my mother followed, her sunglasses glinting. Claude had taken her arm in his, like those couples from movies set in previous decades, strolling down a promenade. But they seemed stiff and awkward, and I wondered what my mother was thinking.

"Sometimes," I said.

We entered the air-conditioned bubble of the mall. Claude took us first to a furniture store and pointed out a new set of bedroom furniture: a canopied bed, a matching dresser and desk. There was also a small sofa and beanbag chairs, bookshelves, and a trunk to hold "memories." The entire set cost more than four thousand dollars. Each time Claude suggested another piece of furniture—an armoire, a princess chair, a trundle bed for sleepovers I'd probably never have—I sought my mother's disapproval; these were things I could not accept. But she stood mute.

"What do you say? Do you like what you see?" asked Claude.

"I don't need any of this," I said, yet I pressed my hands down onto the duvet. I wanted every pillow, every satiny sheet.

When I turned to Alex, he shrugged as if to say, *Why not? Don't fight it.*

"Tell you what," said Claude. "I'll have the store hold it for now. You think about it. If by the end of the day you haven't changed your mind, then that's that, okay?" Claude spoke with easy confidence, and although it appeared to be a question, it wasn't. He turned to speak to the salesman hovering nearby and whispered in his ear, handing the man an envelope. He finished by clapping the man on the back.

My mother pulled me over to one side. "Don't be stupid. Take it."

"I can't."

Memories of our apartment were plain on her face—the tiny rooms with small windows, the secondhand furniture, my bedroom with the mattress on the floor, and the plans she and my father shared while huddled together on the threadbare sofa. They would often share dreams of their own house, where my mother had a studio for drawing and my father could afford an entertainment center, a luxury car, a pool in the backyard. I would have a room with a bed that wasn't a mattress on the floor in the corner.

Next came the clothing. In the department store, Claude sought out the expensive labels, the overpriced dresses or designer jeans, all of it splendid, awesome, perfect. All of it the kind of clothes I envied on others.

"You want to look good for that first day," he said, dangling an outfit in front of my face; I had seen similar clothing in teen fashion magazines—the jacket and jeans, the pretty blue button-up blouse. It had cap sleeves and little eyelets in the fabric. He nodded toward the dressing room, waiting until I took the clothing and followed the store attendant. My mother came with me into the stall and we stared at each other until I stripped down to my underwear. She helped me into the shirt, held out the jeans. She buttoned buttons.

The clothing fit, but the labels taunted me. *Guess what?* I always wanted to ask when Sofie had worn her one Guess shirt that her grandmother bought at a consignment store. My father could never have afforded it. Two hundred dollars for the jeans alone.

I hadn't expected it to look so wonderful, for it to feel so right.

My mother fixed my collar, straightening the sleeves. She brushed hair from my face, smoothing the wild loose strands. "He doesn't have to buy you anything, you know."

"He thinks he owns you. You and me. Is this why you married him? Because he makes more money than Dad?"

She kept fixing the collar and smoothing down the folds of the blouse over my stomach. My hips flared outward like hers, no longer the straight-as-a-board silhouette of a little girl. Her lips thinned, and she shook her head. "No, it's not the money."

"It costs too much," I said, not meaning the clothing or the furniture. "Being with him; it costs too much."

"Whatever the cost, it's already been paid," she said. "You might as well accept it. This looks good. It's perfect, actually. I've never seen you look better. I'll go and tell him."

After a small pause at the door to the stall, she left. I stared at my reflection, trying to pose like one of those girls in the clothing catalogs—my hand on my hip as a photographer caught me in mid-laugh, always so happy and dressed to have fun. No matter how hard I tried to fake my laugh, I knew none of those girls ever looked like I did, with the jut of stubbornness set around my jaw, the dark glower in my eyes.

The buzz of the fluorescent lights grew stronger, then stopped. Dead silence. Bit by bit, my father's ghost formed—first the open wound, then the blood. I was careful not to move, afraid that if I leaned back even an inch I would feel his cold flesh. The mirror fogged and blurred, but then he came into sharp focus. The sad blue of his eyes matched the blue of my blouse.

This was the first time he had followed me outside the house. Had he come with us in the Mercedes? Could he follow me anywhere? He trapped me inside the dressing room. Each time I began to feel like I knew what to expect with the ghost, he changed the rules on me.

"Do you remember," he started, "how your mother hated going to work? She took forever to get out of bed in the mornings. I had to drag her, literally drag her, and she'd complain the whole way, 'I don't want to, I don't want to,' like a child. Worse than you, but you were always a good little girl. Even when you didn't want to be. Ready for school exactly when you should be. Anxious to be on time. 'Come on, Daddy. Come on, Mommy.' Do you remember?"

My breath came fast and shallow as I tried to swallow, but he didn't wait for my answer.

"I had to get the shower going for her. I had to make breakfast for all of us, and your lunch. Dahlia couldn't do any of it because it took her so goddamned long to get the hell out of bed. But I didn't mind; I didn't mind."

I put my hand against the mirror for support.

"She'd get so angry, already late, and then she had to take you to school. Do you remember? We used to fight about it, late at night when you were asleep so you couldn't hear. Sometimes, though, I knew you heard every word.

"But one day she quit her job because her boss made her cry. Or maybe they fired her—I can't remember. She came home, yelling at me even though she was the one who lost her job. How did she expect me to pay for everything? Did she care? The rent, the bills, they were all overdue. She started cooking, pulling out a newspaper, looking at want ads. Cooking and circling ads, right on the counter, next to the stove. She left the paper there, got distracted by something else, by you or me. I said to her, I said—"

"You're gonna kill us all one day." I spoke at the same time as the ghost, our voices matching harmony. Transported back in time into that kitchen, I tasted the thick, black smoke, and my eyes watered.

"God, you started choking, crying and choking, just a kid, no more than two or three. It felt like hot needles slowly inserting into my eyeballs—"

"Dad," I said, but whatever he was, he couldn't hear me.

"—straight to the back of my skull, twisting around and around. I had to fix it. Goddamn it, I had to shut you up—you were screaming. You're gonna kill us all one day—"

"Dad," I repeated.

"And she was yelling at me, and you were screaming your head off, and—"

He fell silent and our eyes met. I saw it there, finally, what he was trying to say, written in the depths of his endless stare.

I remembered: my mother's shocked cry of pain, her white face, and the way she fell back against the refrigerator. And the smoke in my throat as I screamed.

"You hit her," I said.

He shook his head, as if he wanted to get rid of a bug. Get it away, deny that it ever happened.

"You hit her," I said again, but it was harder to say a second time.

The ghost was crying now.

"No, I didn't, no, I didn't. It wasn't my fault," he said. "God, my hand was bleeding, blood everywhere," he whimpered. Then his voice turned hard. "We needed that money and she knew it. What did she think I was supposed to do? How was I supposed to play the game and work at the same time? I was out there, every day, trying to make our dreams come true, goddamn it; I couldn't take a fucking job. Only small-minded assholes take hourly jobs. The truth is she didn't want to work. She was lazy. It wasn't my fault. I bled so fucking much."

I realized what made the ghost appear at the mall—it was the clothing; it was the new bedroom furniture; it was the thinness of my mother's lips when she remembered why she left him.

"She forgave me," he said, but I knew he was trying to convince himself. I had to look at him again. "You saw the whole thing. Do you remember?"

"I remember," I said, and he disappeared.

I sank to my knees. My arms went over my head the way they taught you in school in case of an earthquake.

"Honey, you okay in there?" asked one of the salespeople.

I fumbled with the buttons of the blouse, tripping as

I kicked off the jeans. It took a moment to find my worn shorts and T-shirt, and then I was bursting from the stall as if I were escaping the swelter of hell, tumbling into the freshness and light of the open store.

My mother and Claude stood by the jewelry counter. When he saw me, he stopped talking to the saleswoman, a laugh caught on his face. His eyes went from me to the clothing in my hand. "Did it fit?"

"Such a lucky girl," said the saleswoman, her eyes lined with black, lipstick on her teeth. "Did you like that? There are other styles."

My mother brushed the hair from my face. I flinched.

Noticing that something was wrong, Claude stepped forward. He mumbled thanks to the saleswoman, dismissing her and bending down to my level.

His hand felt heavy on my shoulder. I wondered if the ghost had followed from the dressing room. Maybe he watched as Claude knelt down before me, offering comfort, offering to buy anything I wanted, everything I wished. I would accept the clothes and the furniture that Claude bought. And he would know that I did that. He would understand that I was taking Claude's money and that I wanted him to go away.

"I've been thinking," I said. "If you're still . . . If it's okay, I would like the bed. And the clothes."

Claude's face lit up. He smiled, not laughing or boastful for having won, and took the jeans and blouse from my hands. "That's great. After we finish here, how about we all go to the food court? And then afterward, ice cream."

"Can I change back into the clothes? Right now? I want to wear them right now."

"Okay, sure," said Claude, obviously confused but taking out his wallet to pay the sales attendant.

The pile of clothing included dresses, skirts, a few shirts and another pair of jeans, and more that I hadn't tried on. Underwear my mother said I needed. A new robe and pajamas. The sales attendant folded each article of clothing with her long nails clicking on the counter. She was taking too long, so I fished out the jeans and blouse as soon as she scanned them.

"You don't have to change into them now," said my mother.

"I want to."

"All right," she said. "I'll come with you."

Together, we started back for the dressing rooms, but then I stopped. "No," I said. "Not there."

"Rosaura, I don't understand," she said, beginning to get frustrated, but all I could do was shake my head. I wasn't going back into that dressing room.

Alex pointed somewhere outside of the store, into the atrium of the mall. "There's a bathroom over there," he said.

In the stark lighting, I started putting on the new clothes. My mother sighed but didn't say anything. Instead, she took hold of the tags on the jeans and jerked hard enough for the plastic to snap.

Women and children entered and left, sometimes staring at me or at my mother, her sunglasses still perched on her head, the diamonds a little ridiculous in the barrenness of the bathroom.

She took the shirt from my hands. I shivered in my bra.

"I'm sorry," I said as she snapped another tag off the shirt.

"What for?" she asked.

"I'm sorry." I said it again, not moving. "For Dad, for . . . everything."

She continued to hold the clothing, played with the buttons on the blouse, but her eyes were unfocused. "It's okay. No one blames you," she said. Then she turned to the sinks, as if there might be something for her to do there. "Do you need to use the bathroom? We better hurry; they're waiting."

I took the clothing from her. What had fit before now felt uncomfortable, either too loose or too tight.

When we emerged from the bathroom, there was a crowd gathered in front of the department store. Mall shoppers slowed down as they walked past; a few joined the crowd. Claude's shaggy head was in the center.

A woman stood in front of him, talking very fast, beginning to yell, her voice rising above the noise of mall music and the ever-constant thrum of shoppers.

I couldn't see Alex anywhere.

Claude held his hands out in front of him, trying to smile. "I'm afraid there must be some kind of misunderstanding," he said.

"There's no misunderstanding. I know who you are," she insisted.

"Lady, I don't know what you're talking about."

"You're Claude Fisk, aren't you?"

"Yes, but—"

"My name is Helena Myers. My husband is Raymond Myers. He came to see you a few months ago."

Claude reached into his back pocket and pulled out his wallet, tugging out a business card. "Here, take my card. Give me a call. I'm sure we can figure this out. But I'm here with my family."

"I've tried calling," she said, pushing his hand away. She would have been pretty except for the lines of exhaustion etched deep into her face, with her mismatched clothes and dark tangled hair pulled back into a ponytail. "I tried sending letters, but I don't get a response. I don't get anything."

The words were different. The people were different, but it was like a scene from my past, back when my father was alive. The memory came, sharp and clear, of my mother yelling like this, yelling at my father. "Why did you do it? Why can't we live like normal people? Just get away; just leave me alone. I can't do this anymore. Tell him you can't do it. Tell Claude you changed your mind."

I expected my mother to be upset, but she watched the scene with only a slight crease between her eyebrows, as if trying to place the woman in her memory. There was something familiar about the woman—in the shape of her eyes, in the roundness of her face—I couldn't place.

"Don't you walk away from me. You have to listen." She came after Claude, using her hands, using her body, and Claude stumbled as he tried to get out of her way. From off to the side, Alex appeared leading mall security. They bustled over and the crowd began to disperse. One security guard tried to lead the woman away, but she fought and dragged her heels until she saw Alex. Then she seemed to collapse.

"You won't get away with this, either of you. Stay away from her, stay away from us, leave me alone," she cried as they disappeared through a side door.

The other security guard came up to Claude along with a man dressed in a suit like a manager. They asked if Claude knew the woman, if he recognized her, if he'd done anything or seen anything that could have triggered such behavior.

"I've never seen her before. She clearly needs help," said Claude, passing a hand through his hair. "Thank God you came. I was beginning to fear she'd hurt herself."

We waited while the manager took Claude's name and number, asking more questions before thanking him. When they said he could go, Claude wasted no time ushering us out of the mall. There would be no visit to the food court, no ice cream for the birthday girl.

Inside the Mercedes, no one spoke.

When we arrived at the house, Claude didn't even get out of the car. "There's something I have to take care of," he said in the driveway.

My mother protested. "But what about—"

"I'll be back later." He cut her off, barely waiting for us to gather the shopping bags before he put the car in reverse and backed into the street.

Alex was the first to move. "Let's put these in your room," he said, taking my bags and waving them toward the door to get me walking.

Once inside, I headed to the kitchen for a drink and a snack, since I hadn't eaten anything, but Alex stopped me.

"First your room," he said.

Together, Alex and my mother herded me toward the stairs. "But I'm hungry," I said, not trusting their strange expectant smiles.

They stood in the hallway as I entered my room. The door had been left wide-open, and I stopped at the sight of the canopy bed fully assembled, veils billowing in the breeze from the open window.

"Surprise," said Alex. "It was done while we were out."

"But he just bought it," I said, the bed's presence sucking me in. The wood felt slick; the knob on the bedpost fit into my hand. It answered every wish I had when I was six, or nine, or twelve. Rapunzel, Rapunzel, let down your hair.

The matching dresser was there too. My clothing no longer lay stacked around the circumference of my room. Against one wall stood a small bookshelf for my magazines and books, and against the other wall beanbag chairs sat like fat Buddhas.

Alex leaned against the doorjamb. "Dad arranged it, a couple of weeks ago," he said.

A couple of weeks ago Mrs. Wilson fell down the stairs. A couple of weeks ago, we had Child Protective Services visiting.

The bed overflowed with perfection. Some other girl's flowered sheets, some other prisoner's ruffled cage. Claude had known I would refuse but had bought it anyway. The trip to the mall was just for show—I never had a choice. Not in the furniture for my own room, not in the clothes I would wear. He had known I would say yes, and I realized how lightly he had manipulated me, how I played into his hands. He did the same for my mother, even if it came in the shape of a diamond bracelet or an original art print framed and hung on the wall.

"Do you like it?" she asked, passing her hand over the smooth wood of the new dresser, and once again I remembered our old apartment. "Now you no longer have to have your clothing on the floor."

I hadn't thought she cared, but I guess she had. The top dresser drawer opened smoothly. I'd never had drawers that opened with such ease. Each drawer was packed with my missing T-shirts and shorts and underwear and socks.

"It's perfect," I said, even though I would have thrown

all of it out the window. But I had no more fight left, and I didn't want to disappoint her.

My mother leaned over and brushed her lips against my forehead. "Happy birthday," she said. "Be sure to thank Claude when you see him next."

She left, leaving Alex and me alone in the room.

"It's not so bad," said Alex, still leaning against the doorjamb, thumbs hooked into his front jeans pockets: the image of a young rock star on an album cover. "You get used to it. Dad always likes to have things done his way."

From Alex's tone, I couldn't tell if he believed what he said even if it was a lie or if he stated fact, inevitability. Was it a warning? Accept it or else. Either way, I had nothing to say.

"You can have my old stereo; that's my birthday gift to you. I'll bring it in and set it up. If that's okay."

He left without waiting for an answer, and I went to the bathroom to hide, leaving my new blouse and jeans crumpled on the floor. In the shower I sat on the floor of the tub and let water pound down my back, plaster my hair to my skull, and didn't leave until my skin felt scoured. Wobbly from the heat, I brushed my teeth, brushed my hair.

As promised, Alex had the stereo all set up and playing some punk album I recognized from my time spent in his room. He was sitting in a beanbag with his guitar across his lap, lost in the sea of ruffles and ribbons, strumming along with the music until I entered wrapped in my towel.

"Turn around," I said, not waiting for him to do so before dropping my towel to stand naked. Ignoring the new shopping bags on the floor, I pulled open a drawer and found an old T-shirt that fell to the tops of my thighs, and some underwear.

As I passed him, my nakedness once again covered, he

picked up the thread of his song and I climbed into that big bed so I could watch as he plucked the strings of his guitar.

"Who was that woman at the mall?" I asked.

He continued playing with his eyes focused on his fingers switching from one chord to another.

"It was weird. Like she knew him. Like she knew you. Have you seen her before?"

He paused, mid-pluck, resting his hand against the wood of his guitar, fingers tapping, pinky to thumb. "No," he said.

"What does he do, anyway? How come he always has so much money?"

"What does it matter?" He got up from the beanbag holding his guitar and came over to sit next to me on the bed.

"You're not answering my question," I said, turning to look at him.

"Here, take this. I'll teach you a chord." He handed me his guitar and guided my left hand to the fretboard near the top and forced my fingers where he wanted them. "This is C major."

He took my other hand and scraped across the strings. We strummed a couple of times. Then he forced my fingers into another position. "G major," he said.

"Why don't you want to talk about it?" I asked. The soft pads of my fingers began to hurt. "That woman was so angry."

"Stop thinking." He pressed my fingers even harder against the strings and the wood of the guitar. I tried to pull my hand away.

"But—"

Alex kissed me. The guitar banged against my knee.

Since first meeting Alex, I had wanted this, but for some

reason as he pressed against me I remembered a tattoo that José had on his upper arm. José and I used to make out in the laundry room of our apartment building, surrounded by the ticklish smell of detergent as the dryer clanged. On his upper arm he had a tattoo that his older brother made him get, of a skull with a bleeding heart in its mouth. Sometimes I kissed José's tattoo; I kissed the skull, right on its painted lips.

I held on to Alex's shoulders, wondering what tattoo Alex might choose to get. Would it be a different skull, one with flowers in its empty eye sockets or a rose in its mouth?

He pushed me down, lifting my shirt. His hands were cold, his breath soft and slippery.

Then his weight was ripped off me, and I gasped to see Claude shaking Alex between his big hands. He stood in the center of the room like a polar bear on hind legs, white and growling.

"What do you think you're doing?" Claude bellowed so loud I felt it in my teeth.

Tossed onto his back, Alex stood to face his father. Claude slapped him with the back of his hand. Alex's head snapped back, and I screamed.

"Jesus, fuck. Take it easy, Dad," said Alex, mumbling around a busted lip.

"What's wrong with you? She's just a kid." Claude had turned a color to match the pink frills in my bedroom.

Alex checked his jaw. He started laughing, wiping at his mouth. "Aren't I just a kid?" Alex asked. "Aren't my friends just kids? And Mrs. Myers, couldn't she be a kid herself? What about her daughter?"

Claude lunged at Alex and I screamed louder, but he didn't hit Alex again. He clamped his hand over Alex's mouth and dragged him from the room.

My mother came running but stopped when she saw Alex struggling against his father. She moved past them both, taking in my half-dressed state. I tugged my T-shirt down over my bare stomach.

"What did you do?" she asked, glancing back at Claude and behind him at Alex, who stood in the hallway, a hand covering his busted lip.

"Nothing, I swear," said Alex.

"Get out of here," yelled Claude, and then I heard Alex's bedroom door slam shut.

My mother pulled me toward her, but when Claude came back into the room, I retreated to the other side of the bed.

"Claude, leave," she said, her voice shrill.

She tried to get in front of him, but he ignored her. He grabbed hold of my shirt and dragged me across the bed.

"Leave her alone," cried my mother, pulling at his arm to get him to stop. "Don't you dare hurt her."

But he wasn't looking at her. "Are you okay? Did he hurt you?" He was strong enough to dangle me like a doll.

My breathing was rapid, my heart pounding so hard I felt lightheaded from too much oxygen or blood, panting like a rabbit in the grip of a bear claw, tense and watchful, waiting for when I needed to bite or kick.

Claude's eyes grew sad. "I didn't mean to scare you," he said. "Alex shouldn't have done that."

He let me go, and I slid down onto the plush softness of my new bed. My mother gathered me to her chest.

"Please leave," she said to Claude. "I'll talk to her."

Claude took a step toward my mother but stopped when she stiffened. He turned to leave, and I buried my face against her chest.

CHAPTER NINE

I wanted to walk down the hallway to Alex's room. I had wanted to go to him the previous night after Claude had left, but my mother wouldn't let me. He'd left his guitar and I wanted to give it back to him. She said I shouldn't allow Alex near me like that anymore, and she took his guitar with her when she said good night.

Morning light played across the canopy. I slid from my new bed and went to the stereo Alex had given me. The album he had left had a giant purple X on the cover, and the record was still on the turntable. It took a moment to figure out how to drop the needle, but once I did, I turned up the volume as loud as I could stand it. The lead singer was a woman and I liked that. I liked the way she sang, scratchy and loud.

Maybe the music would bring Alex to me, like a siren.

As the album played, I dumped the bags of new clothing on the floor in front of the bed, then turned to the dresser and emptied each drawer. Some of the clothing went in my new trunk, some of it I stacked in the bookshelf, and the rest I hung in the closet. The leftover possessions from my previous life—books, magazines, old stuffed animals—went into the dresser drawers. Mix and match, everything in a different place, everything in a weird place.

When I picked up my father's camera, I hesitated but then gave it a place of honor in the bottom drawer. It would be safe there.

With the big canopy bed taking up all the space, my room felt smaller. Before, the room had seemed like acres of space, more than enough for cartwheels. Now there existed a narrow, crooked path around the room.

A knock on my door made me jump. Before I could answer, Claude entered and walked over to the stereo, where he turned the volume down.

"You should know he's forbidden from entering your room," he said in the sudden silence, and although he wouldn't look at me, I felt the weight of his attention, the heaviness of his guilt.

"It wasn't him—"

He lifted a hand. "I don't want to hear it. You're a pretty girl, Rosie, and all the boys will be after you. That's fine; that's how it should be. If you want to throw yourself at them, follow some crazy idea you have that it's revenge against your mother, or me, nothing's going to stop you. Although I hope you'll be smarter than that. But not Alex, and not in my house. Got that?"

He narrowed his eyes for long sweaty moments, but his face softened as he glanced around the room. "I hope you like your birthday present."

I didn't say anything, and so he left. A few seconds later the house shuddered; Claude had gone to work. A crosswind lifted the fabric of the canopy up like white arms reaching forward.

It was a pretty bed. But with the bed came new rules. Forbidden from talking to me, forbidden from touching. Had Alex protested? Had he stood before his father, sullen but with that wonderful arrogance that meant he obeyed because he had no choice?

Alex came out of his room, and I ran to the door to see him. He stopped as he caught sight of me. If he had any bruises, they were hidden in the shadows of the hallway.

I waved, but the next moment my mother came down from the third floor and Alex crossed to the stairs and was gone.

She glanced at where Alex's presence lingered with the heat. "Leave him alone," she said.

"What if I don't want to?"

She sighed and held out her hand. "Please, Rosaura," she said. "This isn't a game. You're a child; you'll ruin your life if you're not careful."

I wanted to ask if she'd ruined her life but said nothing. With both Claude and Alex gone, my mother and I rattled around the house. I took my camera and went out into the garden, and I made her sit on the low brick wall that circled the fountain, taking her picture until she complained of the sun and the brightness and the heat. Toward the evening, she cooked dinner, and from the faint determination in her face, I knew she thought she had to, that Claude expected it. I remembered her many sketchbooks and how she used to draw with her colored pencils in the evenings in those in-between moments when my father's attention went elsewhere and I went to José's and left her alone. But she didn't draw in the evenings anymore.

Alex returned moments before dinner. He sat down in the seat next to mine and ate everything on his plate, pausing only to take big gulping swallows of water. He didn't look at me; he didn't look at anyone. When he finished, ahead of the rest of us, he asked to be excused. Claude was slow to nod, but as soon as he did, Alex disappeared up the stairs and into his room. So I asked to be excused, then disappeared into my room, too, listening until I heard Alex moving through the hallway and into the bathroom. Then I went into the hallway and pressed my ear against the bathroom door, listening when the toilet flushed and hearing the protesting pipes when he started a shower. I imagined him naked in the shower, with cascading water all around.

When I heard him approaching the bathroom door, I scrambled back to my room to lie on my new bed, staring at the overhead fabric and the shadows it created, remembering the shock of his hand on my stomach. I thought I heard footsteps outside my door, imagining that he listened for my movements as I had listened for his.

He was going to follow the new rules. He was going to avoid me, no matter that he was the one who had kissed me. I wanted to get up, walk down the hallway, and push his door open, hard, so that it banged against the wall. But as soon as I decided to get up, Alex entered my room, holding a now familiar bag from the camera store. He dropped the bag on my bed, right next to my hand. He paused, and my skin blossomed with goose bumps. I moved my leg, then my arm, but he left, closing the door behind him.

CLAUDE GAVE ALEX AND ME a ride my first day of school. "I'll pick you both up. Wait for me."

"Yes, sir." I saluted, but it only made him grin.

"Don't be a smart aleck." He grabbed my backpack, holding me back. "Before you go, Rosie, I want to say something."

I waited, one leg out of the car. Alex had bolted the moment Claude shifted into park, sprinting across the parking lot.

"You'll do fine," he said.

It galled that he thought I needed reassuring. "Not afraid I'll run naked through the football field?"

He smiled again, although it didn't reach his eyes. From his pocket he took out a business card. "If you need anything, that has my office number."

I refrained from reminding him that he had made me memorize his cell number. I wanted to refuse the card, but I stuffed it into a pocket in my bag.

"Go on, get out of here," he said, waving me out of the car. "Go before you're late."

The air was still, the sky a solid, unchanging ceiling of blue. I turned to face Canyon High School, which consisted of several low, flat buildings that took up the entire block. It was nothing like my previous school, which made it easier to march into the building.

Alex waited on the steps. "Do you know how to find your first class? Where to go?"

"I can figure everything out on my own."

Students zigzagged past, pushing me closer to Alex. "If you need me," he said, already walking away.

"I won't," I said, even though I did need him, want him.

The first warning bell rang and he was gone, swallowed by the crowd of students and backpacks and teachers.

A big white sign with green lettering swung over a couple of tables set up in front of the building: "Welcome, Freshmen." I got into the right line for my last name. A woman with a stuck-on name tag that read "Mrs. Chung" handed me my schedule.

"There's a map right here," she said, pointing to one of the sheets of paper she had given me.

The second bell rang, but I still hadn't found my class. It was in a building across from the main courtyard, at the end of a hallway. When I got there, the classroom door was shut. I knew my mistake as soon as I pushed the door open. The room fell silent, and the students turned en masse to look at the new intruder. No freshmen, no friendly homeroom, only a rotund chemistry teacher scribbling equations on the blackboard.

"Sorry," I said, backing out and shutting the door.

"Wait," said a soft voice, and I turned to see a familiar girl get up from her front-row desk. It was Tina, the girl whom Alex had brought to his room, the girl who'd picked him up in the VW Bug.

"Are you lost?" she asked. The teacher didn't stop writing on the blackboard, and the rest of the class returned to their notes.

She didn't wait for my answer but stepped outside the classroom, holding the door open with a foot, and took the schedule from my hand. Glossy lips, hair braided down one side; her eyes were ringed with makeup. I wanted to take her picture. Maybe I could discover her secrets if I had her picture.

"Mrs. Lombard. She's just over there." She pointed down the hallway. "First classroom on the right."

I took the schedule back and mumbled my thanks.

When I located the correct classroom, I found disorder. Conversation crescendoed as I entered, with students milling around a pile of magazines left on a couple of the desks at the front of the room. It took a moment to find the teacher, who was stuck in the middle of the fray.

"Oh yes," she said. "I'll mark you as present, but be sure to be on time tomorrow or I will have to mark you tardy. Three marks and you drop one letter grade. Go ahead and grab a few magazines. Your assignment is written on the board."

She handed me a used social studies textbook. The assignment was to use modern-day cultural images to create a visual essay, a collage. It was due in one week. Pick a theme and tell a story. It could even be "What I Did on My Summer Vacation."

All the good magazines like *Vogue, Glamour,* and *People* were taken by the time I picked a desk and set my bag down, leaving several *Highlights for Children* and a few *Time* and *Newsweek* issues. Without caring, I grabbed whatever I could and went back to my desk.

My new classmates laughed and talked with easy familiarity. They all knew one another already. The *Highlights* magazines were old, with their covers dangling by loosened staples. I flipped through one of them, stopping when I found the *Goofus and Gallant* cartoon. They made me think of Alex, but was he Goofus or Gallant?

THE FRONT OF THE SCHOOL faced a line of rocky hills, left barren and undeveloped. Near the entrance, I sat on the hot cement curb, waiting for Claude to pick me up. My book bag slumped on the ground, full of the textbooks I'd collected throughout the day.

To pass the time, I took out one of the *Highlights*. Not far away, Tina also waited, leaning on the chain-link fence that circled the campus. She kept searching the street, shifting weight from one foot to the other. I had my camera and took her picture but from such a distance I lost the details of her face, her freckles, the braid in her hair.

The camera clicked loud enough for her to hear. I hid it and tried to look like I hadn't been staring. After a moment, she walked over. "Hey," she said. "How's it going?"

I had to squint to look up at her. She moved to block the sun, then sat next to me on the curb. I shrugged, not knowing what to say. "I found all the rest of my classes," I said.

She smiled, moving closer so she could read the *Highlights* with me. "I remember these," she said, tracing the *Goofus and Gallant* cartoon.

I wanted to say they weren't mine, I didn't read kids' magazines or anything, but the familiar VW Bug spun around a corner, screeching to a halt, the sound of music and laughter braided together.

Alex sat in the passenger seat. He opened the car door, walking over with a secret smile that made him that much more a rock star. It was the ease with which he lifted his chin to say hi, the smooth way he waved at some other kid who called his name, not important enough for Alex to fully acknowledge. These things made him different from the boy who slept in the room down the hall from my room, who liked only to listen to music, always so silent and withdrawn.

"Tina," he said, calling to her as he walked over.

The smile on Tina's face slipped away, as if the heat radiating up from the asphalt had melted all the animation in her eyes and lips. "I was waiting for you."

Alex shrugged. "I'm here," he said, glancing in my direction.

"Come on," said a black girl from the driver's side, impatient. She had a wide smile and breasts that spilled out of her halter top as she wormed halfway out the window. The radio blared. "Both of you, let's go."

It could have been a moment taken out of a movie or an after-school television special. I drank it in, transfixed by this picture of the idyllic high school scene, watching Alex—the face I knew, the hands that had touched me—interact with others, with these strangers who claimed him as their own.

"See you later," Tina said before climbing into the front seat. Alex bent toward me, and for one wild moment, I thought he was going to kiss me, but he whispered in my ear, "Tell him I'll be home before dinner."

Then he got in the car, and I heard someone say, "Let's get out of here." The car rocked down the street, disappearing with another near-capsizing turn around the corner.

The *Highlights* had fallen facedown. A moment later, the Mercedes purred its way up the street. It must have passed the VW Bug on its way up the hill. It did a slow three-point-turn before coming to a halt right in front of me.

I stayed seated on the curb.

Claude leaned over and opened the door. He didn't raise his voice or yell, but it still came out a command. "Let's go."

Funny how he sounded similar to the other girl who'd said the exact same words. My legs obeyed before I could stop them. I sank into the front seat and stuck my tongue out, but it only made him smile.

"Is Alex coming?"

I shrugged, reluctant to relay Alex's message. Claude sighed and put the car in gear.

I DOZED WHILE LOOKING AT magazines, those that I'd gotten from Mrs. Lombard plus the ones I already owned and a few more that my mother had. They lay scattered over the bed. The light outside dipped into that dusky blue of evening, with the music of crickets outside my window and the flapping of the canopy tickling my bare legs.

Formed from dust and light, my father's ghost appeared at the end of my bed, crossed-legged like a genie.

"No," I said, shaking my head. "No more. Not again." I kicked the mattress with both my legs, making the magazines bounce, making the bedsheets bounce. After his last visit, what more could he possibly have left to say? "Get out, get out," I said in a whispered cry that no one could hear.

But he didn't say a word. He held a magazine in his hands and started looking through it, one page at a time, as if he were a patient in a waiting room. He turned pages faster and faster, too fast to be reading them.

He tossed the magazine aside, angry that it hadn't contained what he wanted, and picked up another one, looking through that one just as quickly. Then he stopped and raised it so I could see. "This one," he said.

It was an advertisement for jewelry—diamonds. A woman stood, mostly unclothed, the lines of her body blurred and indistinct as she faced a window. Her back was to the camera, but her face was turned in profile to reveal her expression of restful longing. Behind her, a man, fully clothed but with his face hidden, stood, fastening a diamond necklace around her neck.

"I don't care." My tone became sullen, but my heart beat hard and my blood was ice in my veins. "Whatever it is you're trying to say, I don't care."

The house creaked and shifted, settling into evening. The ghost stopped, cocked his head, then continued at the same agitated pace.

I tried to leave, but he picked up another magazine and did the same thing, turning pages fast before finding, at last, what he was looking for. He held the magazine up so I could see. This time it was a cartoon—a line drawing, meant to be humorous and relevant to some political statement, but all I could see was that it showed a man lying on the ground with a shocked yet comical expression on his face and a knife sticking out of his chest, illustrated blood dripping over the side of the wound. "This one," said the ghost, and he pointed at the drawing, directly over the wound.

Again he continued riffling through the magazine.

He held up a third picture, but I didn't want to see it. I wanted to bury my head under the duvet till the ghost left to go someplace where he could molest as many magazines as he wanted on his own without me as witness.

"This one," he said, holding the picture up in front of my face until I had to look. It was a full-page close-up of a man screaming, his eyes scrunched shut, his mouth open and stuffed with hundred-dollar bills that were choking him. It was the sort of picture that accompanied a lengthy and in-depth journalistic article, with quotations highlighted in large bold letters, telling the woeful tale of someone else's misfortune. "This one," repeated the ghost, holding the magazine too close to my face.

The light faded to a thick, layered haze. My mother said

my name and I jumped, surprised to see her standing in the doorway. Her eyes were brilliant and shadowed, wide with panic, but then she focused on me. "Claude should be home soon," she said, one hand on the doorknob. "Help me with dinner."

The ghost was gone, a tumbled pile of magazines left on the bed.

All through dinner, I thought of the collage. I thought of those photographs the ghost had chosen, and what I would do, so preoccupied I forgot to wonder where Alex was until he came home just as my mother got up from the table to start clearing dishes.

Silence descended. I thought Alex would bolt up to his room, but he stood there while his father eyed him up and down.

My mother picked up Claude's dish and her own. She said my name with a nod at the table, and I knew I had to help her instead of sitting in the middle between Claude and Alex and whatever confrontation they were going to have. I got up and took my plate into the kitchen, but as soon as I put the plate down on the counter I pushed the door open enough so that I could see and hear.

Claude sat back with his right arm laid across the seat next to him. "You missed dinner."

Alex moved a step closer to the stairs and his escape. "Just doing what you asked." He met his father's gaze. "That *is* what you wanted," he said.

Not quite a question, more of a challenge. For the first time I saw a resemblance between the two of them.

Claude opened his mouth to answer but shut it again. With a sigh and a nod, he waved his hand in dismissal, allowing Alex to disappear up the stairs.

I didn't know what it meant, this strange tide and under-tow of their father-and-son relationship. I thought, if Alex had his way, he would never leave his bedroom. Or maybe one day he wouldn't come home at all.

My mother pulled me away from the door and over to the sink, where the dirty dishes were piled. "It's not polite to eavesdrop."

It took a few minutes before Alex's music drifted down from the second floor. He chose a violin concerto, its harrowing voice spiraling down through the sticky night air. I didn't know who the composer was. The music induced an ache deep in my belly of unfulfilled want, of desperation.

Claude entered the kitchen, causing both my mother and me to pause. He carried the rest of the dinner things, and without further words, the three of us finished washing the dishes while the violin continued.

I brought the magazines down to the living room and camped out on the carpet. With tape and a cut-up cardboard box, I created scenes in a play: my father handing Claude his money and a gun. My mother, diamonds, escape. Alex and me and a garden. I cut out the three pictures the ghost had given me and used them like centerpieces. I used my own photographs as well as those cut from magazines.

Sometimes Alex was Goofus; sometimes he was Gallant.

"What've you got there?" asked Claude. He was sitting on the couch, working on his own projects, his own array of papers, folders, and books.

"Something for school," I said, angling my body away from him so he couldn't see what I was working on.

But he got up off the couch and came around to watch while I worked. There were three panels to the collage, like a medieval painting: heaven, limbo, hell. Claude's blue eyes lingered over the scene of my father's death. Maybe he held his breath, maybe he became very still, very quiet, but maybe it was my imagination. He murmured that it was very creative but went back to his paperwork.

CHAPTER TEN

Claude didn't ask to see the final product. As he drove me to school, he didn't look at me at all.

In class, my heart buzzed with the anticipation of revealing so much to the world. But when the different collages were set up side by side, mine blended in with the rest and no one said anything.

After praising the entire class, Mrs. Lombard made us carry the collages across the courtyard so they could be pinned up on bulletin boards in the main building. Students leaving the other classrooms when the bell rang walked past, talking and laughing without looking at the collages. Perhaps they had the same assignment as freshmen and didn't care.

But I liked my collage, and after classes ended for the day I went back to look at it, not caring that Claude would have to wait. A couple of teachers, a man and a woman, took their time examining each collage like they were pieces hanging in a museum.

I held my breath as the female teacher reached my collage.

"Looks like a story," she said, and spent several minutes staring at it. She lifted her glasses. "It starts here," she said, pointing to the gun. "Or maybe it starts here." She pointed to pictures of big houses pieced together.

The man joined her. He shook his head. "That's too violent," he said. "Guns and death. It doesn't belong in a school. This is the sort of thing we all have to watch out for. Flora should have said something."

"Well, I suppose," said the woman. "No, you're right." She didn't protest when he took down my collage. I stepped forward, but a hand clamped around my arm. Alex was standing next to me.

I wondered how long he had been there and if he had seen the collage. Could he tell who the characters were? Could he see what I had done?

"If you demand it back, they might send another social worker," he said. "Make a different collage. Talk to Mrs. Lombard in the morning."

I twisted my lips. But I knew he was right.

That night, I made another collage using pictures cut from *Highlights for Children,* a photo story of Goofus causing mischief with a smirk.

When Alex was in the bathroom, I went into his room and placed the new collage on his bed. I wanted him to see it. I wanted him to know that the boy in the collage was him. He never said anything, but the next morning I found the collage back in my room, left right in the middle of the floor, in front of the canopy bed.

I gave the new collage to Mrs. Lombard and said it was my stepbrother's idea to put the pictures of the gun in the first one. I asked for it back. She said she'd talk to Mr. Bucholtz, but I knew I wouldn't see it again.

ALEX DIDN'T PARTICIPATE IN THE Key Club or the marching band. He was everyone's friend and no one's. He slipped through each day like water through my fingers, held for a moment. I wanted to find his secret, to crack his code, dissect his insides for inspection. But all I could do was take his picture.

At school, I sat on a slick picnic table, shivering in the sudden October dampness, cross-legged. I took pictures of students when they weren't looking. Through my camera lens, I tracked Alex as he picked a spot to sit and eat his lunch. A tall kid with headphones joined him. They listened to music together. Another boy with jeans and a baseball cap slapped Alex's hand in a complicated series of snaps and fist bumps. The members of the football team sat nearby. They teased Alex, called him "Cobain," which made him scowl. They shook his hand, clapped him on the back. Soon he had a crowd around him.

Tina sat with Alex and then looked up to see me. She ventured over the ground littered with sodden leaves like a brave wanderer through foreign lands.

"Can I ask you something?" She stood in front of me, her nose a delicate shade of pink from the cold. Seaweed eyes, foam-white skin. She had a ribbon in her hair that fluttered into her eyes.

"Sure. Can I take your picture?" I asked in return.

"Okay," she said, surprised, but stayed still, a slow smile spreading across her lips.

"Look over there." I pointed to where Alex sat in the

melee of lunch. The wind struggled to catch her hair, strands threading across her face. "Tell me what you see."

"Lunchtime. Chaos. Rain."

She was a hidden poet. I snapped a picture. "What else?"

I caught her in the target of the lens, focusing on the freckles that tripped across her nose. "Why are you always taking pictures?"

"Because I want to." *Snap.*

"I've asked Alex about you."

When she said his name there was a catch in her breath, a dip in her sparkle. It was strange to think of Alex talking about me when I wasn't there. "What has he said?"

"Nothing." Tina tilted her head in an unconscious mimic of Alex.

I lowered my camera. She brushed her hair away from her face. I wanted to hate her, but I liked that she'd painted her nails with pale, frosted glitter, and I liked the way she kept trying to get the hair out of her eyes.

"Are you guys going out?" I asked, trying to keep my jealousy from my voice, trusting my camera to hide my resentment. Focus on the longing, on the splash of pain in the raindrops falling on her face. *Click.* I wondered if she was talking to me because she thought it might get her closer to Alex.

She wrinkled her nose and lowered her eyes. Alex watched us, standing tall in the whirlwind of students. I took her picture again. End of roll.

"It's all right," I said. "You can tell me. Alex and I tell each other everything." My ears grew hot from the bold-faced lie, but I wanted to reclaim my hold on Alex from her, even though I never had any sort of hold on him to begin with.

"I know about his mother," she said, her voice weak against the strength of the cold.

My hands stopped halfway through rewinding the film, forgetting that she hadn't answered my question. "What about his mother?"

"You don't know?" She lifted her chin, upturned nose pointing to the sky. "She wasn't married to Alex's father. I don't think he even knew he had a son until she showed up one day and left Alex with him."

I held my breath, wondering how I had missed this key fact, but there was so much that was never spoken of, so much kept hidden. "I've seen her picture, his mother's. He looks like her. Does he visit her?"

"I don't think so. I don't think they've seen each other since she left. He doesn't talk about her." Her gaze shifted with curious sea-green intensity.

"Yeah. I noticed. How long have you known him?"

"We were all in preschool together." She licked her lips and took a quick, short breath. "When he first showed up, he cried every day. Quiet-like, in his chair. He wouldn't do any of the work; he wouldn't play. A few of the boys made fun of him, but he just kept crying. He let them tease him. They got rough, pushed Alex around, and still he did nothing. He let them hit him. It was so weird. I tried to stop them. One of them pushed me down and I fell to the floor. I wasn't hurt, but Alex took hold of Tom's shirt and threw him onto the floor so hard he broke Tom's arm."

"What happened after that?" I asked, mesmerized by the story and her distant, searching expression.

"All our parents had to meet, and Alex had to see a doctor. They almost sent him away after that. Everyone was half scared of him, and at the same time they wanted to be his friend. They still do. That was the first time my parents met Alex's dad." She added the last almost as an afterthought, wrinkling her forehead.

Behind Tina, Alex was moving toward us. When she saw Alex approach, all her feelings, her emotions, blossomed, more open than the sky above, ready for plucking.

He held his hand out. Tina smiled, radiant. They walked away and left me shivering.

THAT WEEKEND, WHILE I WAS out for a bike ride, it began to rain. I pedaled home as fast as I could, wiping the raindrops from my face, dumping my bike outside and running up the stairs when I heard the front door open and close without the bustle and bang that accompanied Claude's typical entrance. I knew it had to be Alex. He stopped in the downstairs hallway, and I heard the tone of an open phone line. A moment passed, and then several more, before he put the receiver back.

"Who do you keep trying to call?" I asked.

He spun around, blond hair darkened by rain, skin flushed red from the coolness of the weather. He stepped forward, and I saw the way his eyelashes clumped together. "A phone-sex line," he said, deadpan.

I laughed but blocked his path when he tried to scoot past. "Can I come up to your room? Borrow some records?"

"I don't think that's a good idea."

"Why not? There's no one here but us."

Claude had taken my mother with him that morning. He did that every once in a while, disappeared with her for the day, only to return in the evening with a shopping bag or two. It had been weeks since that night when Claude had caught Alex in my room, and slowly the new rules were being forgotten.

"Maybe your girlfriend's coming over. What's her name again? Was she who you were trying to call?" I asked, even though I knew her name and knew that he hadn't been trying to call Tina and that he wouldn't say whom he had tried to call no matter how I asked.

He leaned against the wall of the staircase. "What if it was?"

Frustrated, I let out an exaggerated sigh and stomped up the stairs. "Just say you don't want to hang out with me."

He called after me. "I didn't say that."

I stopped near the top of the stairs but then continued on to my room, shutting the door. It wasn't until later, when I left my room to come down to dinner, that I found a stack of albums in front of my door.

THE MEAL WAS ONE MY mother cooked often because it was easy: chicken baked in rice. It used to be one of my favorites, but even though it tasted the same, it now got stuck in my throat and made me gag. The familiar taste brought memories of eating with my father at the kitchen table in our apartment. I pushed my plate away and drank all of my water.

Alex sat across from me. He took a big breath, as if gathering strength for an arduous task, and said, "There's a football game tomorrow. Against Newhall." He spoke to no one in particular.

Claude leaned back in his chair. He finished chewing before speaking, his tone casual. "Sounds like a great idea," he said. "We should all go. You'd like that, wouldn't you, Rosie?"

I looked from Claude to Alex to my mother. My mother wasn't eating either. She fiddled with a piece of chicken before setting her fork down. She got up and started clearing the table.

"I'd like to go," I said, because I did want to. I had never gone to a football game before. Claude smiled, but Alex didn't. It was strange. Although Alex was the one who brought up the football game, I got the impression that he had no desire to go, that he suggested it because he had to, an obligation or a duty.

Claude sat back and winked at me. "That settles it. We'll all go."

My mother came back into the dining room from the kitchen. "You have fun," she said, as she took my plate and Claude's.

"No," said Claude. He took the plates from her hands and set them down, kissed her cheek. "We all go together. You're going too."

I looked to see Alex's reaction, but he had retreated behind his usual mask of cool disdain. He nodded to his father, turning to run up the stairs, and a moment later I heard the door close and his music begin.

My mother tried to smile and went back to clearing the table. Claude squeezed my shoulder, and I was struck by an urge to give him a hug and let him hug me back. To hide the heat in my cheeks—from horror, from embarrassment—I went into the kitchen to help my mother with the dishes.

By the next day, I began to regret saying I wanted to go to the game. It took place in the evening and didn't start till seven P.M. Alex wanted to meet us there.

"You'll come with us," Claude told Alex, who had become a living statue, like one of those street performers who stood so still you wondered if they were mechanical rather than living flesh and bone.

My mother made us late. She had chosen a dress with a noisy print of big tropical flowers. It swished around her legs. I remembered the dress; she'd worn it a few times with my father, on those rare evenings when they'd left me alone to go together for dinner or to some event. But when she came downstairs, Claude halted, and his brow creased when he tried to hide his cringe. She blushed, then went back up the stairs and changed into a blouse and slacks, returning clutching a designer handbag of brown leather. Her hair fell in easy waves of honey, a woven shawl wrapped around her shoulders. This apparently met with Claude's approval. He smiled at her, but she hesitated before smiling back.

Once we arrived at the high school, parked, and made our way through to the football field, I began to feel better. The air was fresh and crisp. It had drizzled earlier, but the sky was a dark inky blue with the requisite smattering of pale stars. The crowd buzzed, alive, pulsing with energy. This was what high school was about, with the added scent of cotton candy and roasted peanuts. The four of us sat in the bleachers, halfway up on the home-team side. Claude busied himself getting refreshments and a large bag of popcorn. We chewed our popcorn and sipped our drinks, Claude a beer, the rest of us soda. My drink was so cold my hand hurt to hold it, but I sucked it up until my head throbbed and my chest felt tight because of the gas bubbles. The game started with announcements before the teams ran onto the field. They slapped one another's hands, falling into their first formation. I knew nothing about football.

A few minutes into the game, Alex sat up straight in his seat. He reached across and touched Claude's arm. Claude followed Alex's gaze. They were looking at a group of adults, two couples, as well as a few teenagers I recognized from school, standing at ground level in the walkway meant for foot traffic.

Claude swallowed the rest of his beer. "All right," he said, setting his cup down.

Next to me, Alex held his breath and sank into his seat like he wanted to slide off and down between the slats of the bleachers. There was a closed-off, dark expression on his face, and then a brief flash of disgust before he sprang up and made his way down the steps.

Claude grabbed a fistful of popcorn while my mother watched a young couple and their little daughter. The girl was maybe two years old, trying to climb up the stairs of the bleachers by herself. She kept falling. Oopsy-daisy. One small leg slipped, but her mother held her hand and let the child dangle until she found her feet again.

"Where's Alex going?" I asked, picking up my camera and searching through the viewer for a good picture. The football field, the lights, the crowds. *Click*.

Claude turned and held out a kernel of popcorn, opened his mouth to indicate I should do the same. I copied him, and he tossed the kernel into my mouth. Grinning, he did it again. "He's talking to some friends of his," he said, holding another kernel. I opened my mouth again, with one eye out for a familiar blond head.

Alex was leaning in close to the two teenagers, who went to our school. One of them turned to another adult, an older man who must be his father. They introduced Alex. Alex shook the father's hand. He leaned in close again to be heard. He looked back at Claude as he spoke, waving at us. The man waved too.

That was Claude's cue. He got up. "I'll be right back," he told my mother, then took the stairs two at a time, joining Alex and his friends.

I watched everyone shake hands. Introduce themselves. Laughing. More leaning in; then business cards were passed around. More talking. At one point, Claude cupped his hands around his mouth and called for my mother. His voice carried over the noise of the crowd; she wasn't paying attention, still looking at the small family with the two-year-old daughter, but her eyes were unfocused and she wasn't seeing them anymore. I nudged her.

"Claude wants you." I pointed to where Claude stood talking to the parents of Alex's friends while still trying to get my mother's attention. The father had graying hair and deep-set raccoon-ringed eyes.

My mother sat up straight and watched Claude, who waved at her again, flicking his fingers in the universal sign for *Come here*. She hesitated, her eyes moving as she saw whom Claude was with: the gray-haired man, his wife, and the other couple, the teenage children. She shifted to the edge of her seat, paused, then said, "I'd better go."

Claude met her at the base of the stairs, put his arm around her, guiding her to where the others were milling around. He introduced her. Several rows up, I heard him say, "This is my wife."

Apparently I wasn't required to shake hands or receive pats on the head. I picked up the half-empty bag of popcorn, but it had become cold, chewy, and greasy.

I couldn't help but notice that the dress my mother had started out in would have been inappropriate. Next to the other wives, she looked pretty and stylish, younger than they were, but these women were open with her, willing to include her as one of their own. One put a hand over my mother's and leaned in close to say something funny. My mother was stiff at first but loosened up as she returned with a joke, and the women laughed. Claude beamed. I had never seen her like this before: belonging, at ease with others, making friends.

Alex was no longer there. He had slipped away.

The game continued, and I wondered what was the point of going if people stood around and talked instead of watching. Someone made a touchdown and the Canyon High cheerleaders did flips and cartwheels and split jumps. Canyon High wore green and white and gold. Newhall wore black and red. I liked watching the team huddles, with everyone's arms around one another, sharing secrets that might win the game. The team burst apart with friendly slaps, ready to fight; then the football twirled in the air in its giant, majestic arc, caught in the cradling arms of its savior.

Near bursting after drinking my soda, I left the stands to go find a bathroom. Daunted by the long line, I decided to go farther onto the campus, where there might be fewer people. The school was a different place at night, with strange shadows that moved with the wind. I went all the way across to the far end of campus.

Alex was leaning against a graffitied cinder-block wall where the Dumpsters were kept, talking to a boy I recognized from that time in Alex's room. I was too far away to hear what they were saying, but whatever it was, Alex didn't seem interested. The boy was agitated, gesturing with his hands, and then he stopped. He looked Alex up and down and said something real quiet-like, a curse, a swearword. Alex shook his head, said something that appeared to satisfy the boy. They spoke for another moment before Alex shook his head again, and the other boy stood there a second before slouching away.

I took the boy's picture as he shuffled across to the far chain-link fence that marked the border of the campus. He hopped over the fence and then shuffled down the street to where a big, boat-like station wagon was parked.

"Take good pictures?" asked a warm, low voice. Alex sounded annoyed.

In answer, I raised my camera and took his picture. He blinked from the flash.

"I have to pee," I said.

Alex took the camera from my hands, lifting the strap from around my neck. He fingered the back of the camera. "You should ask permission first."

"I never have before."

For a moment I thought he would open the casing and expose the film, but he returned the strap to my neck, placing the weight of the camera against my chest. "When you get these developed, I'd like to see them."

He had never asked to see my pictures before. It was against the new unspoken rules. Even though I wanted to be mad at him, I smiled.

He waited while I found the bathroom.

When we returned to the game, Claude and my mother were still talking to the gray-haired man and his wife. I wondered if this was how it had happened with my father, with Claude shaking his hand and laughing at a shared joke.

CHAPTER ELEVEN

The prescription drugs came in the same kind of plastic bag as my photographs: store logo on the front with cutouts at the top as handles. My mother left them on the dining table next to her purse—I thought she had brought home my latest developed roll of film, but instead I found a white paper package with her name on it. The bag tore when I opened it, and an amber vial fell into my hand.

"What are these for?" I asked.

She took the bottle before I could read the drug's name. The pills rattled when she thrust them into her purse, fumbling enough that she dropped her keys. Then her sunglasses fell from the top of her head and she had to pick those up too. "Something to help with my headaches. It probably won't work. I don't know why I bothered."

She went upstairs, and I didn't see her for the rest of the day. I didn't see her the next day either. A week after the football game, she finally came down to make a dinner of

pasta and homemade sauce, but she overcooked the tomatoes and left the spaghetti too long on the stove.

"It's all right," said Claude when she turned away, one
hand covering her face, the diamond ring on her finger
trembling. "We'll get takeout."

Claude talked to my mother in quiet murmurs, inching
closer until she let him put a hand on her shoulder. "Why
don't you go upstairs? Let me take care of it. I'll bring up
some food for you. Go and get some rest."

Her face was white when she passed me in the hallway.

In the kitchen, Claude was rummaging in a drawer. He
pulled out a stack of menus and fanned them out like playing cards. "What'll it be, Rosie?"

I picked one from the middle of the pack: Chinese food.

"My favorite," said Claude. "Why don't you call? Order
whatever you like, enough for all of us."

I took the menu but stayed to watch Claude pick up the
saucepan. He looked at its contents before turning it upside
down over the sink. The condensed tomatoes plopped with
a wet splat against the porcelain.

Alex showed up for takeout, but as soon as he swallowed
the last of his food, he vanished into his bedroom, leaving
Claude and me alone in the flickering light of the television
with the volume on low.

I retrieved a stack of my photographs and sat cross-legged
on the carpet, laying the photos side by side so I could see
them together: pictures of my mother, of Alex surrounded
by his friends at school, pictures from the football game. I
noticed that the carpet needed vacuuming, crumbs and hard
bits of dirt sticking to the palms of my hands.

"Can I see those?" Claude asked. As usual, he had his
own puzzle in front of him: paper printouts, file folders,

glossy brochures overlapping like conversations where no one was listening. He came to the edge of the sofa so he could get a better look.

"No," I said, attempting to hide the photos with my body and arms. "This is none of your business."

Claude laughed, moving from the couch to sit next to me. He picked up a couple of photos. "These are great," he said, admiring a photo of my mother standing by the window in my bedroom, a cigarette dangling from her lower lip and a wreath of smoke flowing behind her like a wedding veil.

He put the photo down and started flipping through the others. He stopped when he found the photo I'd taken of him and Alex and my mother talking to Alex's friends and their parents at the football game. He froze, then held it up so he could get a better look.

"Why'd you take this one?" he asked, with no inflection to his voice.

I shrugged, not wanting to say how I studied Alex, searching for why he was different with his friends than he was with me. "Because I wanted to."

"What kind of reason is that?"

"I don't know." I tried to snag the picture, but he held it out of my reach. "Give it back."

"Not until you tell me why you took it. A real photographer plans each shot, frames the picture, and considers her subjects and how she wants the photograph to come out. Otherwise you're wasting film."

"It's my film to waste."

Claude's smile didn't reach his eyes. "Can I have it?" he asked.

"Have what?"

"This picture. Can I have it?"

"Why?" I tried grabbing the picture again, confused. If he wanted a photograph, it should have been one of my mother.

"I want a few of these." He pointed to the rest of the photos and picked up another one, of Alex talking to his friend by the cinder-block wall. "They're very good," he said.

I gathered the rest in a messy pile before he could get his hands on any more. "Well, you can't have them. What do you know about photography anyway?"

"More than you. I used to be quite the shutterbug. Worked on the school newspaper, lo these many years ago."

Incomprehensible to think I shared anything with Claude. "You couldn't have been very good."

He barked a laugh, and he was back to the same Claude. "I like you, Rosie. Here, judge for yourself."

From the bottom of the bookshelf he pulled out a crusty binder. The spine crackled as I opened it to find newspaper clippings, all yellowed to the color of old bruises, pasted onto thick black paper. The first article showed a picture of a man, wrinkles crisscrossing his face, sitting on a park bench wrapped in a threadbare, dirty blanket. Caption: *A vagrant admiring the sun on a Monday morning*. On the next page a little girl cried, her gap-toothed mouth hung open, her hand offering a busted balloon while behind her a Ferris wheel turned. She held the torn bits of plastic as if they were a precious but dead pet, perhaps her first loss. The next photo, a long shot of a street littered with trash, and a lone figure trying to sweep with only a broom. Another, of a group of men at a podium pointing into an unseen crowd, and behind them stood a second row of men in military uniforms holding automatic machine guns. A closer inspection

revealed that the last picture was of a stage production, cos-
tumes and props and artificial scenery.

They were horrible—and beautiful. He liked to photograph terrible things, things in which I couldn't find evidence of the happy-go-lucky, blustering Claude who loved
to joke and laugh. But I remembered how he had been when
he had caught Alex in my room, and I remembered the hard
way he asked why I had taken his picture at the football
game.

The final clipping was of a woman with a long face and
straight hair that fell well past her waist, exaggerating her
height and her bony, exposed shoulders. She stood onstage
to the left of the conductor, in front of an orchestra, one big-
knuckled hand wrapped around the neck of a violin. Tall
and imperious, she dared the camera to take her picture. I
realized that I knew that arctic dare.

My finger traced her face, the thinness of her arms, the
curved lines of the violin. With a jolt, I understood; it was
the sound of her violin that seeped from underneath Alex's
bedroom door every day. Her glare drew my attention.
The angles of her face were so severe that I could have cut
myself if I'd touched her, sliced my hands open to bleed on
the carpet. The caption below the picture read, *Violinist
Catherine Craig takes the stage with the Los Angeles Phil-
harmonic.*

"That's Alex's mother," Claude said, no longer smiling.

My tongue stung with questions, surprised that he had
volunteered the truth and intrigued by the flare of remorse
in his eyes.

"I met her that day for the first time"—he nodded at the
binder in my hands—"when I took her picture."

"Did you love her?"

"Oh yes," said Claude.

"What happened?"

"She didn't love me back. Not enough, anyway. I wasn't enough for her. It was a long time ago." Claude held his hand out for the binder, snapped it shut. Back in its place, the dust crowded around it protectively. He stood over me, so tall I felt the bones of my neck grind together as I looked up. "You know, I'd build you a darkroom, if you let me. It'd be better that way. Keep everything in house, close to home. You wouldn't have to wait to have your photos developed."

I went back to stacking my photographs by subject matter, returning them to the envelopes they came in. "Why do you always have to buy something?"

He reddened, and it made me think of the overcooked tomatoes flushed down the drain. "Who do you think gives Alex the money to buy your film? And who asked him to buy it for you in the first place? Tell me to stop and I'll stop."

I'd finally succeeded in making him mad. But it was a quiet anger, cold and reserved, and once again I marveled to see the similarity between father and son.

"I don't know how to use a darkroom," I said softly.

He considered this. "If you'll give me this picture, I could teach you," he said, and bopped me on the head with it, trying to be playful again.

Before I could respond, Alex came down the stairs, pausing when he saw the two of us. "Can I borrow the car?" he asked Claude.

He had never asked for this before, at least not while I had been living with them. Father and son stared at each other. Push me, pull me.

"What do you want it for?" asked Claude.

"There's a party."

A silent conversation took place, questions asked and answered in the open space between them. Claude walked over to the kitchen, rummaged around in a drawer for the second time that evening.

"Take Dahlia's car," he said, tossing the keys. I recognized the green key chain; it was a dahlia flower, a gift from my father.

I caught the keys before they reached Alex, snagging the key chain in my right hand. Alex tried to grab them, but I dodged him.

"Can I go to the party too?" I asked. Going to a party was something normal teenagers did. I wanted to see what Alex would do if Claude said that I could go.

Alex reached around one side of my body, then to the other, but I elbowed him in his belly.

"You're not invited," he said, exasperated, annoyed.

It didn't surprise me that he didn't want me with him, but now I was determined. "But I want to go.

"If you let me go to the party, I'll let you have those photographs," I told Claude, who was leaning against the kitchen doorframe.

Alex stopped trying to grab the keys, noticing for the first time the photographs in Claude's hand. "What photographs?" he asked.

Claude hadn't moved. "I think that's a great idea," he said, and then shifted his attention to Alex. "Why don't you take Rosie with you?"

My heart stopped, breath trapped in my chest like a great big ball of wonder. I hadn't thought he would say yes.

"But I can't—" started Alex.

Claude looked at me. "Wouldn't you like to go?"

He had turned it around and made it his idea, as if I

hadn't been the one to ask to go. As if he knew I hadn't been serious before and now he was calling my bluff.

"Well?" Claude asked.

"She doesn't want to go," cut in Alex.

"Let her say that. What will it be, Rosie?"

On the mantel in the living room a clock ticked, doling out time by the fistful. It was past eight on a Friday night. All over Southern California, hundreds of teenagers were getting ready to go to parties. My mother would have wanted me to go; at least the version of her that had existed before my father's death would have wanted me to go. My father would have wanted me to stay. Alex wanted me to stay.

"I'll go," I said.

Alex sighed and took the keys from my hand.

I thought Claude might grin in his usual triumph, but that hard look returned as he pinned me down in close scrutiny. "Then you'd better get ready," he said, by way of dismissal.

The command in his voice had me already running for the stairs, but I stopped when Claude said my name.

"Why don't you leave those photographs here, so I can go through them?"

I knew I didn't have a choice, not if I wanted to go to the party. Not if I wanted that darkroom. And I did want to go, despite Alex's clear annoyance. After another hesitation, I handed over the envelopes that held both the photographs and negatives before running up the stairs. But I stopped on the top step when I heard Alex speak.

"What are you doing?" he asked.

"Just taking a look," answered Claude, but when there wasn't a response, he continued. "Can you explain this?"

Silence, then Alex said, "It was nothing. I was using the phones and Tom was there. That's all."

"We have enough problems, Alex."

"I know."

Another long silence followed before Claude spoke again. His tone changed back to his usual fatherly sternness. "She's been here for months. It's good for her to get out of the house."

"But I thought—" said Alex.

"I trust you." There was finality in Claude's words, in his tone, that made me wonder if he trusted *me*. "Or can't I?"

Alex paused long enough for me to fill the silence with desires and hopes unspoken. "Of course you can," he said.

"Then what's the problem?"

"Nothing. I'll take her. It's fine."

After a silent moment, I heard the front door open and close, and then the soft complaint of the couch as Claude sat back down again.

As I stepped into the hallway, I climbed up the stairs to the third floor, where my mother was resting. I realized that I wanted her opinion, that I wanted her to know I was going to a party. The stairs creaked with each step. In her room, the moon shining through trees made a patchwork design across the floor.

She lay on her back with one arm flung across the other pillow. Maybe she sensed that I was there because she tossed her head, slurred my name, and made as if to open her eyes, but it was like they were glued together. "What is it?" she mumbled.

A collection of amber-colored medicine bottles sat in a row on the bedside table. I picked up the first one. The label read "Benzodiazepine" in bold lettering. It was a pretty string of letters all together. Some of the pill bottles were larger. Some smaller. "Take with food. Take with water. Do not operate machinery. Do not drive."

I called her one more time, but she turned onto her side, facing the wall.

Alex honked the horn, telling me I was taking too long. I left her sleeping and went down to my bathroom, brushing my hair until it crackled with electricity, the ends rising like a mad scientist's. I twisted it into a ponytail and then applied ancient makeup handed down to me by José's sisters years ago. "Take this," they had said. "Take this, girl, you need color." With lipstick I looked like a clown with too wide a smile. I took a bit of toilet paper and rubbed the color off until my lips were raw.

Claude appeared in the doorway of the bathroom.

"What's wrong with her?" I asked, speaking into the silence that braided between us.

"Nothing," he said. "She's tired."

"She's always tired." I tried to find the truth in his eyes, but all he did was wave me out the door.

"Go," he said. "Have fun."

IT WAS STRANGE TO SEE my mother's car parked in front of the house. Claude kept it in the garage, along with other forgotten things my mother and I had stolen from our old life. Unlike the Mercedes, which purred, this car growled and hiccuped while it waited. The hood was dented, the blue paint chipped and rusted.

When I climbed in, Alex was sitting like a statue at the wheel. He wouldn't look at me.

"If you don't want me to go, it's okay. I'll stay home,"

I said, reaching for the handle, but he put his hand over mine.

"No, it isn't that. I have to pick up Tina. I mean, I offered to pick her up."

His breath hung in the air for a moment before disappearing. I looked through the rain-splattered windshield. "Of course."

Alex drove, one hand on the steering wheel and the other tapping on the gearshift with a rhythmic beat; his fingers were always busy. I concentrated on the familiar movement of the car, the smell of the ashtray, choked with crushed cigarette butts smeared with lipstick. My mother had left a trail of burn marks over the dashboard and the seats. There was one deep scar in the pleather of the passenger-side seat, a gnarled old wound. I remembered when it happened. She had the car in reverse and hadn't seen how close she was holding a lit cigarette to my leg. It burned through my jeans to my thigh, and when I cried out her hand jerked and she dropped the cigarette. It burned a hole in the seat before she picked it up. I still bore the scar, a circle on the side of my thigh.

Alex turned the car onto Eveningstar Road, then coasted down the street until he parked underneath a big, overhanging tree. The tree dripped fat drops of rainwater, pinging the roof of the car.

"What are we waiting for?" I asked.

"She's meeting us here," he said.

"On the street?" I looked at the houses, but they were dark and quiet. A moment later, I saw a flash of movement beneath the intermittent streetlight. Tina did a half walk, half run across the street. Alex exited the car but left the door open.

As Tina got closer I saw that her coat covered something that glittered red and gold. "I was watching through the window," she said as she came up to Alex. "I saw the moment you came up."

Then she noticed me sitting in the passenger side. She looked from me to Alex.

"She's coming with us," said Alex, apologetic. I felt my cheeks burn.

"Oh," she said. "That's cool."

An awkward moment passed. I knew I was supposed to move to the backseat, but I couldn't make myself do it. If Alex wanted me to move, he needed to ask.

"We should get going," said Alex.

"Wait, come back to my room first." Tina tugged on his arm. "I want to show you something."

"I can't go to your house," he said, digging in his heels. "That would be a really bad idea."

Tina shook her head, tugged on his arm. "No, it'll be all right, I swear. They're watching television. They won't notice. They don't even know I'm gone. I climbed through the window. Please. Please," she said again. "It's important."

Alex hesitated. "But." He bent down to look at me, still sitting in the passenger seat. "What about—"

Tina didn't say anything, and I knew she didn't want to say that I should wait in the car. I also knew Alex didn't want to ask if I would mind waiting, either. I could have let it drag on, neither Tina nor Alex asking and me not offering. But Alex cocked his head to one side and gave me a lopsided smile.

"Whatever," I said, sighing. "I'll wait here."

"Ten minutes," he said. "We won't be gone long."

I refused to look at him as he shut the door and disappeared into the dark across the street. Drops of water weaved drunken paths down the passenger-side window, distorting the view of the beleaguered front lawn of the house on the corner. The house had a fat fake turkey marching across the lawn, its ceramic feathers fluffed and bold, and a scarecrow sitting on the porch next to carved pumpkins lining the railing. I realized it must be near Halloween.

I was left alone with my memories of driving and waiting in this car to keep me company. Alex's presence had kept the memories at bay, but now they pushed and shoved like they needed a ride, some in the backseat, some in the front with me, like live things, with pulses and heartbeats.

And some memories stood outside and tapped on the driver's-side window. The ghost's face pressed against the glass.

"Open up," he said in my father's angry voice, fiddling with the car door. When it wouldn't open, his hand slapped hard against the glass. He came around to my side, but I climbed over the gearbox to get away. He tried that handle, then slammed his body against the door. The car rocked, back and forth.

"Open the goddamned door or I swear I'll kick it in," he yelled, pounding on the window. "Look what you're doing. Look at her; you're making her cry, you're scaring her. Let me in and we'll forget this ever happened."

The ghost paused, as if someone was responding and speaking to him. Even though I knew I was alone, I looked in the backseat, but it was empty. All I saw were cigarette burns and the stuffed ashtray.

The banging stopped. I was breathing hard. The windows had fogged, making it difficult to see through the rain to Tina's house. Maybe he had given up; maybe he was gone.

Then a deafening crack shook the entire car. I bit my tongue and tasted blood. Through the fogged window I saw the ghost standing by the hood of the car wielding a baseball bat. He slammed it down on the hood. The car reverberated.

He came around to the passenger side. "Sweetie, open the door. Open it," he coaxed, the way you do with a small child to get them to do what you want. But when nothing happened, he yelled, "Open it! This is your fault; you're making me do this."

The baseball bat shone in the meager light of the streetlamps. The ghost held it with both hands above his head. "Get away from the window," he said, with dead calm.

I backed away as far as I could, pressing up against the opposite door. He swung the bat and I put my arms over my head, curling into a ball in the front seat, screaming into my chest. The door opened and I fell, tumbling from the car, splashing into a puddle.

Alex helped me up from the ground. I struggled between breathing and gagging. Next to him Tina held an umbrella. I hadn't noticed her gold headband before. Her coat fell open. She wore a red bustier and starry blue hot pants. They sparkled in the streetlight. Alex had changed out of his old T-shirt into a blue shirt with a Superman logo on the front that he wore under his jacket. In a flash I understood: She was supposed to be Wonder Woman. She must have made him change into the Superman shirt.

He had been calling my name, his lips moving, but I hadn't heard him. Sound returned with the splash of rain on my face.

"I'm fine," I said, struggling to stand on my own, holding on to the car door and Alex for support. The window wasn't smashed. The hood of the car had the same dents it always had, but now I understood how they got there. My mother had tried to run away before. Years before. She had tried and failed.

"I fell. When I got out," I said, wanting to climb into Alex's arms. Tina watched both of us, a crease between her eyebrows.

He looked uncertain. "I should take her home," he said to Tina.

"No." I pushed his hands away, adjusting my blouse and jacket, which had twisted with my frantic motions in the car. "No, please."

Alex wiped the rain from my cheeks. "If you promise me you're all right?"

"She doesn't look well," said Tina. The noisy rain drowned out her voice, but she touched Alex, tugged at his jacket. The cold brought color to her cheeks. "Maybe we should take her inside."

I rubbed at my damp and dirty knees. "Really, I'm fine. It was just a little weird alone in the car. Halloween, I guess."

After considering me for a moment, Alex said, "She's okay. We should go."

He stepped aside and held the door open for Tina. She hesitated before sitting down.

Alex held the back door open for me as well. I didn't want to return to the car, but after insisting that we continue on to the party I had no choice.

The seat was cold. Alex shut my door; then he shut Tina's door. Our eyes met in the rearview mirror, but he turned his attention to the drenched street and started the car. Tina was peering out her window. She wiped at her eyes, and I wondered what she had to cry about. He was going to the party with her.

CHAPTER TWELVE

The party glittered at the butt end of a cul-de-sac, on a street called Calypso Court. The house was perched on the side of a hill and lit up like a beacon for wayward teenagers dressed as cowboys or punk rockers. Floodlights illuminated the ghouls and goblins greeting Alex with high fives. Witches and fairies clustered around Tina, cooing with delight over her Wonder Woman bustier. Costumed strangers mingled near a damp barbecue or formed a crooked line for the keg. Lawn chairs were scattered around the yard like rocks in a lake. Alex disappeared, buoyed into the house as if carried by a strong current. I wished for a mask to hide behind. Perhaps a harlequin clown or a Zorro mask and bandanna.

Inside, the house was a honeycomb of rooms. Like Ariadne in the labyrinth, I picked up a string made of music and walked from room to room, encountering monsters and princesses around every corner, bodies flailing and laughing. Looking for Alex's blond head became futile among the rubber faces, witches' hats, and Halloween streamers dangling from the ceiling. I met ghosts in every room, but these were ordinary ghosts, solid and familiar, with holes cut out of bedsheets or greasy white pancake makeup smeared over bright faces. These ghosts lacked gaping bullet holes along the sides of their heads. They didn't carry baseball bats.

In the kitchen an alien with bouncing antennae handed me a plastic cup of thin, urine-colored beer. It was bitter down my throat, but I drank most of it like water before refilling. I wandered around, looking at pictures that belonged to the family who lived there. The shiny, happy faces reminded me of Mrs. Wilson's handbag with its countless pictures. A young man in a cap and gown, fat babies and rosy-cheeked toddlers perched on laps and told to look at the camera. Look at the camera! Say cheese! The walls were mint colored with chocolate chip accents, and the carpets plush and spotless. It was a house for rich people—clean and pristine.

A twang of a guitar followed by a smattering of drums caught my attention, and shouts of Alex's name. "Come on, Alex, just one song."

People crowded the living room. Squashed into a corner, a band had set up their equipment. Alex resisted, but a man with a bandanna tied around his forehead thrust a guitar into his hands.

I found a spot where I could watch away from the crowd. I'd seen him play so many times it should have been familiar, but there was something different in watching Alex on a stage with an audience of more than one. He'd taken his jacket off and his Superman T-shirt hung loose on his slender frame. He tuned the guitar, the pick held between his lips.

At his feet Tina sat with her girlfriends crowding around her, whispering and giggling. The girl I recognized as Tina's friend who drove the VW Bug hooted and hollered, her hair teased big and buoyant. She was dressed as a Dallas Cowboys cheerleader, her breasts spilling over the lip of her top. "Come on, stud," she said, whistling through her fingers.

Alex smiled, lopsided. He liked the attention.

It was a song I had never heard him play. A ballad. A love song. A pretty melody, sidling around the room to make love to all the girls, to make the boys envious. Sung for Tina, I thought, who looked up at him with adoration. Next to Tina, her friend in the cheerleader costume rocked and swayed to his music.

I dug my fingernails into the flesh of my palms. He kept his eyes on his fingers as he played but then lifted his gaze to meet mine. Even separated by the length of the room, by the many bodies of strangers, I felt naked in front of him. With the twang of his last chord, I noticed that Tina was no longer pouring devotion up at Alex but had turned to see where he was looking.

The crowd applauded, wanting more, but Alex returned the guitar to its bandannaed owner. Before I could get close, Tina grabbed his hand and led him from the room.

I followed, weaving through the party. They slipped farther into the smoky labyrinth of the house, through the kitchen to the backyard.

The wooden deck behind the house opened up to a pool that was encircled by a string of paper lanterns creating an oasis of light, conversation, and music thumping from a sound system perched on one of the tables. Around it sat a pirate talking to a devil who held his forked tail over his arm like an accessory. A black-nosed, fuzzy-eared kitty cat danced with the same alien who had poured my cup of beer, his antennae bobbing in a mismatched rhythm. Beyond that circle of light lay the promise of lush, damp darkness. Alex and Tina glided through the chaos unnoticed except by me, disappearing off the edge and tipping into the unknown.

She took him farther into the garden, where the light could not penetrate. It felt like a betrayal. The garden had been ours, mine and Alex's. I stood on the edge of the deck, wanting to follow, not wanting to follow. I wasn't certain what I wanted. Their shapes moved farther into the darkness, until all I could see was Tina's gold headband with Alex's blond head bobbing beside her.

I turned away and collided with Tina's friend in the cheerleader costume as she stumbled down the stairs that led to the kitchen. Both of our beers sloshed everywhere, splashing my shoes and her chest. Through her damp top, I could see the outline of her breasts.

"How drunk are you?" she asked, laughing, clutching my hand to keep her balance. She'd chewed off her lipstick and had clumpy mascara on her lashes.

"I'm Joey," she said. "I'm the queen of this party. I'm the best fucking lay. I'm . . . I'm—"

She trailed off, glassy-eyed and vacant. Then, with urgency, she asked, "Have you seen Tina? I need to find that girl. I need to talk to her."

"No," I said, not knowing why I lied.

But she plunged ahead. "Are they fucking?" she asked in an exaggerated whisper, her beery breath washing over me before she covered her mouth and scrunched her eyes as if the answer to that question was the most hilarious thing she'd ever heard.

"Stupid girl," she said then, pinching my hand, which

was still held in hers, and I didn't know if she meant Tina or me. "Stupid fucking girl." Then she stumbled the rest of the way down, clutching the cup of beer in her hand.

I threaded my way back through the house. The front door banged open and a man stood silhouetted by the light from the street. His sweatshirt hung crooked, weighed down in the front pocket by something heavy. Shaggy hair, pale skin, and sticky blood dripping down the side of his face, to his neck, to the collar of his sweatshirt. My heart slammed in my chest, but the door opened wider and light fell on his drunken smile. A teenager, pulling out bottled beer from where he'd stashed it in the front pocket of his sweatshirt. It was fake blood, a fake wound. He had vampire teeth in his mouth. He moved past me, shouting a greeting to his pals, already spitting out the fake teeth and guzzling down his beer.

The ghost look-alike jumped up and down to the music, tripping and spilling his beer. He jammed his fake teeth into his mouth and pretended to bite the neck of a girl dressed as a seventies hippie. She squealed, then punched him in his shoulder, but he rocked back on his feet with a laugh, drinking more beer. Suddenly, the wind swept in through the open door, bringing with it prickling drops of rain. I backed away from the look-alike, who in full light looked nothing like my father. I needed to get away—outside, into the soft drizzle, down the steps—and I ran from the house. The rain brought a soft, diffuse glow to everything. The farther I went, the more the noise of the rainwater rushing down the street masked the pounding music of the party.

I climbed onto the hood of my mother's car and lay down, still holding my plastic cup and what was left of my beer, wishing that I had gotten more. The front of the car faced the house. Perhaps the entire high school was there, every person in one form of disguise or another. Even I wore a costume—part ghost's daughter, part crazy stepsister—it was just harder to see than the others.

I imagined Tina undoing Alex's jacket. He knew where to put his hands. Through her thin bustier he could feel the bones of her rib cage. If he squeezed too hard she might bruise. But she wanted rough. She wanted hard. She wanted those bruises. Her fingers reached beneath his T-shirt.

When I opened my eyes, two skeletons stood next to the car.

"This is perfect," said the first skeleton, tall and skinny and just as a skeleton should be, apart from his long red hair and smeared makeup. "Can we sit with you?" He didn't wait for an answer, and the hood bent farther and buckled under his weight. "You don't mind, do you? Come on, climb up." He waved to the second skeleton, offering a hand.

We all fit if we sat cross-legged. I scooted to one side.

I studied the other skeleton. He had a cheaper costume, the kind you found in discount stores: a plastic tunic and plastic mask held by a thin elastic band. He lifted his mask over his head and wore it like a hat. I hid my surprise behind my cup of beer, recognizing him as the boy from the football game, the boy from Alex's room. The boy whose picture had caught Claude's interest. I had seen eyes like his before; they belonged to a man who lived in the apartment building next to ours. His windows had always been covered with newspaper and aluminum foil, and his apartment smelled like *gato* piss.

"I'm Aaron," said the redheaded skeleton, offering his hand. His toothy grin stretched across his face. "And he's Tom."

I shook Aaron's hand, but Tom only lifted his chin in a quick nod. I wanted to ask Tom if he remembered me, in an effort to find out what he and Alex got up to, but he turned away and I changed my mind.

"You're Alex's sister," said Aaron.

"Not his sister." I sipped from my cup. The beer tasted like recycled laundry water, but I liked the way it made me feel.

"Not his sister," repeated Aaron in a disbelieving tone. "But you take his picture all the time, right? I've seen you, sitting by yourself."

"I don't take just his picture," I said, even though they were mostly of Alex. But I didn't want to think of Alex right then, not when he was with Tina. "I like taking pictures. Do you have a problem with that?"

"No, ma'am," he said, shaking his head. "But where's your camera?"

"I didn't bring it."

"Didn't bring it?" Outraged, like it was the most preposterous thing he'd ever heard. "What kind of photographer doesn't bring her camera?"

I made a pretend camera, squinting one eye, made a clicking noise.

"Oh wait, I wasn't ready. I think I blinked. Let me fix my hair. Do it again." Aaron tossed his hair back, adjusted his position, pretended to fix his makeup, smeared to a streaky gray all over his face.

I laughed, and it felt wonderful. Wonderful to laugh, no matter how stupid it was.

"Now one with Tom," Aaron said. "Come on, we have to look pretty."

He pulled Tom so that he faced me as well. Aaron fluttered his eyelashes. Tom managed a slight upturn to his lips.

"Will you take our pictures for real?" asked Aaron.

"Sure."

He took my hand, fingers hooked together in the start of a secret handshake. "Like this," he said, bending my hand to copy his: he butted our fists, slid the palms together, fluttered the fingers, snapped the thumbs. "See, now we're bound for life, you and I. In some cultures, we might even be married."

I laughed again.

"Promise?" he asked.

"Yeah, okay."

"Good. Hey, where's your costume? You gotta have a costume."

I spread my arms wide. "I'm wearing it. Can't you tell what it is?"

He folded his arms. "You think you're clever. Don't say some bullshit like 'I'm a sociopath or a secret agent in disguise' or whatever. That's lame."

Tom glanced at me with his rusty stare. "She's got her costume," he said, and then looked away again.

"Don't mind him," said Aaron, leaning close as if to tell a secret. "He's crotchety. He needs his medicine. Come on, Tommy. Time to dose up."

Tom leaned back and lifted his plastic skeletal tunic so he could dig a bag and a lighter out of his front pocket. He took out a joint, cupped his hand around the lighter, lit up, and inhaled, holding his breath as he passed the joint to Aaron, who did the same thing. He then handed it to me.

"You ever smoke before?" asked Aaron.

I took the joint between my fingers, thinking of that time I had my mother's cigarette and stood before the stove, unable to light it. It made me think of Alex and the way he had looked when he lit the cigarette for me.

It was Tom who moved closer. "You don't have to," he said, pushing Aaron away.

"No, I want to."

"I tell you what," said Aaron, taking the joint again. "We'll do a shotgun. I'll blow it in your mouth. Like this." He took a hit from the joint, waving Tom closer. It was like a kiss, with Tom's mouth clamped wide over Aaron's. Tom sucked, and Aaron blew, passing the smoke back and forth like a ball, a strange game of catch, until they parted. Tom held his breath, face turning the barest bit red before he let it go, misty smoke into the air. "Your turn?"

I wanted it. I wanted it with Alex, but I had only this skinny skeleton. Aaron took another long drag; then he grabbed my face between his hands.

It wasn't kissing; it was both more and less. The sweet smoke passed into me. I inhaled as if yawning, deep as I could. Like a vampire, sucking in Aaron's soul, taking it deep inside. Time glowed orange like the tip of the joint. My fingers tingled, my toes went numb, and I wanted to keep sucking as much of his soul as I could.

Aaron ran out of breath. He pulled away and smiled.

"Hold it," said Tom, warm, marijuana-sweetened breath close against my ear. Aaron still held my face between his hands. I listened for Aaron's heartbeat and also Tom's on the other side, the three of us linked. I let the smoke go and breathed in a shock of cold air. Aaron laughed and leaned in. His lips had just touched mine again when he was yanked away.

Alex had Aaron by his skeleton costume and had dragged him down to the curb. "What are you doing to her?" he yelled.

"Nothing," yelped Aaron, trying to get loose, but Alex punched him in the face.

Tom launched himself from the hood of the car, and all three went down onto the slick wet grass and mud. Alex grabbed Tom around the waist. They scrambled in the muck. Tom climbed on top of Alex, pushing his face down. Alex's arms flailed; his legs kicked. Aaron tried to pull Tom off.

I jumped down from the car, uncertain what to do. As a crowd gathered, I saw Tina push her way to the front. Her Wonder Woman headband was gone.

"Do something," I yelled at her, but the crowd was egging Alex and Tom on. Tina acted as if she didn't hear me. I went over and grabbed her arm, intending to drag her to Alex and Tom, but she twisted out of my grasp.

"You shouldn't get involved," she said with an edge of accusation, and I knew she thought this was my fault. "They always fight. They won't hurt each other."

Alex pushed Tom off him and rolled onto his hands and knees, struggling to stand, a streak of blood across his face. Tom was bent over, panting, with Aaron beside him holding him up.

"Come on, let's go," Aaron said to Tom. "Let's get out of here." But Alex had lunged again, knocking Tom to the ground with his elbows and his weight.

Tom grunted. Aaron swore and then jumped on top of Alex.

A loud horn rippled through the air. Searchlights covered the crowd, coming from the street, from a police car.

Aaron swore again. He grabbed Tom's arm and yanked him to his feet. They bolted, leaving Alex on the ground.

The police car door opened, its revolving lights blinding

as they shined on our faces. I squinted until I could see a uniform, brown over brown. The policeman approached and lifted my chin. He turned it from one side to the other, then fixed his flashlight on Alex. Then the light moved on to the rest of the crowd, which was beginning to disperse.

"Deputy Mike," I said, breathing his name.

Deputy Mike seemed displaced from the scene, like a cutout from a magazine or a pop-up book. "All right," he called, with his voice carrying over the bedraggled costumed crowd. "Time to go home."

The party was over. My hair hung heavy from its ponytail; my fingers were like ice. I balled my hands into fists and crossed my arms. Damp partygoers left in twos and threes. The keg was rolled away under the baleful glare of Deputy Mike and his partner. Alex, Tina, and I waited on the porch.

"You," said Deputy Mike, pointing at Alex. "What was the fight about?"

"Nothing," Alex said, then added a belated, "Sir." Blood stained his cheeks. He was as tall as Deputy Mike, maybe even taller. "A misunderstanding."

Beside me, Tina stood tense and shivering in her skimpy bustier and bare legs. "I'd like to go home," she said, and inched closer to Alex.

"Looked pretty serious to me," Deputy Mike insisted.

"Can you take me home now?" Tina asked again. I sensed that she might be trying to help Alex get away from Deputy Mike, but neither paid her any attention.

"Nothing important," said Alex, and I wanted to stomp on his foot. I wasn't anything important. Tom and Aaron weren't anything important.

"Who was the fight with?" asked Deputy Mike.

Alex hesitated, showing the first sign of unease.

"I asked a question."

Alex shook his head with a stubborn, mulish expression, but he glanced at Deputy Mike before speaking. "Tom," he said.

Deputy Mike swore under his breath, unzipping his jacket.

He must have gotten a new one, because I still had his old one in my closet. Sometimes I even wore it to school. Behind me, the screen door banged open and more people left the party, most of them casting a nervous glance at Deputy Mike before crossing the yard. Joey tumbled from the front door. A princess and a kitty cat tried to get her to walk, but her knees buckled and they couldn't carry her.

Alex watched Joey slip and fall a second time. She laughed, raised her arms like a small child asking to be lifted, but he did nothing. Tina made a move to go to her, but Alex held her back.

The other officer shined a light into Joey's face. She flinched, waved her hands in front as if she were blind. He spoke to her, helped her to her feet, and led her from the house and around the corner.

"Have you been drinking?" asked Deputy Mike, pulling Alex's attention away from Joey.

"No, sir," answered Alex, easing up on his hostility.

"Your father know you're here?" Deputy Mike eyed Tina and me. We were standing like two Alex satellites, but he was uninterested in our teenage love triangle. I shifted toward him and was rewarded with a hand on my shoulder.

"He gave me the keys to the car," answered Alex. "You want to call him?"

They held each other's gaze long enough for the rain to soak my shoes, for my face to prickle with spittle bouncing

off the nearby window. Deputy Mike nodded. "All right."
He waved everyone off the porch. "Get going." With a nod
at Alex, he said, "Get them home."

Alex took his jacket off, holding it over Tina's head, and
they ran to the car.

I stayed where I was. Deputy Mike beamed his flashlight
through the thickening rain, following the slow departure
of the party.

"The fight was about me," I said.

He pointed his flashlight at the various ghouls and fairies crossing the lawn. Then he pointed the flashlight at my
face and I had to shut my eyes.

"I doubt that," he said, returning to observing the party
exodus.

"But it was," I said. "Alex got mad, and I was—"

Deputy Mike looked straight at me, and I fell quiet,
intimidated by his nearness. The wind swooped down.
Quicker than an intake of breath, the downpour that had
been threatening began and the rain fell in thick veils,
louder than a thousand drummers drumming.

He took his jacket off and put it over my head, the same
way Alex had with Tina. Together, we moved across the
yard. Water sprayed into my eyes despite the shelter of his
arms. He hauled me against his chest, his gun belt digging
into my side. When we got to the car, he pushed me inside
with Tina, shutting the door before I could say anything.
Alex remained outside, listening and nodding to something
Deputy Mike was saying.

Tina had turned in her seat, wiping the rain from her
face and watching Alex and Deputy Mike with a searching
expression. I wanted to shake her and imagined pushing her
out of the car so that she floated away with all the debris

that washed down the street. That might shock Deputy Mike and Alex and get their attention. "Do you think he's in trouble?" I asked.

She wiped the rain from her face. "He's always in trouble."

Before I could ask her what she meant, the car door opened, bringing in noise and rain. Alex slid in. He looked at Tina and then at me. The shadows in the car made the bruises emerging on his face seem grotesque. Cold, hard silence wrapped around us. He started the car.

It wasn't until after we had dropped Tina at her home that I realized I still had Deputy Mike's jacket: another one, to add to my collection.

THE CAKE HOUSE WINDOWS WERE glowing with golden light when we got home, a warped hint of the warmth inside. I wondered if my mother had woken up. She never rested easy during rainstorms; the thunder was too loud, the lightning too bright.

Alex pulled into the garage and turned the car off, the heat from the vents fading away. Lightning flashed, with thunder hard upon its heels. The rain beat a constant tribal rhythm against the roof of the garage.

"Stay away from Tom," he said. "And Aaron."

"Why?"

"Just do it. They're not—" Gingerly, he licked his lip where it had split open again. "They're not good friends for you."

"And you are? If I said stay away from Tina, would you do it?" I asked.

"Leave her out of this."

"Why?" I demanded, wanting to hit him at the same time that I wanted to make him tell me what he was feeling. I was frustrated with his evasions, the way he came close only to push me away again. "You kiss me, then you kiss her; I don't know what it is you want. I don't know what's going on in this house. Why did Claude want my photographs?" I fell silent, but he wasn't looking at me.

"Tina's none of your business. It's not what you think. It's complicated."

"Then tell me. Sometimes I think you like me. But maybe you're just playing? What were you doing with Tina at the party, in the garden? I followed you, you know. That Joey girl said you were fuck—"

Alex pushed me against my seat, his arm across my chest. "Don't follow me," he said.

"All right," I said, trying to dislodge his arm, but it wouldn't budge.

He pressed harder, and my chest and collarbone hurt. "Don't fucking follow me."

"I said all right." I dug my nails into his flesh until he snatched his arm back.

In the poor lighting, his chest rose and fell, and the bruise stood out like a stamp over his eye and cheekbone. He said, "Joey should keep her mouth shut."

The rain continued. I suppressed a shiver.

"But were you?" I wanted him to look at me, so I took his hand in mine. "Fucking?"

His fingernails were rough, brutally hacked away, calluses like unsung songs mapped across each fingertip.

"Now who's playing?" he asked, but he didn't let go of my hand.

Our mingled breath hung in the air, visible in the cold. I

could see the small boy he used to be in the shape of his face, in the way his hair curled around his ears.

The drumbeat of rain stopped as quickly as it had started, and the absence of noise was like a sudden loss of hearing.

"What about you?" he asked. "You're normal one minute and then completely fucking crazy the next. What is it that you see?"

I opened my mouth in shock. He couldn't know. He didn't know that the mere mention of my father frightened me. But he had noticed; he'd paid attention and had seen something that wasn't right. It made me shiver, to know how closely he had been watching and that maybe, with time, he could see the ghost. I licked my lips, wanting to tell him about the ghost, but I remembered how the ghost looked wielding the baseball bat outside the car. Before Alex could ask again, I kissed him and tasted his blood. Cold air blew through a crack in the rear window. I ran a hand under his damp shirt, as I had imagined Tina had done earlier, up against his chest where his heart beat fast. He trembled, but maybe that was because of the cold. He took my other hand and pressed it flat against his stomach, against his crotch. Not gentle, but desperate, and strange.

A muffled bang and crash pulled us apart. I heard my mother's voice, loud and panicked, and I struggled to unlock the car door as Alex said, "Wait up."

I burst into the house. The front room was empty and I took a deep breath. No blood on the walls, no body on the floor. I had expected the ghost to be crouching in a corner, upset that I had been kissing Alex, or upset that I was afraid of him, but there was nothing.

Claude and my mother were by the stairs, facing each other like someone had pressed pause and they stood frozen in their current positions. She was dressed in her nightgown but had her coat on with slippers on her feet. A suitcase lay at an angle across the last few steps, with clothing exploding out of it. Neither my mother nor Claude acknowledged my existence, or Alex's.

Then she took a long, shuddering breath and wrapped her coat across her chest. "I wear what I want to wear," she said, her voice raspy. "I stay home if I want to stay home. If I don't want to meet your"—she swallowed—"your friends, I don't have to."

"Absolutely," said Claude, his hands held before him. "Whatever you say. Whatever you want."

My mother's eyes fell on her scattered clothing. With an awkward jerk forward, Claude bent to pick up the suitcase, stuffing the clothing inside. My mother's eyes wandered to where Alex and I stood.

"You went to a party?" she asked, coming over to pass her hands over my hair, down to my shoulders. She smiled. "I'm glad. Did you like it?"

Alex headed for the stairs, but Claude stopped him and peered at his face. Alex tried to duck his head to hide the bruises.

"Care to explain?" Claude asked Alex.

"Not really," said Alex.

Claude frowned but let him go.

I looked from my mother to the suitcase and then to Claude.

"Are we leaving?" I asked. Every morning, every day since my father died, this was all I had wanted from her. Only now I wanted to go back to that interrupted moment in the darkness of the garage. I wanted to follow Alex up the stairs and into his room.

My mother breathed in and closed her eyes. "Go to bed, Rosaura. Everything's all right."

She and Claude remained where they stood, locked in their silent conversation. I left them and went up the stairs to the dark hallway. Alex waited by his door. I started for him, but he held his hand up and I stopped. Perhaps he waited to find out if my mother and I were leaving as well. He didn't say anything, and a moment later he went into his room and I went into mine.

CHAPTER THIRTEEN

The rain worsened overnight, and the Cake House had let in water. We woke up to coffee-colored stains on the carpets and a leak dripping down the walls. It had started in the roof, seeping through each floor to my bedroom, buckling the plaster by the closet, then down to the first floor. But the storm damaged the back room behind the staircase the most, where a window had been left open. No more than a closet, barely large enough to hold a table, a couple of chairs, it wasn't good for much except as a storeroom for Claude's old filing cabinet and boxes of paperwork.

I opened a box filled with computer printouts of names and addresses faded and barely legible, then stepped back to let Claude lift it, the bottom dissolving into mush, spilling paper like a ladder. The sight of Claude holding a rotted cardboard box with the bottom flapping like a torn wet paper towel made me laugh.

"I don't see what's so funny," he said, looking at the mess at his feet.

Damp hands on my hips, I kicked another spongy box to the side. "You're going to have to get rid of everything in here."

"Is that your expert opinion?"

"Definitely," I said.

Claude sighed. "It's probably for the best. I should have gotten rid of this stuff ages ago."

I bent down to pick up a handful of disintegrating documents with the letters "K.I.S., LLC" written on the letterhead. The logo—a mountain, a half circle that maybe represented the sun—was familiar, but I couldn't place it.

Instead of going through the rest of the boxes, Claude made a fist and knocked on the wall, inspecting the structure of the room. "If all this has to be cleared out, it'll be wasted space," he hinted. He knocked the wall again and then turned toward me with a "so what's it going to be?" expression. He wasn't going to say it. It had to be my decision, my desire.

"We could make it a darkroom," I said.

"Is that another expert opinion?" he asked.

"Yes."

I yelped as he spun me around in the small room.

"Get your coat. There isn't a moment to waste," he said, ushering me out to the living room. He took a set of keys from his pocket and handed them to me. "Do me a favor? There should be an envelope in that desk over there," he said, pointing to the rolltop desk in the corner. "Get it for me."

He didn't wait for my answer but pulled his coat and an umbrella from the downstairs closet. Before he could change his mind, I unlocked the desk, eager to see the treasures it held. But inside was nothing other than unorganized stacks of bills, receipts, and a few floppy disks and CDs inside jewel cases. The photographs and negatives Claude had confiscated were shoved in against a folded manila envelope, my payment for the darkroom.

The manila envelope weighed as much as a book. I undid the metal clasp and turned it upside down. Two stacks of hundred-dollar bills fell into my hand.

"Can I trust you, Rosie?"

I hadn't noticed Claude's approach. The night before, he'd asked Alex the same question. Instead of answering, I handed him the money.

He slipped out a few bills for his wallet, then returned the rest of the money to the envelope. He locked the desk. "All set?"

"What else do you keep in there?" I asked as Claude ushered me toward the front door. I realized that he wanted me to see his money. Or maybe he wanted to say that this money was as much mine as it was his, that I was a part of his world now and that I belonged to him.

"My secrets," he said as we walked to his car. He stopped before I got into the passenger side of the Mercedes, and for a second I thought he was finally going to tell me the truth, but instead he looked bashful, rubbing at his jaw before speaking. "I wanted to thank you. For letting me build you a darkroom. Means a lot to me. More than I can say."

"You don't need my permission to build anything you want."

He suddenly looked aged. "You'd be surprised."

At the camera store, Claude asked what brand of enlarger I preferred. He wanted my opinion on paper stock and how much of each chemical we should order. He deferred to my choice on trays and squeegees and aprons, and even to the color of clothespin. By the end of the two-hour shopping spree, I couldn't stop smiling; my blood pulsed hot and strong. I realized, as Claude pulled out his wallet and paid the attendant in cash, that until that moment I had not thought once of the ghost.

THE DARKROOM WOULD TAKE A few days to finish. After the boxes were removed, the room had to dry out, the carpet had to be torn up, and a sink had to be installed to provide water for the developing processes. But Claude had bought me a box of black-and-white film and said I should get started.

That Sunday, I sat on the front steps with my camera. The laundered blue of the sky unfolded and expanded to every corner, pinned to the heavens by the sun. I shivered in my sweater and thin pair of jeans, taking pictures of the front yard full of puddles.

The Mercedes lurched into the driveway. Claude and my mother had gone for a drive. She was smiling when she exited, dressed in a new camel-hair coat with a fur-lined collar that nestled around her neck. They held hands crossing the lawn, but my mother lingered in the front yard as Claude went inside. It was as though the storm had swept the tired and sad Dahlia away. Her eyes bright, her expression clear, she sat next to me and brushed the hair out of my face.

"It's gotten so long," she said.

"I like it long."

"Come up to the room," she said. "We can still trim it."

I followed her up the stairs into the bathroom on the third floor. She held my head beneath the faucet. Water dripped cold down my neck and into my eyes and nose before she sat me on a chair facing the mirror. From such a low angle, all I could see was her reflection. She rubbed my head with a towel before placing it around my shoulders. Taking a comb, she pulled it through my hair. My head dragged back. Before, when I was younger, I had resented that she cut my hair herself instead of taking me with her when she got her hair done, but now I was relieved that we weren't going to a fancy salon, that it was just the two of us. "What were you and Claude fighting about the other night?" I asked, wincing.

"We weren't fighting." She put the comb down and reached for a cigarette, struggling with the lighter. Then she drew in a long drag and set it on the edge of the porcelain sink before picking up the comb again.

"You had your coat on. And you'd packed a suitcase."

She parted my hair down the middle. "I was confused when I woke up."

I knew she hated storms. "Were you scared?"

"A little," she said, now wielding a pair of scissors. As wet clumps of hair fell to my lap, she added, "If there's one thing I've learned, it's this: The life you have is the life you choose."

I made a face at her. I didn't choose to be haunted by my father's ghost, or choose to live here in the Cake House with so many secrets. But the more I thought about it, the more I wondered if I had. After all, I had chosen to go to the party. I had chosen the darkroom. Maybe I had even wanted my mother to leave my father.

After this thought, I looked for the ghost in the mirror's reflection, but there was nothing. More wet clumps of hair slid down to my waiting hands.

"I didn't choose any of this," I said.

"Maybe not," she conceded. She came around to kneel in front. "Should we give you bangs? What do you think?" Without waiting for my answer, she took the comb and scissors, cutting away at the hair over my eyes. "That's better." She took the towel from around my shoulders and dusted the hair off my lap, wiping at my neck. "It's still long," she said. "I didn't cut too much."

I looked at myself in the mirror, wanting to understand. "What about this life did you choose?"

Her fingers fiddled with my new bangs, brushing them over to one side, then back to the other. "We have to live with our choices, Rosaura. And I'm trying to live with mine. Or at least, taking some control over it. I've made a decision."

I watched her through our reflection in the mirror. She reminded me of crystal, both fragile and strong. I wanted to run far away from her, and I wanted to be just like her. She placed her hands on my shoulders and squeezed. She had made a decision. I didn't ask what it entailed, but I thought of the manila envelope full of money.

The moment passed. She pressed her lips to the top of my head before letting go, picking up the cigarette. Most of it had burned away, leaving a long, crooked finger of ash that crumbled into the sink.

"I'm going to lie down," she said, with a brief return of the Dahlia from the week before.

She left the bathroom, trailing smoke behind her. As she went under the shadow of the doorway, it seemed as if the smoke took the shape of a man that reached for her, grasping for her shoulder, missing by mere inches.

———

MONDAY MORNING, I HEARD ALEX'S footsteps and hurried putting on the rest of my clothing to meet him before he headed downstairs and left for school. He hadn't come home till late the night before, and I hadn't had the chance to talk to him, to see if he noticed my new haircut. He was standing by the open door of his bedroom.

"Where were you last night?" I asked.

He didn't answer but paused as he was putting on his jacket. I suspected strongly that he'd been with Tina.

"Whatever you're doing, you should end it." I was thinking of what my mother had said, about this being the life we choose.

"What?"

"With Tina. Break up with her."

His features were devoid of expression. "What makes you think we're even going out?"

I folded my arms. I couldn't tell if he was serious or not. "She believes you are."

"Then why should I break up with her? Give me one good reason."

The demand left me speechless. There were so many reasons why he should break up with Tina, I wasn't certain I could name them all. Because she deserved better. Because he didn't love her. If he did, he wouldn't kiss me. He wouldn't look at me the way he did.

"Because I want you to," I said, then turned and left his room.

Claude didn't comment but quirked his eyebrows when I came downstairs and demanded, "Can we go now? I don't want to be late and I want to take some pictures before class."

"Whatever you say." Claude followed me out to the Mercedes.

Eager to have a stockpile ready to develop in the soon-to-be-completed darkroom, I took pictures of the empty campus, the dew-glistening football field with its sleeping clusters of daisy-chain flowers. With the temperature cold enough for my hands to ache, I sat near the football field and took pictures. I could have gone inside one of the warm buildings, but I preferred to be outside with my camera and catch the start of the new day on film.

The broken focus of my camera made objects in the distance blurry. I trained the lens on two fuzzy figures in the distance moving closer. By the long red hair and skinny skeleton silhouette, I knew one of them must be Aaron. The other, Tom.

Aaron came into focus first, the bruise below his right eye having faded to a mottled yellow with green around the edges. Without the skeleton makeup, freckles crowded across his nose. They both plopped down to the ground next to me.

"If it isn't our very own intrepid photographer," said Aaron. Tom lay on the grass.

I had been wondering if I would see them again, if perhaps they would emerge from the sea of faces in the hallways at school or remain onetime apparitions from the party.

"Does it hurt?" I asked, sorry for the bruises and cuts on both of their faces.

Aaron smiled a little. "If I say yes, will you kiss it?" His smile slipped away as the first bell rang for class.

"Let's get out of here, go for a drive," said Aaron. He stared down at the grass. "I have my car. We can go wherever. Take the day."

My first thought was that Alex would know. Not only

that I ditched classes, but that I went with these boys in particular. I looked at Tom where he lay with an arm shading his eyes. The skin on his knuckles had split but was already scabbed over. Most of Alex's animosity during the fight had been focused on him. And yet they were friends enough for Tom to be invited into Alex's room. Some dark impulse of mine wanted Alex to yell at me, come after me, to answer my questions when I asked him what he was doing with Tina. Anything but ignore me.

"Forget it," said Aaron. "Forget I asked."

"Let's go," I said.

Aaron grinned. He slapped Tom on the shoulder. Tom peeked from under his arm and let Aaron pull him up on his feet. The three of us slipped between buildings to an opening in the fence, then scurried over to Aaron's station wagon, an old Buick with bench-style seats that smelled of aftershave, engine grease, and, weirdly, bananas. I sat between them.

The mountains made a jagged silhouette in the sky. We drove on Soledad Canyon Road past horse ranches and riding stables then onto the highway, the windows cracked open, the wind whistling a strange tune. Bushes dotted the way like spots on a calico cat as the road hugged rock walls and sheer cliffs. Aaron turned onto a smaller path, and we drove high up to a mountaintop covered in billowing wheat-colored grass. Below, over the side of the mountain, I saw houses and ranches, open fields. Aaron parked the car beside a large rock formation.

The wind lashed my hair across my face.

"Stand with him," said Aaron, trying for my camera as he pushed me next to Tom.

"No—first the two of you, over there," I said, wanting

the first picture taken to be of them. Tom leaned against the hood of the station wagon and pulled Aaron to sit next to him. Aaron squawked, thrown off balance, but he settled next to Tom and flung an arm around his shoulders. Aaron turned awkward under the camera, grinning like a child at a birthday party, all teeth and cheeks and bright smiles, while Tom could have been a professional model, posing with stormy eyes focused on some distant skyline.

We took turns, each taking charge of the camera until another claimed it. Tom got creative, forcing Aaron and me to bend and contort into ridiculous poses. Aaron, on the other hand, wanted action scenes: Tom jumping off the hood of the station wagon, Tom carrying me on his back. Aaron swung my arms up and down, hyperactive and unstoppable. "Who's a winner?" he asked, laughing, then flung my arms up and took my picture. "You are!"

Aaron led me to the rock formation, tugging off his shoes until he stood barefoot. My shoes and socks followed. He started climbing, and I placed hand and foot into the same holds Aaron used, until I teetered at the top with him.

I turned back to help Tom, but he remained sitting on the hood of the wagon. "You're not getting me to climb that rock. I'll fall over the side. Crazy mofo," he scolded.

"Party pooper," Aaron yelled. But the merry light in his eyes vanished when Tom rolled off the hood and crawled into the backseat of the car.

I squeezed Aaron's hand.

"Raise your arms. Up, up. That's it," he said, whooping out loud and hopping up and down in a comical war dance, his voice carried away, echoing into vastness, bouncing from one side of the valley to the other. "Your turn," he said.

"No way." I shook my head, dizzy from the altitude.

"Come on, let it out. Let the wind take it. Give it up to the gods of sun and crabgrass." He grinned, then wrapped one of his long arms around my middle and made me stand in front of him. "Trust me."

He put his hands on my shoulders. I closed my eyes, tipping forward as if I might dive off the rock, legs swaying, but he held me against his chest. I barely breathed, my toes gripped into the rock as if I had claws like a bird. I lifted my arms, felt his arms line up along mine. And then there it was, a long, single note spilling from my throat and out into the open valley, not very loud but building louder until it was all I could hear.

When my voice failed, Aaron kissed me, lips and teeth and saliva, wet and slippery, smooth like the wind-polished rock face, clinging like the tough grass. We sat on the rock, facing the valley.

"What about Tom?"

Aaron didn't answer, spreading his legs so that I could sit between them as he wrapped both of us in his jacket. The station wagon was the only immediate reminder of civilization. I couldn't see Tom through the windshield.

"What's wrong with him?" I leaned back and pressed my cheek against Aaron's chest, my butt already numb from sitting on the hard rock.

Aaron's breath was warm on my scalp. "You want a list? Jeez, where should I start? He likes Pop Rocks for one thing. And by 'like' I mean 'is obsessed with.' He's a Pop Rocks fanatic; it's the weirdest thing. Demands I drive him all over creation to buy the damn things. I find them stuck in the seat of my car, in my *hair*. Everywhere. And he thinks Van Halen was better *with* Sammy Hagar. I don't even know what to say to that one."

I laughed and Aaron put his cheek next to mine. From his front pocket he took out a joint and a lighter. The smoke floated away, carried by the wind.

"Are you scared of Alex?" I asked.

"Nah. Your friend Alex is a . . . chump," he said, nodding as if that gesture added weight to his word choice.

"I've seen Tom with him," I said. "Are they friends?"

Maybe that was what irritated Aaron, that Alex might be friends with Tom, usurping his position. But Aaron snorted.

"Alex isn't capable of having friends," he said.

"What does that mean?"

"Only that he doesn't view people the same as you or I do. He doesn't have friends. Unless they're rich."

"You're wrong," I said.

Aaron's expression cooled. He slid off the rock, then made a motion that I should do the same. He caught me when I jumped down, my feet raw and frozen. We walked back to the station wagon.

Tom almost fell out of the backseat when Aaron opened the door. He had been sleeping with his head tucked against the window, the sleeve of one arm rolled up. He was bleeding from the inside of his elbow.

"Hey," Tom said, struggling to open his eyes.

Aaron crouched next to him, out of hearing range. I inched along the grass, straining to listen without intruding.

"You said you didn't have any more." Aaron held Tom's face between his hands.

"I'm sorry." Tom nodded, his head falling forward.

———

THE STATION WAGON FLEW DOWN the mountain, careening around the curves of the winding road. Once again the chatter of the wind through the open window was the only conversation in the car. Tom sat in the middle this time, regaining consciousness every so often like a kite yanked by a strong wind. Aaron propped him up and I stared at the golden mountains until the school came into view.

"How long have we been gone?" I asked. For the first time I took note of the sun sunk low in the sky and the lengthening shadows.

"All day," said Aaron. Tom blinked like a baby as we drove up to the main entrance, where a few students still loitered by their cars. It looked like the last class had ended some time ago, and that particular desolate, post-school, end-of-the-day quiet had settled over the campus. Neither Aaron nor I had a watch. It was possible that Claude had even come and gone.

The VW Bug was parked on the opposite side of the street, close to the residential houses behind the school. The passenger-side door was open and, as if he had been kneeling, Alex's blond head rose into view.

We coasted to a creaky stop several feet away. I pushed my door open and heard a muffled crying, the kind of crying that came from south of your heart. Through the windshield I saw Joey sitting in the driver's side. Then I saw a third person, partially blocked by Alex. A flutter of a ribbon, dark hair pulled back in a low braid. Tina sat in the passenger side. When she saw me approach, she covered her face with both hands before pushing past Alex and running across the street toward the school.

The driver's-side door opened. "Tina, wait," called Joey.

She ran around the car, pausing to say something to Alex in a fierce whisper before running after her friend.

I wanted to ask what had happened, but Tom, who had sobered somewhat, beat me to it. "What did you do to her?"

Alex tensed, and I expected another fight, but instead Alex sighed. "It's better this way."

Tires squealed, and I heard the familiar rumble of a Mercedes. Claude pulled up on the other side of Aaron's station wagon. Without a flinch or a flicker of emotion, Alex turned and got into the backseat.

CHAPTER FOURTEEN

Every evening after school Claude and I worked together to finish the darkroom. He boarded up the window; I painted the walls. He hired a plumber to pipe water into the room from the downstairs bathroom. I directed several more trips to the camera store. He bought a drafting table with a stool, another set of shelves, a pushpin board, a light box, more basins, more of everything.

One night Alex helped clean and sand the floorboards. I hadn't seen much of him since the breakup with Tina. I burned with questions and with an uncomfortable awareness of the scent of his sweat as he worked the sander over the wood.

Claude stabbed into the drywall to get at the electrical wiring, teetering on a stool as I handed him a second overhead light. He showed me how to wire a third light outside the room and mount it on a sawed-off piece of two-by-four. I hammered the extra lightbulb to the door beam.

"This is safelight," he said when I finished hammering.

He held a set of lightbulbs colored red, screwing one into the new light fixture. "That's what you use when printing to paper. You have to do it in safelight or you'll ruin the photograph. The next thing to buy is a developing tank, so you can develop your own negatives. It's a bit complicated, but then you'll be able to do everything yourself."

We were done. He toggled the switches. Normal light flipped over to the deep red of safelight, like new blood, enhancing the wrinkles that crowded around the corners of Claude's eyes. "Shall we develop the first photo together?" he asked, gathering the stack of negatives I had collected so far. "Pick one."

I chose one of my mother standing before a full-length mirror. His hands guided my hands through each step, while he murmured instructions, patient and attentive. How to thread the film, how to focus, how to choose the right grade of paper, dip in one chemical bath, wait for the image to emerge, dip in another to stop the process. A slow, careful dance.

Her head appeared first beneath the watery veil, then the line of her shoulder, the sway of her back, and the rest of the room with the sunlight streaming over the carpet and the bed unmade behind her. She was putting on a dress, her head turned to one side, her arms contorted, attempting to reach the zipper. A lit cigarette balanced in an ashtray on the dresser nearby, smoke floating from the tip in whorls that wrapped around her feet and around her neck like hands or chains.

Claude held the dripping photo. "It looks like a man," he said, pointing at the cigarette smoke that encircled my mother. "See? The head is here, and the body."

Within the folds of smoke I saw a pair of eyes, a mouth,

and a wound to the side of the ghost's head. The more I studied the photograph, the more his shape solidified behind her, taller than she was by a couple of inches.

"Maybe it's a ghost," Claude murmured, distracted as he pinned the photo to the clothesline.

My stomach clenched. "You see it too?"

The darkroom felt too warm, having no window to let in a breath of fresh air and a towel stuffed underneath the door to block the light. Claude's cologne was thick in the air.

He creased his forehead, then cursed under his breath as he held my shoulders between his hands. He flipped the switch and flooded the room with bright, electric light. With a push of his hand, he ushered me to stand before the dripping photograph hanging on the clothesline. In the full spectrum of light, the picture was simpler: a woman dressing, careless with her cigarette in a messy bedroom. Nothing remarkable. Nothing unnatural. Smoke twirled as smoke should.

"This house is no more haunted than anything else," he said. "She smokes too much."

"When I was a kid I stopped eating, trying to force her to quit," I said.

He laughed and squeezed my shoulder. "That sounds like you. You shouldn't be scared of a make-believe ghost, anyway."

After he left me alone to learn on my own, I flipped the switch back to safelight and selected another photo at random, this one of Claude and my mother standing together in front of the sliding glass doors, the full expanse of the garden behind them.

"No, you don't scare me," I said, but it wasn't for Claude.

I said it for the absent ghost, who had been missing since the night of the party. Perhaps the darkroom angered him. Or perhaps he waited in the invisible ether, ready to pop out like a jack-in-the-box. The next image emerged beneath the chemical bath: Claude, my mother, and the swirl of smoke that blurred their smiles, a smothering embrace.

LATER IN THE EVENING, MY mother knocked on the door of the darkroom. She examined the equipment Claude and I had set up, passing a hand over the bottles of chemicals.

"You've been busy," she said, and I couldn't interpret her threadbare smile.

"Isn't it great?" I asked. I loved the shelves the best. They held more than photography things—also brushes and glue and glitter and metal trays.

"It is." She fiddled with the two photographs I had developed. They swayed on the clothesline. "I've hardly seen you all week."

There was a note of sadness in her voice. "I've been here."

"So many things," she said, walking to the shelves. "I remember when you didn't want Claude to buy you anything."

I didn't know what to say. She had been the one to tell me to say yes when Claude wanted to buy my bed and my new clothes. The darkroom answered all my wishes, my unlooked-for dreams—it was a better birthday gift than the bedroom furniture.

"Should I have said no?"

"Of course not." She smiled with a shake of her head. "Come on," she said. "Help me with dinner."

In the kitchen, she handed me a cutting board and a zuc-chini. "Tell me everything," she said. "I want to know what you do for so many hours with no light and no fresh air."

I supposed, after all those summer days spent outside in the garden, it must seem strange to her. "Just photography stuff," I said. "Claude's teaching me how to develop pic-tures. It's cool."

Her lips pursed, and I knew I shouldn't have mentioned Claude. But after a few silent moments of her stirring a pot on the stove, her expression softened, and she said, "Your father loved that camera. That must be where you get it from."

"Maybe," I said. My father had taken an endless num-ber of pictures, at least a drawerful, but he never bothered to put them into albums or frames. "What happened to his pictures?"

"I think they're in the garage," she said, watching the flame as she set the soup to simmer.

After dinner, I took a flashlight and went outside to the garage. The box of my father's photographs was somewhere shelved and mislabeled among the forgotten detritus of Claude's life, and Alex's, not to mention the fragments of my mother's and mine. I found the switch for the overhead light and walked around the Honda, my fingers caressing the blue metal like an old friend. My reflection flashed in the glass of the passenger-side window: new haircut, new dimensions to my face.

On the corner beam overhead, a pretty bird with rose-colored feathers watched, one black pearl eye tracking my movement, its head cocked. No twittering, no chirping, only silence.

The first box I looked in held my mother's clothing. I

picked up one of her blouses—beige, the underarms darkened by use, and the sides pilled and thinned where it had
become worn. It used to be one of her work blouses, worn
with a blue suit and a paisley scarf pinned down to her collar with a bit of fake jewelry, but now it looked like a rag,
with its cheap fabric and loose buttons. It still held hints of
her smell, jasmine and cigarette smoke.

In the next box, I found old broken toys, a Barbie with
tangled hair, a snow-cone machine, and children's books
with the corners chewed up or the binding hanging by a
thread. A smaller box contained my watercolor set, the red
all gone but for a faint ring of color left embedded in the
plastic oval cup. Unbound colored pencils rolled around,
mixing with a few broken crayons. At the bottom, I found a
book of Mother Goose nursery rhymes bought secondhand
at a garage sale. What are little girls made of? Sugar and
spice and everything nice.

Some of this hadn't come with us in the car when we
had run away. I wondered who had returned to that distant
apartment, who had gone through our things and packed it
all in boxes.

I pulled down box after box stuffed with Claude's
papers full of long-worded financial forecasts and graphs
with jagged lines in a steady incline. Most were for Global
Securities, but there were several decrepit, moldy financial
statements with the heading "K.I.S., LLC" over the top.
Every now and then I came across tattered album covers of
Catherine Craig's violin concertos: Brahms, Mendelssohn,
and Sibelius.

The side door to the garage opened and Alex entered.
Startled, I dropped the album for Catherine Craig as soloist
in *Scheherazade*.

"Sorry," he said, letting the door creak shut behind him. "You weren't in your room. Or in the darkroom."

I bent over, as much to hide as to pick up the album and return the scratched record back inside its sleeve. It had been almost a full week since his breakup with Tina. Except for that one time when he'd come to help in the darkroom—where I couldn't speak with him while Claude was there watching and listening—he had made himself absent.

"Not that it's any of your business, but I'm looking for my father's photographs. They have to be in here some-where," I said, setting the album aside.

Dust billowed around Alex's head, caught in a stray beam of light. It made him glow. He shrugged. "Can I help?" he asked.

I started to say I didn't need his help, but he pulled down a box, poked inside, then put it aside to pull down another one. He was much quicker than me; he didn't need to linger over each piece of clothing or broken toy.

In less than a minute, he found a box on the top shelf and set it on the long metal worktable. "Is this what you're looking for?"

I jumped up to sit on the tabletop next to him and opened the box. My father had taken pictures of me as a baby: in my crib, on the couch, in my mother's arms, in my high chair. And more of my mother in various stages of undress. He was like me in that he tried to catch her unveiled, but he defeated me in quantity—so many pictures, several ruined by a thumb over the lens or the top of a head chopped off. There were no pictures of him. He had never stood still enough to have his picture taken.

Better than the photographs were the envelopes of nega-tives: a treasure of precious, unknown gold.

Alex trailed a finger down my arm. My skin puckered with goose bumps; my ears grew hot. I stared at the curls that formed at the base of his neck.

Despite the chill, he wore a short-sleeve T-shirt, the words "Mellow Yellow" written across his chest in buoyant, round letters. His breath warmed my cheek.

"You ditched class the other day," he said, close enough for me to see the trapped specks of gray in his eyes. "I could tell my dad."

"Go ahead." I knew he wouldn't. "You're a few days late, anyway."

Alex's almost smile had sharp edges. "Who'd you cut with?"

"Aaron and Tom," I said without hesitation.

He shook his head. He had already known but had asked to see if I'd answer. "My dad will lose his shit if he ever finds out."

"So don't tell him."

I realized it wasn't just Alex who would be upset if I cut class and became friends with Aaron and Tom; Claude would be angry too. Alex was once again acting on his father's behalf. Was it Aaron or Tom or both who would make Claude angry? But I knew the answer to that question, or I could guess, thinking of Tom unable to remain conscious for two seconds together during the drive back to school.

"You've been spending a lot of time with him."

It took me a moment to realize he meant Claude. Something in the way he said it reminded me of my mother.

"Has he asked you to do anything?" Alex's tone was casual.

"Like what? Like ask me to make friends with rich kids?"

He narrowed his eyes. "What do you know?"

"Nothing," I said. It had been a guess. "Not enough, so don't worry. Your secrets are safe, whatever they are."

He dusted his hands and jumped down from the worktable. "Take your pictures. Say no to anything else."

Before he could leave, I reached for the waistband of his jeans. "What happened with Tina?" I asked.

"What do you think happened?" He grabbed my wandering hands, held them together.

He must practice this, how to answer questions with questions. It was like a game to him, a slow way to bind me to him by acting as though he was interested. Acting as if I mattered, making me think I was special, important. Until he pushed me away afterward and left me wanting more.

"You broke up with her."

"Isn't that what you wanted?" he asked, so honest yet so cold.

I tried to wrench my hands free, but he wouldn't let go and at the same time wouldn't let me take hold of him. Suddenly he kissed me, knocking teeth together, biting my lip. I opened for him, took him in until he let go of my hands. I scraped my hand down his stomach and under his shirt, wanting to meet his challenge. He sucked in his breath, hissing from the shock of my chilled fingers.

I thought he would kiss me and then leave, walk away back into the house and barricade himself in his room like he had done before, but he put his hands around my waist and lifted me from the worktable. He carried me to the car, fumbled to open the door, and we tumbled onto the backseat.

He sensed my uncertainty and squeezed my hand, turned

my palm over to expose my wrist, scraping my skin with the calluses on his fingertips—his way of saying it was my choice to go or to stay. I brought his hand up to my cheek, to my neck.

The pleather seat was as cold as it had been the night of the party, but I sought the warmth of his skin, the hidden pockets of heat. He worked my jeans down, and I lifted my torso up so he could take my shirt off. He kicked his jeans aside, pushing my legs open with his knees.

"Wait, wait," I said.

Rising onto his elbow, he traced my eyebrows with the tip of his finger. "Do you want to stop?"

"No," I said. His stomach pressed down against mine with each breath. I didn't want to stop, but I wasn't certain I wanted to continue either.

"Are you sure?" he asked, bringing his hand between my legs.

I wasn't sure about anything. Not about him, or about the garage we were in, or about the house. I sighed when he slid a finger inside my body and teased until I gripped his arms and pushed onto his hand.

His eyes brightened with urgency. He had a condom.

"It'll hurt," he said. I spread my legs wide, faint from the reality of what we were doing.

"It's okay." I breathed into his mouth.

His forehead pressed against mine and I couldn't look away.

The pain blinded. I let him mold me, turn me over in his hands, rewriting my knowledge of everything, anything. The pelvis stretched, the bones re-formed, he pushed until I had all of him. I bit his shoulder and left a ring of teeth marks embedded in his pale skin. He moved within me, panting into my ear, hard and fast, and I let him. I wanted it. I wanted it all.

When he finished, he didn't move and I put my arms around his back, fingers finding each knobby point of his spine.

"Maybe it isn't Tina who I should stay away from," he said.

It took a moment for my brain to engage, to comprehend and understand what he had said. It hurt that he brought Tina into this moment. I pushed at his chest until he slid off to one side. It was awkward, seeing him naked from the waist down, his wet penis brushing against my thigh.

I turned to find my shirt and underwear. Pulling my jeans on, I slipped on my shoes, then climbed over his body, searching for balance. The car door shut behind me, unable to latch because it bounced against Alex's extended legs. The bird sat in its nest, watching.

The side door to the garage banged open, and Claude walked in. "Rosie," he said. "It's late. What are you doing in here?"

Alex was lying down on the backseat. I didn't dare look at him or at the car door only partly closed, or anywhere but at Claude. Could he see the stain of blood on my fingers?

"This box," I said, moving to the worktable. "My dad's photographs. I was looking for them."

He stepped back. "Good idea," he said, and held the garage door open for me, and I had no choice but to go through, with Claude following.

AFTER CLAUDE AND MY MOTHER had gone to sleep, I left my room and stood outside Alex's door. I put my hand on his doorknob, I even turned it, but it was locked.

———

THE NEXT MORNING I SAT in the living room and waited for Alex to come down the stairs, perched to block him as soon as he emerged. He had been in his room all morning, and it was close to noon before I heard his footsteps stomping down the hallway. I met him at the base of the stairs. He stopped when he saw me.

"Hi," I said, choking on that one simple word. "Can we talk?"

A car honked. He looked toward where the front door was, then back down at me. He put his hands on my shoulders and moved me out of his way.

"Later," he said, not cold but without patience, with avoidance, and I knew there would be no "later." Before I could stop him, he left through the front door.

I went to the bay window and pushed the curtain aside. Alex strode across the street, heading for the VW Bug parked under a tree.

"Hey," said Alex as he approached the car.

The person in the VW Bug spoke—I didn't know if it was Tina or Joey or both—but I heard only a few words: "How come" and "invite," followed by a laugh.

"Don't be stupid," answered Alex, opening the car door. "Just drive."

Hollowness expanded within my chest as the car pulled away. It seemed to match the soreness between my legs, the bruises that ghosted the insides of my thighs. My fingers and toes felt cold, and my mind searched for an explanation. I was certain Tina was in the car. Why had he left with her when they were supposed to be finished, when he and I had had sex the night before?

I went to the bathroom, stripped naked, and sat at the bottom of the tub with the water pouring down my back. It had started to cool when my mother knocked and entered the bathroom. She opened the shower door. "How long have you been in here?" she asked, holding a towel. "Do you feel okay?"

She touched my forehead, but I yanked my head away. "I just took a shower," I said, wrapping the towel around myself, afraid she could see the loss of my virginity on my skin. "I'm going to feel warm. Don't worry, I'm not sick."

"Claude wants to ask you a question," she said, and wouldn't let me go until I dressed and followed her.

Downstairs, Claude was at the dining table reading his newspaper. My mother settled in next to him with a sketch-book and colored pencil, staring at the blank page as if figuring out her plan of attack.

"Do you know where Alex went?" I realized Claude had been watching me. "Anything going on I should know about?"

I froze. Claude leaned back in his chair, nonchalant but for his penetrating stare, fingering the small key that opened the rolltop desk. It was that small, nervous action that betrayed Claude and allowed me to breathe. He was nervous about his money and whatever it was that Alex did for him. He wasn't asking because he knew what Alex and I had done in the garage.

"He doesn't talk to me."

Claude smiled and spun his keys on a finger before putting them in his pocket. "He's a teenager," he offered as an excuse, as if I weren't a teenager as well.

"You can spend the day with me," my mother said to me, her colored pencil still hovering over the blank page. She hadn't been paying attention. "Tell me what's going on in your life. Just you and me for a change."

"I need to go into the office today for a couple of hours. I should be back by three or so," Claude said, not waiting for my answer. My mother kept her eyes on the blank page.

"Can I go with you?" I asked before I thought about it. I wanted to get out of the house. I didn't want to be near Alex's room or near the garage. I didn't want to be waiting when he came home so he could ignore me again. "You said I need a developing tank. I made room for it in the dark-room. And I need that special paper to print color negatives black and white."

My mother's head finally came up. Her silence pulsed from across the table.

Claude was slow to answer. "I have to go into the office."

I shrugged. "Maybe I can help with things."

"Rosaura," said my mother, "Claude's been helping you all week. Isn't that enough? Do you have to bother him at his work, too?"

"Nonsense," said Claude, oblivious to her pale-faced alarm. "Sure, she can come. And then I can pick up the things she needs."

With great effort, my mother bowed her head, gripping her pencil with white-knuckled rigidity. She refused to watch as I followed Claude out the door.

I was silent during the drive to the camera store. My body was a constant reminder of the previous night, the way my flesh slid against itself in new and different ways, the way it felt like I had a hole inside me.

"Everything all right?" asked Claude as he drove.

"Why wouldn't it be?"

He took my sullenness in stride, going over the complicated process of developing my own film. It had to be done in total darkness; not even the red of safelight was allowed, everything done by touch, by feel.

"It won't be hard for you," Claude said, with a confidence that I didn't share.

At the camera store, we had to order the developing tank and the paper because they didn't have any in stock, so I walked through the different aisles. But there wasn't anything more I needed. Requesting to go to the store had been an excuse, and Claude had humored me. I loved looking at the different cameras, the lenses and stands and umbrella light bounces, while Claude explained how they worked and how they differed from one another and told stories from when he used to work for his school's newspaper.

I stopped listening but neither did I stray too far. At the back of the store, I found a few bookshelves with every sort of photography book imaginable. I picked one with the title *Photo Development: The Art of Image Manipulation*. It was a paperback, with a glossy cover of a woman standing in a bathroom looking at herself in the mirror, the only light coming from a bare bulb swinging fast enough to blur in a bright arc of light.

"I had a similar book when I first started playing around," said Claude.

I flipped through the pages, skimming over each page full of diagrams and samples. He put a hand on my shoulder and I leaned against him. The tears came before I could stop them.

"Rosie, Rosie," he said, bending down. "What is it? What's happened?"

I opened and closed my mouth like a fish trying to

breathe, but no matter how much I pushed, the words wouldn't come.

"Okay," he said. "It's all right." He rubbed my back, and I pressed against the scratchiness of his sweater. "Whatever it is, it'll be okay."

"Claude," I said, wondering if it was the first time I'd said his name out loud. "Thank you."

Instead of smiling or saying "you're welcome" or giving me another hug or doing any of the things one would expect, he closed his eyes before he took the book from my hand.

"We'll buy this. An early Christmas present. Anything else you want?"

"No," I managed, wiping my face on the sleeve of my jacket.

Ten minutes later we were riding an elevator to the sixth floor of Claude's office building, which was dominated by gray carpets, beige walls, and dark wooden doors with ornate plaques displaying businesses' names. We walked to the end of the hallway. The plaque next to the door read: "Global Securities, CEO Claude Fisk."

Inside was a bright set of rooms with prints of famous paintings on the walls: one of naked women lying down on a hillside and another that had swirls of a blue-and-yellow sky over a village. Leafy plants nestled between the chairs and couch in the waiting area, where a coffee service and water cooler hummed in a corner and plenty of magazines sat on the coffee table. The receptionist's desk was empty, with a sign placed at an angle: "Please take a seat. The receptionist will be with you in a minute." Past the receptionist's desk, I saw a pantry with a microwave and a refrigerator.

Claude flicked the light switch, then stood in the middle of the room looking like he didn't know what to do with me.

Despite the appearance of habitation in all the rooms—cluttered desks, scattered file folders—it felt empty, abandoned by its employees. I followed Claude to the largest office, his office. He had two picture frames on his desk. One was perhaps last year's school portrait of Alex, from the shoulders up, his smile showing that same hint of arrogance he always carried. In the other photo, a young Alex stood next to his father with a large costumed cartoon animal on the other side. The cartoon had his arm around Alex's narrow shoulders, its wide, vacant, plastic eyes staring straight ahead. Beneath the cartoon's head was a grate where the human underneath must have been sweating and counting the minutes until his workday ended. Alex's eyes were cast to the floor. He looked uncomfortable in his shorts, with one sock pulled over his calf and the other bunched around his ankle. Such a miserable little boy. I put the photo back on Claude's desk.

Unlike the rest of Global Securities, Claude's office thrummed with his energy. It smelled like him. His big desk contained files and notepads, a dried-up plant. A computer took up a chunk of space off to the side. Two chairs faced the desk, and I suddenly had a vision of my parents sitting in this office, meeting with Claude, with my father standing up, coming around the desk to give Claude a handshake, to slap Claude on the shoulder in camaraderie.

"You might be bored," Claude said, sounding uncertain.

"I won't get in the way. I can help."

Tilting his head, he led me to a small room—part copy room, part storage area, packed with open boxes filled with unsorted piles of paper. He sat me down before a large machine with metal toothy grooves on top and buttons down its side, pushing a box of paperwork over.

"You can shred these," he said, pointing to disorganized stacks of folders and documents. "I've been putting it off. This'll be a big help."

Photocopied forms, fill-in-the-blank questions with the answers given in handwriting. "Have you ever invested before?" "Do you typically invest large amounts or small amounts?" "How much do you have available in liquid funds?" "How did you hear about Global Securities?" The forms were signed by Bob Anders, Xavier Villalobos, Desiree Robinson, Raymond and Helena Myers.

"You don't need these anymore?"

He grinned. "I'm happy you're here," he said. "No, I don't need them anymore."

As I started feeding the machine sheet after sheet of other people's lives, Claude made coffee and went into his office, putting on the radio. He kept his door open, and I could see him sitting at his desk. We both worked in silence and strange camaraderie as the shredder hummed and chewed.

The phone rang and Claude answered, changing from the man who could sit with me in the darkroom into Claude the businessman, Claude the charmer. On the phone, he used words and phrases that were meaningless to me: future trading, high-yield investments, acceptable losses, and on and on. How do you trade the future? What was an acceptable loss? In a strange way, it was similar to the cop language I had heard Deputy Mike use the day he found me riding my bike naked. I wondered who was on the other end of the call. Was it a colleague? Or was it a client, someone whose name might be on a form in the pile I had in my hands, moments away from being fed to the shredding machine?

I paid closer attention, not only to the words he spoke but to the way he spoke them.

"You don't want to do this," he said. "*Listen to me.* This isn't one of those penny-ante mutual funds handled by some anonymous manager. I personally watch every dollar I invest on behalf of my clients—I sweat over it. If you cash out now, you're throwing away an immense advantage."

Silence.

"I see," he said in a darker tone. "No, of course, I'm sorry to hear that, but listen, the market is changing, daily, believe me, you don't want to— All right. I can see I won't change your mind. I just don't want you to blame me later, when you look back and realize the colossal mistake you made. No, it's all right. It'll take some time. Six to eight weeks, per our terms of service, and penalties, of course."

I turned back to the machine. The machine's hunger never ended, its stomach emptied into black garbage bags. It vibrated, growled, shuddered. I ran my hand down its flank where its heat was expelled with static electricity, my hair rising on my head, sparks shooting from my fingertips.

Claude entered the copy room to share a candy bar and a soda. Our fingers shocked each other, jarring all the way up my arm. He watched me tear the wrapper from the candy bar.

"How's it going?" he asked.

I bit off a mouthful and tried to smile. "Fan*tas*tic."

He smiled at my sarcasm, sipped his soda, and stared at the wall, lost in thought. I handed him back the rest of the candy bar. He was the one who looked tired.

"Bad day?" I asked.

His eyes shifted to me with a sudden unguarded intensity.

I jumped when the office door opened with a jingle. Claude pushed the half-eaten candy bar at me and fumbled with his can of soda in his haste to greet whoever had entered, shoving both into my hands. I peeked around the corner; a man older than Claude with gray hair and two deep-set raccoon-ringed eyes stood by the water cooler. It was the man from the football game, with the teenage son who was a friend of Alex's, the same man whom Claude had talked to the entire night.

Claude held out his hand. "Harold," he said in his big, booming businessman voice, and Harold gave an answering grin as they shook hands. "This is unexpected, but it's good to see you." Claude led Harold to his office without acknowledging my presence. "Come in, have a seat. How's your family?" He shut the door, muffling their voices.

The smell of melted chocolate lingered on my fingers. I tried to hear what they were saying as I picked up another fistful of papers. The top one read, "William Stuart, married with one daughter, who heard about Global Securities via the *Santa Clarita Valley Signal*."

The machine hummed, waiting. I stared down at William Stuart's application, thinking of the football game, of Harold, of the smell of chocolate, of Alex at the football game, of the ache and sting between my legs.

Then I saw the signature down at the bottom of the page, in the box reserved for in-office use: Robert Douglas, my father's name, written in his style of jagged lines. The shock of his name made me look up to see if anyone had noticed, but Claude was still secluded with Harold. The rest of the office pulsed in its pervasive silence. I looked at the next form and saw his name again in the box marked for in-office use. And again. How many more? How many times had I unknowingly fed my father to the shredding machine?

He hadn't been a client. He had never had the type of money a client of Claude's would need to invest. No, all this time, he had been an employee. He had worked for Claude. "Claude's the ticket," he had said. "I do this work for him, and we got it made."

The machine roared to life, and I fed my father into its mouth.

CHAPTER FIFTEEN

After Harold left, Claude said he would drive me home and come back to the office. He needed to stay longer than he'd thought.

"Can I ask you something?" I asked as he shut and locked the door to the office, distracted.

"Of course, sweetie," he said, but he didn't wait for me and I had to break into a run to catch up. In the car, Claude glanced in my direction while backing the Mercedes out of its parking spot. "Did you have a question?"

I took a deep breath and thought about how to frame my questions. I wanted to know what my father had done for Claude, the kind of work he'd done. I wanted to know why he'd called it a game.

Before I could speak, Claude patted my leg. "Don't worry," he said. "We'll have time to work in the darkroom later. There are a few tricks I know we can do without a developing tank."

As he spoke, he tapped at the steering wheel. It reminded

me of Alex. Claude pushed the Mercedes into traffic, tapping at the steering wheel, gazing into the distance with a faraway expression. He wasn't thinking about me or the darkroom. Those were just words he said because he thought I wanted to hear them.

"Great," I said, and turned to look out the window.

Claude dropped me off at the house. I found my mother in the kitchen, surrounded by groceries. She was unpacking bags, the counter crowded with vegetables and packaged food. "You're back," she said, with a strange, relieved smile. "You can help me with dinner."

I sighed and sat down on one of the kitchen chairs. "Can I ask you a question?"

She didn't look up from where she was pulling out pots and pans.

"About Dad?" I continued.

She stopped and became still, her hand on the handle of a saucepan. When she turned, her face held an expression of resigned fear. Then the phone rang. I jumped, and my mother took in a breath before she left for the hallway. I heard her answer and then say, "Just a moment." Then she called for Alex.

I went out into the hallway to see Alex come down from his room and felt my entire body awaken, wondering how long he had been home and if he had thought of me at all. There was a moment with all of us looking at one another before he took the phone. There were no other phone extensions, no place for him to go for a private conversation, but he picked up the phone and carried it to the other side of the house, as far as the cord would let him.

My mother and I went back into the kitchen, my questions forgotten as I chopped a cucumber into wedges and tried to listen to Alex's conversation.

IN THE NEXT FEW DAYS, Alex acted as if nothing had changed between us. To him, we were the same stepbrother and stepsister who used to listen to music and ride our bikes together, as if he hadn't taken my virginity in the darkness of the garage. At school he was rarely alone, surrounded by his friends or sitting with Joey. The weeks drained toward winter, shrinking the days into stubby, short stumps of limp light. When school closed for the holidays, I spent all my time either in the darkroom or with my camera outside taking pictures, avoiding Alex as much as he avoided me.

On Christmas Eve, my mother wore a patterned dress all in Christmas colors with her hair up in a twist stuck through with a pencil. She looked like someone else's mother, not the woman who had raised me the previous fourteen years.

She came to the darkroom with her hip cocked to one side, wielding a vegetable peeler like a knife. "That's enough photography for one day," she said. "I need your help."

I knew that tone. With a muffled sigh, I followed her into the kitchen. She was planning to cook a turkey, pie, and macaroni and cheese. I started the mashed potatoes, peeling and digging out bruises and gnarled rooted eyes, loving the feel of the potatoes with their brown strips of rough potato skin, the sweet dirt smell of them. The day had turned warm enough for open windows that let in the clean scent of a recently washed world.

"You've been spending a lot of time with Claude," my mother said as she mixed the cheese and macaroni together.

She was trying for a tone of indifference, of idle curiosity. "What is it that keeps the two of you so occupied?"

The potato slipped from my hand and I had to chase it around the sink. I found her unease—or was it jealousy?—difficult to comprehend. Perhaps seeing Claude and me together, like a father and daughter, was something she hadn't realized could happen. That I might choose Claude, that I might choose him even over my father. Maybe she worried that I would learn that my father had worked for Claude.

"I thought you wanted us to get along." I stopped skinning the potato, turning it around in my wet hands. "Isn't that the whole point? Aren't we supposed to be a family?"

"I know, I know," she said. "Of course we are." She set the macaroni on the counter. "It's just that . . . ," she began, then seemed to change her mind. "Have you gone to his office again?"

For the first time, I noticed the few gray hairs that sprung from the top of her head. They were difficult to see amid the honeyed strands, but at that moment the light from the window bathed the both of us in the clarity of midmorning.

Alex walked into the kitchen. He paused when he saw how we faced each other, then continued to the refrigerator to grab a can of soda. As he walked past, my skin prickled and the hairs on my arm rose.

My mother looked from me to Alex, then back to me. She creased her brow and searched my face.

"Something's changed," she said after Alex had left the kitchen.

"Mom," I said, annoyed.

"What is it?"

"Nothing, God. Just—" She took me by the shoulders. I

ducked away, raising an arm to fend her off. But I did know what she meant. Even though I looked the same on the outside as I always did, my hips, my breasts, even my skin felt different. I couldn't tell her what had happened in the garage. "Nothing's wrong. Leave me alone."

She continued her silent inspection of my face. Through the kitchen window I saw the Mercedes pull into the driveway, a tree strapped to its top. Claude honked. I went back to peeling potatoes, afraid she could see the stain of Alex in the heat of my cheeks. Claude honked again, and she moved toward the door.

Carrying one end of the tree through the door, Claude beamed when he saw her. "Merry Christmas," he trumpeted, setting the tree down for a moment to spread his arms wide. She rocked back on her heels when he kissed her, but he didn't notice, picking the tree back up and marching through the living room with Alex holding the other end, trailing pine needles like confetti.

I climbed onto the couch and watched them fit the tree into a corner of the room, its large, spindly branches bouncing as they moved it this way and that way.

"What do you think?" Claude wiped his hands, satisfied. He picked up a bag of white cotton batting and began to spread it around the bottom of the tree. It was fluffy and green, and already the pine scent spread throughout the first floor.

"I think it looks like a tree in a living room," I said.

He gave me a look that said, *Don't be a wiseass.*

"Come on, Rosie, do your part," he said, pointing with his chin to the boxes full of ornaments.

Alex grabbed a tangled mess of colored lights; I grabbed the tinsel. We did a complicated dance around each other until Claude called me over to his side. "Over here," he said, indicating a bald spot on one side of the tree. "Attagirl, get it all covered."

The afternoon flowed into evening, bringing chilled air and a jeweled sky, vast and deep, visible through the sliding glass doors. We ate in the living room as Alex and I took turns decorating the tree.

"I like the red ones." I held a perfect round orb in my hand, seeing my reflection widened, my lips stretched, my nose flattened. I held the red ornament close to Alex so I could see his face distorted, stretched wide and unrecognizable.

Claude hunched over his record collection, picking through carols and old standards with baritone men and soprano women. Like his son, he preferred vinyl to compact discs, and he spun the black records in his large hands before carefully dropping the needle.

My mother popped popcorn. I sat cross-legged with a needle and threaded string. She joined me, threading her own needle. I made her a popcorn crown and necklace to match. She laughed a real laugh. Distracted by the lopsided crown falling over her eyes, she pierced herself with the needle and hissed in pain. A bead of blood formed, squeezed from the tip of her finger. Claude left the stereo and went to her, kneeling by her side.

"It's nothing," she said. "Jabbed myself like an idiot—that's all."

"Give it here," he demanded.

She hesitated but offered her hand. Claude inspected her finger, brought it up to his mouth, and sucked on it. She lowered her eyes.

"All better," said Claude. He took the pile of popcorn from my lap. "Popcorn Queen, come on."

Together, he and I draped the tree. He held his arms out, ready to catch me if I fell while I stood on a stool and put the angel on the top, her cloth hands demurely pressed together, her head bent to one side as if listening for answers.

"It's so pretty," said my mother. She started picking up dishes, bits of escaped popcorn, and tinsel.

"Alex, help your stepmother."

Claude's command hung in the air as my mother froze. Except for that time when he'd lit her cigarette for me, I don't think Alex and my mother ever spoke to each other.

"Yes, sir," said Alex, bending to collect my plate as the record player scratched onto the next song. Claude took my hand, twirled me around.

"Brenda Lee, she's the best," he said, singing along. *"Rocking around the Christmas tree at the Christmas party hop."*

I couldn't help but laugh. The lights blurred, color blending and arcing across my vision. I was breathless, dizzy; the world tilted, rocking to one side. My mother watched, a smile spreading across her face, slow and sweet.

Alex leaned against the doorway in the kitchen with his arms folded—very stern, very cross—but his habitual chill defrosted as he also watched us dance. He clapped and sang along.

Claude spun me around until I collapsed onto the couch.

"And now your turn, m'lady," he said to my mother.

"Oh no." She backed away, shaking her head, coquettish.

"Oh yes," he insisted, his hands clasping hers like big traps.

"You and Rosaura play. I've got work to do," she protested, yet she let him drag her to the center of the room. "No, no. Really. Robert, I can't."

It took only a second to register her mistake. Claude dropped her hands, his smile halting like a windup toy stuttering to a stop.

"Claude, I—" she started.

"It's all right." He held up his hand, the effort it took written in the stiffness of his shoulders. "A slip of the tongue," he said, but his voice was every bit as cold as Alex's had ever been.

He went to the stereo, started flipping through record albums as if nothing had happened. My mother and I didn't move. Neither did Alex. A minute passed before Claude stopped pretending and dropped his head.

"How can you even think of him?" he asked.

She looked to her hands, to her feet, and then up to the ceiling, as if the stucco contained words that might save her. "I don't."

"Don't lie to me."

He moved toward her, and she flinched before she could control it. It stopped him. Sorrow stamped all over his face, he reached for her and took her arm. She breathed deeply, then leaned against him so he could rest his cheek on the top of her head. Together, they started up the stairs.

The music had ended during the previous five minutes without my noticing, and the needle skipped over the label. I stood in the middle of the living room, no longer dizzy, no longer dancing. I couldn't erase that last image of my mother's face with my father's name on her lips.

Alex turned the stereo off. "Hey," he said, and lifted my chin so I had to look at him. Concern warmed his eyes. "Don't worry about them."

Here was my chance. Here he stood in front of me, the two of us alone, without Claude, without my mother, and the well of emotion in the pit of my stomach threatened to overwhelm everything. I grabbed his hand so tightly it must have hurt.

I grabbed his shirt.

I kissed him.

DARKNESS DRAPED MY ROOM, WITH accents here and there from the moon glowing through the window. Something moved in the shadows, and my stomach clenched in anticipation of the ghost hiding in the folds of night, but I refused to fear him, not while Alex stood beside me.

Alex removed his shirt and jeans to stand, bare chested, in nothing but a pair of boxer shorts. The background of darkened shadows made him paler than usual.

Above us, I thought I heard the low rumble of Claude's voice, the quiet susurration of my mother's cries. Alex moved again when there was nothing but the wind, and together we lay on my bed.

"Why'd you drive off with Tina?" I asked.

He drew back. "What? When? Which time?"

"That morning. After you and I—" I couldn't say the words, too shy, too uncertain.

He took a moment to think, and it angered me further that neither Tina nor I was important enough for him to remember. But then he said, "That wasn't Tina. That was Joey."

It hadn't been Tina; it had been Joey. He'd driven off with Joey. Did they get together and talk about Tina? What was Joey to Alex? Was there now a fourth person, to make our triangle a quartet? I didn't know whether to believe him or not, but either way it increased my competition for his attention.

"She's a friend," he said, answering my unspoken question, but I remembered that Aaron said Alex didn't have any friends. "What if I said you're the only one? No one else. What would you say?"

I shifted a little, my blood pumping warm and hard in a thumping rhythm. Smooth; he was smooth and slippery like glass. These might have been the same words he spoke to Tina. But I realized it didn't matter. Regardless of his feelings for Tina, I would still want him and still take him.

"I'd say okay. Show me." The dark obscured his features.

"I should go back to my room, Rosie. I should leave you."

He used his father's name for me. It made me shiver. He shifted closer, a bit of moonlight catching the intensity of his eyes.

"But you won't," I said. I didn't want him to go.

He slid a hand under my top, lifting it up and over. He untied my shoes, removing my socks. My jeans followed. We lay in our underwear.

The house creaked. Claude's voice dropped through the ceiling from the third floor like an unwelcome visitor. We stopped, Alex tense and rigid, but in the silence that followed he smiled, and for once I didn't shiver; for once he made me warm and I wanted to feel his smile on every part of my body. I wanted to unzip his skin and reach between ribs to hold his beating heart in my hand—as if that would tell me where he might choose to give his love.

I licked his lips. I was skin hungry, unable to get enough, thrilled when he shivered and panted and came apart in my hands. He slid my underwear down, parting my legs. I stopped listening for the noises of the house at rest. All I could hear was the music of Alex's breathing.

He filled all of my vision, above me, between my legs.

He paused to put a condom on, then pushed in, and it hurt less than before. He took his time, until he couldn't hold back anymore and I pressed my lips against his neck.

I WOKE IN TIME TO see Alex sit up and slip his boxers on. I trailed my hand down his back. He arched away from the chill of my fingers but smiled when I sat up.

"I better leave," he said.

The bedside clock read a little past six in the morning.

"No one's awake," I said.

I slid my arm across his back. He held himself still this time, knowing that it was me who touched him. I explored the vulnerable skin at the back of his neck, taking the time I hadn't earlier. He shivered, but I didn't let that stop me, tasting down the line of his collarbone, lost in the poetry of his nakedness until he pushed me down against the mattress and kissed my neck, my breast, his hand pushing at my legs.

The house creaked, its weight shifting when a door opened and closed. Alex froze and we both looked at the door to my room. Nothing happened; all was quiet. "It's okay. It was probably the wind," I said, hoping that he would start again, but he pulled away, alert.

"Someone's awake," he whispered without looking at me. He rose from the bed and walked to the door, opening it a crack to look into the hallway, his bare shoulders bone white in the moonlight.

I didn't have a good argument for him to stay. Alex was gathering his discarded clothing but paused when I stood and let the sheet fall away. He watched me cross the short distance.

"See you in the morning," I said.

He shook his head at my crazy naked boldness, and I felt warm inside that he liked what he saw. But with another smile, a quick kiss, he slipped through the door into the darkness of the hallway.

With his absence, I felt a wave of embarrassment to be naked alone in my room, and I slipped my nightgown over my head. I cupped my breasts through the nightshirt, remembering how he had cupped them, tempted to follow him down the hallway, into his room.

I heard a bump and scrape of furniture, then a curse. I stepped out into the hallway, then down the stairs.

Moonlight flooded the living room, spilling into the dining room. All was quiet, but then Claude emerged from the shadows. I took a step back before he could see me.

He was pacing, his briefcase left open with his papers strewn across the dining table. Behind Claude, the desk was open and exposed, pulled away from the wall. It must have been the source of the noise. He paced from the desk to the briefcase, then all the way over to the sliding glass doors, his head twitching, as if getting rid of a fly. A hand swatted, confusion crossing his face. The Christmas tree stood unlit in the corner, the cloth angel silent and observing from on high. The longer I watched, the more I saw a shadow that dogged Claude's every move.

My heartbeat slowed, and my breath with it, and I saw *him*: the shape of the ghost's head, a couple of inches shorter than Claude, his sweatshirt with the pocket weighed down, the wound on the side of his face. I froze, my heart hammering so hard it hurt. Claude continued his pacing, restless: desk, briefcase, then up and down the living room. With each step the ghost mirrored his movements. Each step Claude took, the ghost took one with him. Step. Step. Turn. Breathe. Sigh.

A quiet rasping filled the living room. The harder I listened, the more I understood the words that were not spoken out loud. A hum in the air. A buzz.

The ghost whispered in Claude's ear, saying, *You're worthless.*

Claude twitched; he swatted the air again, but the ghost switched to his other side.

You fail at everything.

Claude paused by the laptop and picked up a few of his papers.

She's using you. She doesn't love you. It's your fault. All of it.

He moved to the desk and the ghost followed.

"What are you doing?" I asked, my voice cracking, uncertain which of them I spoke to.

Claude glanced up and so did the ghost. They smiled in sync, but only the ghost lifted his finger to his lips.

"Did I wake you?" Claude asked. "I'm sorry. I'm . . . working, figuring things out."

He pushed the desk back into position and rolled the top down, used his key to lock it. "Isn't it a little early?" he asked. "I hope you're not trying to sneak a peek at your present." But his chiding grin didn't hold as he returned to staring without focus at the documents in his hand.

"Couldn't sleep," I said, with my gaze more on the ghost than on Claude.

"Oh. Well—" Claude seemed at a loss. He wasn't looking at me but went back to collecting his paperwork into a neat pile. The ghost stood beside him, his shadow.

Behind me, I heard the soft sound of bare feet on carpet and turned to find my mother in her kimono robe standing a few steps above. She came down the remaining steps and entered the living room. The four of us—Claude, my mother, myself, and the ghost—stood in awkward silence.

There was no movement between us, until I saw the ghost lean in close to Claude to whisper in his ear, and somehow, as before, I heard the words as well: *What's wrong with you? How can you stand to look at her?*

Then the ghost detached from Claude, took a step back, then another step, and melted into shadow. With his disappearance, the spell lifted, and I took a big breath.

"You're awake," said Claude, speaking to my mother.

"I thought I'd start breakfast," she said.

"That's good. But I have some work to do." Claude returned to his briefcase. "I should really go into the office. Just for a few hours."

"On Christmas?" I moved farther into the room. Claude startled when I spoke, having forgotten that I was there. I turned from my mother to Claude and back again.

"Just for a few hours," he repeated, and a smile returned to his face when he looked at me.

"You can't go."

"Rosie," said Claude in a reasoning tone, but I could hear the change in his voice and knew he wouldn't be leaving.

"Maybe later, after we've opened presents."

He sighed but nodded. "All right. Why don't you turn the Christmas tree lights on?"

I moved to the tree and plugged in the lights, watching them blink on and off, on and off. Beneath the tree, presents waited to be opened, my name among them. I crouched low to inspect the new ones that had appeared overnight.

Claude moved over to the couch, bringing his paperwork and briefcase with him. "See anything for you?" he asked.

There was a box with my name on it, wrapped in silver

paper and topped by a round, springy bow. I picked it up. It was heavy. Claude smiled as I carefully turned the box around.

"Rosaura, help me with breakfast," said my mother, standing by the door to the kitchen.

"Go help her," said Claude, but without looking at her.

I set the box down, hesitating for a moment, worried that the ghost would reappear with my absence, but Claude nodded toward the kitchen and I left him alone in the gray of morning.

She and I cooked breakfast. "Maybe I should get a job," she said while carefully inserting bread into the toaster.

I stirred scrambled eggs around in a pan and lowered the fire.

"Something part-time, maybe at a store," she continued. "I can't sit here and do nothing all day forever."

Careful not to drop any of the egg, I scraped the pan clean before turning to her. She was looking at me with uncertainty, a quiet plea on her face.

"Sounds like a good idea." I said.

She pressed the back of her hand to her mouth before nodding, turning to the refrigerator, and hiding in the light of its open door.

Alex stood in the kitchen doorway. "Can I help?" he asked.

He and my mother eyed each other, but I took his arm and positioned him by the counter, giving him a knife. "Careful," I said, handing him half an onion to chop. "Don't cry."

Claude appeared at the door, watching as the three of us negotiated the kitchen space.

After breakfast we sat around the tree and I gave everyone gifts. Claude got a bunch of small photos of my mother arranged like a bouquet of Dahlias. He took his time, carefully examining each one. My mother got a photograph of me that Aaron had taken. I wanted to give her something else, something more, but she waved her hand. "I don't want anything," she said. "This is perfect."

Alex received a picture of him and me together, sitting side by side on the low brick wall that circled the fountain. The automatic timer on the camera had been too quick or I had been too slow, because the edges of my body blurred like a ghost. It had been hot that day and though my hair was in a ponytail, most of it had come loose, bits of it netted about my face.

"Will you cherish it forever?" I asked, trying to sound coy.

"If you want me to," he said, cocky, with half a smile. He put his hand near mine, fingertips touching. I looked at Claude, but he had eyes only for his Dahlias.

"Open your present, Rosaura," said my mother.

Alex got up and brought the silver box to me. I slipped a finger under the taped flaps of the wrapping paper, slowly working it loose. The picture on the box showed a shiny new camera, the word "Nikon" printed across the top.

"To replace the broken one. I thought it was time," said Claude.

TINA APPEARED ON THE LAST day of winter break. She was a bit of sea foam, bobbing back and forth at the bottom of the hill, popping in and out of view as if she were waiting for me to go inside or leave before venturing any closer. She remained at a distance until I left the yard and went to meet her. When she saw me, she took a moment to regroup before facing me.

"Is Alex home?" she asked. Her hair was dirty and her lips chapped and bloodred.

"I haven't seen him today," I lied. Alex had come out of the bathroom at the same time that I had left my bedroom. He'd stepped aside to let me enter and we had brushed against each other. But I didn't tell her this.

"Can't you go check?"

I should have told her to leave, but I wanted to understand her. I wanted to take her picture again with my new camera. When I first knew Tina, she was my rival, but now I wasn't so certain what her role was, and it hurt to see her so confused and lost.

"Come around to the back," I said.

She appeared suspicious, but I didn't wait for her to say no and led her down the worn path along the side of the house. The tall grass had turned white like an old man's hair.

"The garden is my favorite part of this house," I said, my bare feet dusty and dirty, hurting a little from sharp rocks and burrs that lay hidden in the grass. "When I first came here I liked to hide in those bushes."

"And you don't anymore?"

"Not since . . ." There was something about Tina as she was in this moment that reminded me of myself those first days after my father died. "Sometimes I see my father's ghost. He died in this house. I saw him down in those bushes not long after."

I spoke of his ghost out loud for the first time, but surprisingly nothing happened as a result: The garden remained exactly as before; the sky and the sun floated above us. I let out a shaky breath.

She didn't look at me like I was crazy. Instead, Tina sighed, as if she knew all about ghosts, had one of her own, or even several. We sat on the brick wall of the fountain.

"Are there fishes?" Tina bent over the rim. "Hey, there they are. I see them."

"You can see them?" I saw nothing but the dark, mossy water.

"Right there." She pointed, dipping her hand into the water. She bent closer, and for a moment I worried that she meant to climb all the way in and sink below the surface. But it was a foolish fear. The water couldn't be more than a foot deep.

We sat on the edge of the fountain, splashing water. Five minutes. Ten minutes, and for all that time we sat together and didn't mention Alex.

"I got a new camera for Christmas," I told her.

She said she wanted to see it. "You're lucky. My parents didn't get me anything. They were promising a trip to Europe, but that's not going to happen now."

I wanted to ask why they wouldn't be going to Europe when Alex appeared on the other side of the sliding glass doors.

"You should go," I said, with a rise of conflicting emotions. She needed to be gone, away from Alex. He was no good for her, but she wasn't any good for him either.

She followed my gaze, but I blocked her view, pleading with my eyes, with my entire body, *go, get away, get away now.* I pushed her toward the side of the house and the narrow path that led to freedom.

"Is that him?" she asked when the sliding glass doors opened.

"Get out of here." I kept pushing until she pushed back and gave me a hurt expression. Too late, I thought, when Alex called for us to stop.

"What are you doing?" he asked Tina, while ignoring me. I wondered how he could stand to have the both of us there in front of him. Were we interchangeable to him? Or perhaps he did not think of us as the same.

I witnessed her struggle as she managed her emotions. "Is your dad home? I thought I could speak with him."

Her question threw me—why would she want to speak with Claude?

"He's not here. And it wouldn't help. Come on, I better take you home," he said.

Reluctantly, she followed. Any second and they would both be gone, back around the house. Maybe he'd take her for a drive; maybe they would park and he'd have sex with her in the backseat. I was jealous, but I was also afraid for her and angry that she couldn't see how Alex would only hurt her more. It had been a mistake to bring her to the garden.

That night, Alex appeared in my room. Bare chested, he slid in against my overheated skin.

"Is this how it's going to be?" I asked. "Will you be hers during the day and mine at night?"

"We only talked."

"Oh right, of course."

I didn't know why I bothered to ask; he didn't answer.

"What happened to her? She's different now, than how she was," I said, even though I risked that he would get up and leave if I kept pushing. But he slid his hand beneath my nightgown, across my stomach, up to my breast, a nipple between his fingers. I started to think that maybe I hated him.

"If you hurt her, you'll never forgive yourself," I said.

All I could hear was his breathing.

CHAPTER SIXTEEN

At school, I began to watch Tina more often, watched her spiral and unravel slowly, an inch at a time. From across the courtyard, I watched her approach Tom. He was sitting against a wall reading a brand-new *Popular Mechanics* magazine, partially hidden from view by a tree and a trash can.

I couldn't hear what she was saying, but he listened. After she finished, he closed his magazine, and then he shook his head, no. Tina, with a jerky nod of acceptance, turned to leave.

"Wait," said Tom. He placed a closed fist over her open palm, then leaned in and whispered into her ear. When she tried to walk away, he held on until she nodded in agreement to whatever it was he had made her promise. Then he let her go. She ran back to her friends.

Tom sat back down in his corner and picked up his magazine.

I crossed the courtyard to sit with him. A mix of bushes

and bedraggled flowers were growing where the cement ended. I picked a buttercup and rolled it between two fingers.

"What was that about?" I asked, offering Tom half of my bologna sandwich.

He took it and chomped off a big bite, speaking with his mouth full. "They're all going out tonight. She asked if I wanted to go."

Without Aaron next to him, something about Tom appeared unfinished, with his skin yellowed and pale like tissue paper, the cuts and scabs on his knuckles, stains below his eyes.

"Did you say yes?" I asked, wondering who "they" were exactly, and if Alex was one of them.

"Nah," said Tom. "They're going to some club. She doesn't want me to go."

"Then why'd she ask?"

Tom rummaged around in my sack lunch and took out a bag of chips. I noticed that his left arm bent at a crooked angle. I examined it, bending the arm back and forth, trying to figure out what was wrong with it.

"That's from when it broke. I was just a kid," he said in answer to my unspoken question, and I remembered the story Tina had told, about how Alex broke Tom's arm when they were children. They had all known one another since preschool. I was the one who didn't fit. I was the interloper, the stranger.

I rolled up his sleeve to reveal the crease of his elbow. "Why do you do this?" I asked, softly caressing the ragged set of track marks.

He smiled. "I'm glad you can ask that question."

My cheeks grew warm. I let his arm go, wanting to ask him what it was like when he was high, but it was like asking how someone liked to have sex. I changed topics. "I've seen you with Alex. Are you friends?"

Tom slapped his sleeve down to cover his skin. "We're not. Friends."

"Then what do you guys talk about? And don't tell me you don't."

He upended the bag of chips over his mouth to eat the crumbs. When he saw that I expected an answer, he said, "We talk about his dad and my brother."

I wrinkled my forehead. Because of his general air of neglect, his exhaustion and unkemptness, I had always thought of Tom as being alone, without family, besides Aaron. Or if he had family, they were as good as nonexistent. I held all sorts of assumptions, that Tom came from a broken home and that was why he turned to drugs. That maybe he was homeless. But of course he had to have a home. He was scruffy and occasionally unbathed, but he wasn't dirty. He wasn't starving. Maybe a single brother wasn't enough.

"Do you have parents?"

He blinked, his eyes dark and bleak. "My dad's dead," he said. Nothing about his mother.

"My dad's dead too," I said.

From where we sat we had a view of the field where the cheerleaders rehearsed, dressed in the green, white, and gold of Canyon High's colors. The girls chanted, over and over again: *And one, and two, and turn around and double step, and kick, and hold, and hold. All right, girls, let's do it again.* They practiced flips and handstands with broad smiles, so perfectly normal.

"Here," he said, and gave me a buttercup flower, slightly crushed.

"Thanks." I added it to the one I already had. He held a second flower, looking at Tina and perhaps thinking of getting up and giving it to her, but Aaron appeared from around the corner and plopped down next to us.

"Is that for me?" asked Aaron, taking the buttercup and putting it behind his ear. "Thanks, buddy."

Tom cuffed Aaron, and they mock-wrestled until a scream ricocheted throughout the courtyard. Tina had fallen, and blood was pouring from her nose. She stared at her hand and screamed again. Several girls ran to her, and Joey took Tina's head between her hands. They picked her up from the ground, helped her walk across the courtyard in the direction of the nurse's office.

From his aloof perch on a picnic table, Alex watched as they passed; then he returned to his lunch.

Tom stared at Alex. He rolled up his magazine and twisted it around and around with his hands.

"Fucking asshole," he said. "He did that to her. That's his shit."

Aaron laughed. He knocked Tom on the shoulder. "Tell us how you really feel. And you're one to talk."

A look passed between the two boys, sharp and filled with uneasy color. "Fuck you," said Tom, and I tensed. Aaron and Tom never fought. They were friends; they cared about each other. "I thought you hated him," Tom said in his quiet way.

"I don't hate anybody," said Aaron with a shrug. Then he smiled. "I'm a lover, not a fighter. I'm all about the love, man."

Tom looked at Aaron like he was crazy but gave a short laugh, and the weird tension passed. Aaron would insist on being happy forever, for every day of his life, until the earth died. Tom settled back with his magazine. "That's what worries me," he said, then closed his eyes.

Aaron watched Tom for a moment, his happy façade slipping away.

"Can I show you something?" I asked, not understanding what had passed. From my backpack I took out their Christmas presents, two photographs, each stapled to thin balsa wood. "I made these for you. One for each." My voice was small and quiet, afraid they would think the gifts stupid.

They were shots of Aaron and Tom that I took on the day we skipped class. In the one I'd given to Aaron, he was carrying Tom on his back and they were both laughing, the edges of the picture blurred, but their faces were in focus. In the second picture, Aaron and Tom sat side by side on the hood of Aaron's station wagon. Aaron had an arm flung across Tom's shoulder, laughing at something, his entire face lit up bright like his hair, leaning over, whispering in Tom's ear, and Tom's mouth was split in a rare full smile, head tilted to one side.

Neither Aaron nor Tom spoke for several minutes, both staring as if they'd never seen photographs of themselves before. "Thanks," said Aaron, although he wouldn't meet my eyes.

Tom took a moment longer before he handed his gift back to me. "You keep mine," he said. "Keep it safe."

I felt as if I'd blundered into a private moment.

Maybe to diminish the unease that settled between us, Aaron poked around in my book bag, finding my collection of photographs developed over the holidays. "What else have you got?"

"Just more pictures." I had brought them to show Aaron and Tom, wanting to share this with them.

Aaron went through the photographs, giving me a sly look each time he stopped at a picture of Alex.

"You need better subjects," he said, then stacked all the photographs together. I tried to take them back, but Aaron raised the stack over his head. "I'm available for modeling," he said with an eyebrow waggle.

I started laughing, still trying to get the photographs back. He bopped me on the nose, and I wrestled him to the ground. He let go of the stack, and the photographs fell in an untidy heap. A strong breeze blew around the corner, lifting the photographs off Aaron's lap. He tried to gather them to his chest, but they fluttered away, out to the field, dozens of faces taking flight as if it were their one chance for escape. Faces on the wind. Aaron and I ran across the field, chasing photographs like chickens on a farm. He dropped back down next to Tom, panting and grinning like a clown with his arms full of faces and bodies and rooms of the Cake House. "This one's been in a puddle," he said, still breathless. "Are they ruined?"

"It's okay. They'll dry out," I said with a laugh. The photographs were crumpled, bent and creased. "Or maybe it just makes them more interesting, soggy and smeared."

Aaron put his hand on my head. "Very wise, Grasshopper," he said in mock solemnity.

Tom wasn't paying attention. He held a photograph, the only one he'd caught. It was one of Tina, turned in profile, her petal eyes searching the distance with such longing. He handed it back to me.

The end-of-lunch bell rang, and the field and courtyard emptied slowly as the students disappeared into the buildings.

Tom kept his arms to his sides as if cold. "Aaron," he said, rubbing at his face, pleading in a language I couldn't understand, asking for something I didn't want to know about.

Aaron nodded, picking up both his and Tom's bags. "Okay, kid. Let's go."

A sad smile, a quick hug, and they left me standing with my arms holding unbound photographs, creased and muddied and bent backward.

ALEX STARTED JOINING ME IN the darkroom, but only when Claude was out of the house. On Saturday, he knocked and asked to be let in. He brought his guitar and sat on a stool in the corner, strumming along with the radio. It was an old battery-operated AM/FM radio with a broken antenna and poor reception of a static-filled Christian talk radio station. I learned how much Jesus loved me and how he would gladly save my soul if I only took him into my heart, but sometimes the neighboring golden oldies station overpowered the preacher's words, giving me a bebop sermon, a rock-and-roll prayer.

Sprawled on a chair, legs up on boxes, Alex sang along with the radio, strumming—*"Johnny Angel, how I love him, he's got something that I can't resist"*—while I made memories come alive out of chemicals and paper.

He stuck his foot out as I tried to walk past, tripping me so I stumbled into the photographic supplies. "Quit it," I said with a laugh, hopping over his feet. Quit it. Do it again.

"Trying to get you to fall," he said.

"That's not very nice."

"Not at all," he agreed, playing at being the bad-boy rock star. "Come here." He set aside his guitar. I straddled his lap, feet dangling, his hands on my hips.

The radio prayed for salvation. Pray for forgiveness at Heartbreak Hotel. Thank you, Jesus. Thank you, Rolling Stones.

He stripped my clothes away like plucked petals from a flower. I gripped his shoulders hard enough to indent my fingers into his flesh, to leave red marks across his pale, white skin—skin like a blank page of photographic paper ready to be imprinted, ready to be transformed.

Claude's voice rang through the house, calling for both of us. He banged on the door. "Rosie, let me in," he said. He opened the door before I had my shirt completely over my head. Alex stood bare chested, jeans unzipped and loose around his waist.

I braced myself for Claude to drag Alex from the room by his hair, or slap him back into the trays of chemicals, everything crashing to the floor. Instead, he did nothing but look at us, his shock replaced by flat, hard anger. Claude gripped the door handle, stepping aside to reveal Deputy Mike standing in the entryway with his familiar calm expression.

"Alex, get dressed. The deputy wants to speak with you," Claude bit out, and then left.

My fingers shook as I tried straightening my top, ashamed to have Deputy Mike see me so unclothed. Was he here to arrest Claude? Was he finally here to shake the house free of its secrets? But Claude had said Deputy Mike wanted to speak with Alex.

Alex zipped up his jeans and picked up his shirt from the floor, then just stood there, ready for anything.

"Out here," said Deputy Mike, taking a step back.

Alex followed Deputy Mike to the front room. As I closed the door of the darkroom behind me, Claude's hard expression was like a slap to my face.

My mother pinched my upper arm and dragged me over to the sliding doors, as far from the front room as possible.

"Please tell me you haven't—" she started.

"Yes, we did. We were careful." She looked as if I teetered on the edge of a cliff. Maybe it wasn't so much my falling that frightened her, but that I fell alone.

She brought the back of her hand to her mouth, and the small lines around her eyes showed. "All right," she said, with a clear attempt at calmness. "We'll talk about this later."

"Why is Deputy Mike here?" I asked.

She shook her head. "I don't know. He and Claude showed up together. They said something about an accident."

I left her by the sliding doors and went closer to where Deputy Mike sat with Alex, so that I could hear what he said. He spoke in a quiet, almost monotone voice. Once Deputy Mike started talking, Alex didn't move. He sat still and quiet and listened with his entire being. He didn't even appear to breathe.

Friday night a group of teenagers from the high school made plans to go to a club in Hollywood where one of them knew the bouncer. The group was comprised of two couples and three more girls, two of whom were Tina Myers and Joey Robinson. They started drinking at Sammy Bolger's house, before they left Canyon Country. Around nine o'clock, they piled into a car, four in the back and two sharing the front passenger seat, leaving Joey to drive.

They made it to the club, and the bouncer, true to his word, let them in. One of the girls said she went to the bathroom and found Tina snorting methamphetamine.

After leaving the club, they stumbled to a nearby twenty-four-hour Denny's to have breakfast and sober up before the drive home. It was two o'clock in the morning. But Tina didn't feel well and went to the bathroom. When Joey went to fetch her, she found Tina on her hands and knees, hyperventilating. Her eyes were unfocused and she was sweating. Afraid Tina was really sick, Joey called the others for help. They carried Tina to the car, arguing whether to take her to a hospital or not, but Tina protested and insisted she was fine. They decided to take her home. Around three in the morning, they began the drive back to Canyon Country. Joey said she was sober and took the keys. Timothy Holden sat with Tina in the front seat.

When Deputy Mike questioned Joey, she was crying so hard he couldn't understand everything she said. She thought she maybe fell asleep at the wheel. She didn't know exactly what happened. She kept saying she only had a little to drink. They were almost home, driving on Soledad Canyon Road, when she closed her eyes for a second. In that second, she didn't see a man step into the middle of the street. He appeared like a ghost, she said, coming out of nowhere. She tried to swerve to avoid hitting the man but lost control of the car, and it crashed into the curb. The car flipped over, then collided with another parked car and a lamppost before coming to a stop.

"Tina's parents didn't know she'd gone out," said Deputy Mike. "She went into her room earlier in the evening and they guess she slipped out the window somehow, or they just didn't see her leaving."

I didn't know what to say. Last night Alex had made me come for the first time. Listening to Deputy Mike, near to

Alex, I could feel the tiny quivers of energy shooting through my whole body. We might have been together at the same time as the car accident.

Deputy Mike sighed, looking at all of us then back at Alex. "I'm here because several people think Tina may have acquired the methamphetamine from you, Alex—" He held his hand up when both Claude and I protested. "Did you have anything to do with it?" he asked, looking directly at Alex.

Alex's gaze had become distant and unseeing, but he focused on Deputy Mike when he spoke to him. "You're asking if I gave her the drugs?"

"Did you?" asked Deputy Mike.

"No."

I should have felt relieved at his denial, but instead the tension in the room tightened.

"Do you know who did?"

A thousand tiny needles pierced down my spine. I remembered so many months ago when Alex had both Tom and Tina in his bedroom, the way Tom had lit a joint for her, and the way he'd stayed by her side. I remembered the day before when Tina talked with Tom at school, the way she'd asked him for something. In an alternate universe, Tom might have gone with them. He might have been in that car when it crashed. But he'd said no; then he'd called her back and had taken her hand in his. Both of his hands over hers, pressing them together.

Alex and Deputy Mike continued to stare at each other, as if the rest of us no longer existed. "Answer the question," said Deputy Mike. "Do you know who supplied Tina with methamphetamine?"

"No idea," said Alex.

Deputy Mike narrowed his eyes, then turned to me. "What about you? Do you know anything about it?"

I was surprised to be questioned. "Sorry," I said. "They're not my friends. I just know them from school. I don't know what they're into." My face grew warm from my lie, although in many ways it wasn't a lie. I knew Tom was not innocent, but I didn't want to say that, and I didn't know for sure. And I didn't know how Alex was involved, but he was, somehow. I'd learned to lie with the truth, the same as Claude, the same as Alex. "How bad was the accident?" I asked.

Deputy Mike's dark eyes were my answer. It was bad.

"Besides Joey, no one was wearing seat belts," he said. "Timothy Holden went through the windshield. He died on the way to the hospital. The others are in critical condition, but they'll be fine, eventually. Joey was unharmed."

"And Tina?" I asked.

He paused before answering. "She'll live. But she hit her head pretty hard. She's lucky she didn't break her neck. The rest of her is banged up as well. That's all I know."

Abruptly, Alex got up from his chair and headed for the front door.

"I'm not done yet," said Deputy Mike, and it scared me how powerful and loud his voice got.

Alex didn't stop, but Deputy Mike was quicker than he was and reached the door just as Alex fumbled with the handle. Deputy Mike gripped him hard and made him turn around. Claude followed but was blocked by Deputy Mike, holding his hand up to stop him in his place. Alex, face flushed, his eyes wide and red, turned away from Deputy Mike, but it wasn't in anger. I watched, horrified, as Alex began to cry. Deputy Mike stepped closer and blocked my view. I could no longer hear what he was saying.

"Were you friends?" my mother asked softly.

I jumped at the sound of her voice, having forgotten that she was there. I shook my head, knowing she was asking if I had been friends with Tina. No chance for friendship between Tina and me, although I would have liked that if things had been different.

CHAPTER SEVENTEEN

After Deputy Mike left, Alex remained in the front room, sitting with a blank, alien expression, so devoid of emotion that I almost failed to notice his balled-up fists. I expected him to run and barricade himself in his room with his music, but he didn't move from his seat, and I knew something was very wrong.

Claude made himself a drink, then sat across from me in the living room, the glass held with his right hand. He appeared relaxed, but I didn't think he was. Ice clinked in his glass. It was unusual to see him with a drink. For all the shady and questionable activities Claude took part in, he wasn't much of a drinker.

"I thought I could trust you," he said.

His disappointment wasn't unexpected, but the way he said it surprised me. I had expected him to give a speech about how I was too young and Alex was off-limits before confining me to my room or forbidding me to use the dark-room. Instead, he wouldn't meet my eyes. I felt confused by the emotion in my chest. What did I care if I disappointed him? I didn't even like him. I didn't trust him.

Claude rubbed at the condensation on the glass. Next to him, almost invisible but for the smoke caught in the light from the glass doors that gave him form, the ghost knelt at Claude's shoulder, whispering: *You disappoint me.* Claude's expression darkened, and he took another sip.

My muscles were slow to respond, afraid to move, as if that might draw the ghost's attention.

"May I be excused?" I asked.

Claude nodded, continuing his close inspection of the whiskey glass. Next to him, the ghost nodded as well. I escaped as fast as I could.

That night, I waited for the sounds of the house to settle, for that magic moment when I knew the house had fallen asleep. I had grown accustomed to waiting for small noises: the creak as my door opened and closed, the soft slide of bare feet over carpet. But Alex did not come to my room as he had before.

I slipped into the hallway. I thought his door would be locked, but it opened when I pushed. He lay on top of the blankets, on his back, wide-awake. I sat next to him, my weight shifting the bed. He put a hand over his face, then another, his palms pressing against his eye sockets.

I touched his chest, then his neck. He felt warm, and the muscles of his throat worked as he swallowed. When he removed his hands from his face, his cheeks were damp.

"I hate this place," he said. "I hate everyone."

Surging up, he twisted us around so that I lay beneath him. He still wore his jeans, and the rough fabric rubbed against my pubic bone. I bit my lip, not afraid, not yet. He started to unbuckle his jeans.

"Do you hate me?" I asked.

His eyes glistened. He stopped fumbling with his jeans and crushed his lips against mine, our teeth banging together.

Then I felt him shaking. He stopped kissing me, his mouth slipping down to my neck, his left hand threading through my hair. I held him as he continued to shake.

"What did you do to her?" My lip was bleeding; I tasted blood as I spoke.

He rolled onto his side, facing the wall. He put his pillow over his head.

He lay rigid, unmoving. I had never seen him this upset. I shook his shoulder to make him turn around, but he was stiff; he barely moved. I said his name, but he had stopped acknowledging my presence. Alex wasn't going to talk anymore. I left his room and walked back down the hallway.

ALEX WITHDREW BEHIND SNOWDRIFTS OF silence. When further questioned by the police, he denied having anything to do with drugs. He didn't deal, he didn't use, he never even gave Tina so much as a bottle of beer. Each time they questioned him, whether Deputy Mike or another policeman or his father, he stood silent and white-faced.

At school, from the moment Alex stepped on campus, he drew stares. The crowded hallways throbbed with silence as he walked to his classes. In the courtyard at lunch no one sat with him; no one spoke with him. He ate his lunch bite by bite, staring with an unfocused gaze at the ground. Tina's friends huddled together, holding hands, with tear-streaked faces, but Alex did not see them or acknowledge their existence. No one dared approach him. Not even me.

The football team wore black armbands. A disembodied voice announced over the loudspeaker that a counselor was on hand should anyone feel unable to cope with the trauma. Bake sales were organized, with the proceeds promised to the families of Tina Myers and the boy who had died. Even the teachers were solemn, speaking in hushed tones, conferring over cups of coffee and saying over and over again, "I can't believe it. How could this happen?"

"So young. Such a waste."

"I just *can't* believe it."

And through it all, Alex remained silent and aloof. It didn't take long for the whispers to grow.

In the hallway, I overheard a girl with jet-black hair say, "It's like he doesn't even care. He acts like nothing happened. That's cold." She shuddered.

"Do you think it's true, what they're saying?" asked her friend.

The girl shrugged. "Tina was messed up in the head. I believe anything."

"She told me her parents were having money trouble. Fighting all the time. She complained about it to anyone who would listen. Probably just wanted to get out of the house."

The first girl shut her locker. "Shit, you wouldn't know it to look at her, Miss Perfect. Why does everybody know her family's problems? That's not anybody's business."

"I don't know," said the second girl. "Damn, give the girl a break. She's lying in the hospital, near-dead."

They walked away. I hid my face in my locker as I took the books I needed for my next class. I hid not from shame but from sadness. From horror.

At the end of that long week, I sat with Aaron and Tom in the courtyard during lunch. Tom looked like he hadn't showered or eaten all week. His eyes were red, his normally olive skin waxy and pale.

Joey was the only one to penetrate through Alex's glacier-like barrier. She went right up to him, into his face, and pushed him with both her hands. The courtyard sank into silence as if a vacuum had sucked out all the sound. He staggered back but otherwise didn't react. She pushed him again. "Where the fuck were you?" she asked through tears. "Why weren't you there?"

"I couldn't . . . It wouldn't have—" But he bit off whatever he was trying to say. His cool façade slipped, his skin flushed.

Joey pushed him again, but this time Alex pushed back, and she fell down onto the bench of a picnic table, crying out. The crowd hushed in shock.

In a flash, Tom jumped forward and slammed against Alex. They both went down hard onto the cement. Alex landed on his ass, catching most of his weight on his hands.

At first I thought that would be it, that Alex would shake it off and leave Tom and Joey and the rest of the lunch crowd and retreat with his anger and resentment. But then Alex leapt up and punched Tom in the face. And then again. Tom fought back, twisting around to sit on Alex as Alex curled in on himself, like a boxer in the ring.

I searched for someone to stop them, pushed at a couple of the guys who were just standing there useless, but no one moved. Joey was crying, still sitting at the picnic table. The crowd seemed stunned into immobility, and there were no adults around. Then I saw Aaron attempt to pull Tom off, but Tom pushed him back into the crowd. Aaron stumbled as a couple of students caught him before he hit the ground. The crowd stepped back, away from Alex and Tom as they rolled around on the hard cement.

Tom grabbed hold of Alex's jacket. Alex swayed, shook his head. He spoke through a bloody nose. "This is your fault, you fucker," he said, voice broken.

Tom wiped his face, his busted knuckles smearing blood. He shook his head, trying to catch his breath. "Bullshit. You hurt her. You know you did. I tried to help." Tom took his bleeding hands and put them over his head. "I should kill you."

"You're such a fucking liar." Alex's voice cracked. "You little shit. I didn't give her any drugs. You did. You kept on giving them to her, even when you knew she couldn't handle it."

The silence in the courtyard ballooned with the collective breath of everyone watching.

Then something in Alex snapped. I could see it, like the flip of an electric light switched on. He took hold of Tom and slammed him to the ground, pressed his knee into the crook of Tom's left arm. Tom cried out, arching with pain, white with it, trying to fight back, but Alex pressed into Tom's throat, cheeks quivering from strain.

Several adults charged in and pulled Alex off, but not before I saw in Alex's face the truth. A moment longer and he would have crushed Tom's throat.

THEY CALLED CLAUDE AND MADE me wait outside the main offices.

"Have you seen Alex?" he asked when he appeared in the hallway, once again big and broad like a ship with a tall mast sailing down a river.

"He's in there." I pointed to the principal's office as a door at the other end of the hallway banged open and two sheriff's deputies entered. I could tell right away that one of them was Deputy Mike.

Claude pursed his lips. "We have to stop meeting like this, Deputy." There was a flash of an amused glint to his eyes.

Deputy Mike held up his hands in a plea for peace. He stopped in front of Claude. "This time I'm here as a civilian. Deputy Peters will take the boys' statements."

Claude frowned. "What do you mean?"

"Tom's my brother, Mr. Fisk. I guess you didn't know that." A strange light entered Deputy Mike's eyes. "This is the second time your son has broken my brother's arm. I guess you don't remember that, either."

Claude stared at Deputy Mike before saying with a strange, almost calm sadness, "What can I say?"

Deputy Mike shrugged. I could see the similarities now: the same shape to their heads, the same quiet, dark eyes. Tom was shorter than his brother, a little beefier, and his skin wasn't as dark.

"Tom's not innocent in this either. Come on. Let's get this over with."

The other deputy opened the door to the administration offices. Claude went in first, but before Deputy Mike followed he turned to me. "Did you know?" he asked.

He didn't sound angry or disappointed or hurt, yet the weight of his gaze carried such pain that, like a coward, I had to look away. "I didn't want it to be true," I said.

I wanted to say more. I wanted to say I was sorry, but he nodded and disappeared into the office.

The squares of lights moved across the floor as the sun sank lower. A class period ended, and students filled the hallway, walking over the squares of light. They held up their hands to shield their eyes from the sun. The bell rang, and everyone disappeared, another class period starting. I continued to wait until paramedics pushed the gurney through the door with Tom lying strapped in, his sweatshirt and T-shirt cut away to reveal his black-and-blue arm in a splint and a jagged open wound right in the crook at his elbow. Deputy Mike walked beside the gurney as they wheeled Tom out. Tom turned his face away from his brother.

Finally Claude emerged, with Alex in front of him. "We're going," he said.

Someone had stuck a Band-Aid over Alex's eye and another along the side of his mouth. Claude walked with his hand on his son's elbow, steering him as if he were a prisoner in the exact same way Alex had guided me through the house in those first days. And maybe we both were prisoners.

Inside the Mercedes, the radio started when Claude turned the ignition. He lowered the volume and let the car idle. I thought Claude must be angry, but as I watched from the backseat, I realized it wasn't anger that made Claude wait while the Mercedes burned gas.

"You can kill yourself over it, to try and make it better," he said to Alex, "but it won't work."

"What the fuck is that supposed to mean?" His breathing was choppy and damp. "Are you saying it isn't my fault? That this isn't our fucking fault? I lied to her. I lied to her parents. She came to me begging to talk to you, begging for her dad. I used her, and I knew I was doing it. Tom at least was trying to be a friend."

"What's done is done, Alex."

"Jesus, do you hear what you're saying? You can't even say the truth to yourself. You take and then shrug it off. No problem, right, she wanted it. She asked for it, they all do. If it hadn't been me it would have been someone else? Is that how I'm supposed to think?"

Claude's expression flattened and he faced front. Besides

the low rumble of the Mercedes, the only other sounds came from Alex, his wet breathing, his snot and tears. With a harsh jab, Claude roughly put the car into gear.

AT FIRST I DIDN'T SEE the different car parked in our driveway. It was a black sedan even larger than the Mercedes, with tinted windows—a real limousine. Forehead creased, Claude slowed down. Alex sat up when he noticed the new car. He wiped at his eyes, and before the Mercedes could fully stop, Alex had the door open and was running toward the house.

Claude paused, each of his actions laborious as he hauled his body from the front seat. He waited for me to exit before locking the car. He didn't speak as he walked toward the house, although I could see uncertainty in his step.

There was a woman in the front room sitting across from my mother, who waited with rigid patience. The woman had long blond hair swept back from her face, and she sat with a stiff, unbending posture, gazing at the artwork on the wall in a vacant, absentminded manner.

"Hello, Catherine," said Claude to the woman.

But Catherine had eyes only for her son. She touched where the Band-Aid cut across his brow, inspecting it as if she were a doctor, assessing it for permanent damage, almost clinically detached. Her fingers were long, bony, and tapered, and she held his chin, turning his face from one side to the other. There was no obvious affection for the son she hadn't seen in years, but she stepped closer and took him into her arms. Alex rested his head against her shoulder. He closed his eyes.

CHAPTER EIGHTEEN

With her thin arms held close to her body and her big-knuckled fingers wrapped around her clutch purse, Catherine Craig seemed out of place without a violin to hold. She dismissed me right away and kept her attention on Alex, whom she looked at as if he were an interesting art piece at a gallery.

Alex resembled her more than Claude, not only in the details of his face—his thin, bow-shaped lips and colorless eyes—but also in his elevation over us. She held refinement displayed in the fine cut of her suit and her delicate jewelry, in the simplicity of her posture. No one asked where she came from. Claude stared at her like a memory made flesh and bone. I wondered if the real Catherine matched his dreams of her.

"You're here," said Alex, breathless with wonder, with a light-filled happiness I had never seen in him before. His expression showed that he hadn't believed she would come, and he gazed at her with worshipful devotion, with the same intensity I had seen on Tina's face when she followed Alex with her eyes.

Ever since I had first met him, I'd sought to understand Alex, wanting to crack his code as if he were a safe with a treasure inside. At night, in my bed, with his sweat on my skin, when he smiled at me, when we sat together in his room or in mine and he sang for me or asked me to sing— these were moments I came close to understanding him but never truly could, not in any way that lingered.

Mother and son existed in their own bubble, excluding Claude and me and the world, and I realized that finally, I'd gotten my wish. I understood him now. It was there, in the way he turned to her with his heart willingly given: She was the key that unlocked Alex Fisk. He had been waiting for her.

"Do you have anything you want to bring with you?" she asked, as if she and Alex were continuing a conversation from earlier, private to themselves.

"Five minutes," said Alex. "I'll be right back." He ran from the front room, his footsteps thundering up the stairs.

It took a moment for me to understand, the dominos falling one after another: Alex's mysterious phone calls, his mother's sudden presence and the car outside, her question to him. Five minutes, he'd said. She was there to take Alex away.

"Dahlia, Rosie, could you give us a moment?" asked Claude. He hadn't looked away from Catherine since walking into the room. I had a momentary flash of anger at this woman who could capture both Claude and Alex so effortlessly.

"Of course," said my mother with a stiff nod as she crossed the room, waiting for me to go ahead of her. I had no choice but to move.

Out of sight, I pressed against the connecting wall. My mother pinched my arm, whispered that I should get away, but I fended her off. After a moment, she gave up and we both pressed our ears to the paint to listen. At first there was nothing, until Catherine spoke again.

"How have you been?" Catherine sounded cool and mildly curious.

"Just as you see," he said. I always pictured Claude's anger like a red squall raging wild and uncollected. But with Catherine, he pulled back; he became small.

"Still the same?" she asked. Like her violin, Catherine's voice struck a strong and sorrowful chord. I pictured how she must look on stage, how she was so compelling you couldn't look elsewhere. "I always wanted to know how you were doing," she continued, her tone honest. "You had such dreams. It was what I liked best about you. Your plans, big and small, and the people you would help."

"I remember you never cared." Claude's voice was flat.

"He's been calling me."

"I know," he said. "I know what he's like when he leaves you a message and you don't return his call. What right do you have, waltzing back in here like you have any claim on him? You abandoned him."

"Don't pretend as if that wasn't exactly what you wanted. I know what I did. I would have come for him earlier, but—" She hesitated, and I heard the first hint of vulnerability. Then, as if she stood straighter, her voice dropped in timbre. I heard the rustle of paper. "He's my son, and he's coming with me. I had my lawyer draw up these forms. Please sign them."

"What is this?"

"They release you from any right to Alex."

"I won't sign these."

She paused. "If you dare fight it, it would only take one phone call. He's told me everything. I know all about your so-called business. Did it never bother you, using your own son? Was it a pride thing? A chip off the block, so like his father. Except he's nothing like you. I'll make sure of that. Do you really want the authorities to know how those families became your clients? And why?"

I remembered Alex's earlier conversation with Claude in the car. Claude lied to his clients. He lied to my mother. Had he lied to my father? Did Alex ever lie to me?

Next to me, my mother stepped away from the wall, her expression turned inward. She didn't look surprised or upset. Instead, she seemed deep in thought as she crossed the room. I watched her leave, then pressed my ear back against the wall.

"You wouldn't risk Alex just to get at me," said Claude, strained but in that dismissive way of his that tried to regain the upper hand in a conversation.

"Well, you're right there. I wouldn't. Risk him, that is. I wouldn't need to, because you'll sign those forms." She paused, then added, with a tone of condescension, "I'm sure he'll call you."

I pushed away and ran up the stairs, bursting into Alex's room. He had laid out a suitcase on his bed and was moving from dresser to suitcase with his arms full of clothing and whatever else he could grab. The suitcase overflowed with T-shirts and jeans, his shoes stuffed around the edges. His music books were zippered into the suitcase's net pocket, as was the framed photograph of his mother.

His room, always so clean and ordered, with nothing on the walls, nothing out of place, and the bed always made. As if he lived in the guest room. He had been prepared to leave, at any moment, after any phone call. It was something I should have noticed and never let myself see.

"Are you leaving?"

"Yes," he answered, without hesitation.

"You're going to leave me here?" I accused, trying to catch his hands and hold him still. He danced out of my reach. If I had ever thought I could hold him, I was wrong. "Why didn't you tell me about her? You never said anything. I would've understood."

He pushed me aside but squeezed my arm. His smile—I always craved his smile, and there it was. He was radiant in his freedom. "I guess I got used to never talking about her. I hated her. I thought I hated her."

"Then why are you going with her now?"

He returned to packing without answering. It hit me then, that I wouldn't see him tomorrow. That if I waited for him later that night, he wouldn't appear next to my bed. This hollow feeling, this rending of limb from limb, must be what Tina had felt that day he broke up with her.

He shut his suitcase and placed his guitar case next to it.

"Wait," I said, desperate to keep him with me for as long as I could. I wanted to give him something, anything that would remind him of me, anything that might change his mind about leaving. My mind raced through everything that I had that I could give him, that could possibly bind him to me, but I came up blank.

He cocked his head to one side as he looked at me. From his back pocket he took out the picture I had given him for Christmas, the one of the two of us leaning against the fountain's brick wall. He held it out for me to see; then he put it back in his pocket.

There was no warmth in his face, no love mixed with his bruises and the bloodied Band-Aid over his eye, which already needed to be changed, but he came close and took me into his arms. I listened to his heart beating, just a little faster than mine. We were off tempo.

There had been moments when I thought I hated him even as I loved him. But now, as he was leaving, I wished only that I could go back in time and relive every second so that it wouldn't end.

"You can keep the records," he said, touching his lips to my neck.

"Why?"

He picked up his suitcase with one hand and his guitar with the other. "Because I don't want to be here anymore," he said, and hesitated for only a moment before stepping into the hallway.

His room was empty except for a few sheets of crumpled notes on his desk, his handwriting near illegible. They were parts of songs he had written, unfinished or abandoned. I folded the pieces of paper, over and over again, into a small square and put it in my pocket. His desk faced the window overlooking the driveway and the street. I didn't have to wait long for Alex to appear below on the front lawn, followed by his mother. A chauffeur took Alex's luggage. A moment later the car drove away.

WHEN CLAUDE PULLED UP TO the curb of the school, I touched the door handle but didn't open it. Claude was hunched over the steering wheel. In the gray morning light, I thought I saw a second face next to his, like a double exposure in a photograph, superimposed, one on top of the other. Which one was Claude?

"Rosie?" he asked when it became clear that I wasn't exiting the car.

"Can I go with you instead?" I didn't want to go where I would automatically search for Alex in the hallways and in the courtyard, where his absence would be keenly felt.

He stared at the other parked cars, looking pained, both of his hands on the steering wheel. "All right," he said. "Just this once."

"Just for today," I agreed.

When we reached his office, I sat on his swiveling chair, passing my hands over the files left there and tapping on the keyboard of his computer. I wondered how many hours my father and Claude shared together in this office. Were they friends? Did they know they both liked to take pictures? I didn't think I would ever know the answers to all my questions.

"This is where you meet your clients?"

Claude stood facing me, his back leaning partly against a filing cabinet.

"Yes," he said.

"This is where you talk them into giving you their money."

"Rosie," he said, shaking his head. "What are you trying to get at?"

I spun myself around and around, and faster and faster, pulling my knees and legs close to keep them from hitting the desk drawers.

"Stop it. You'll make yourself sick."

"What are you supposed to do with their money?" I asked.

"I said stop it."

Toes on the ground to stop my spinning, I waited for his answer. He passed his hand over his hair again, longer than it should be and grown almost to his ears. I was surprised he hadn't made me leave his office yet.

"I invest their money for them. I help people," he said. "I give them hope, make their dreams come true."

In his world, he helped his clients by taking from them. Did he have a patchwork bag of his own, made from the pictures of those he helped? I thought of Mrs. Wilson with her wide, purple-tinted glasses, the grip of her strong hand on my shoulder.

"But you don't give their money back. Did my father help people too? Did he have an office here where he met clients too?"

"Rosie," he started, then paced a little, but he was like a caged animal and couldn't go very far. "He didn't . . . he helped . . ." Claude faltered, stopped moving. Our eyes met across the office.

"He worked for you. I know he did. Don't lie to me. I know he worked for you."

"Enough," said Claude, and he slammed his hand down on the filing cabinet. It banged, a loud metallic *clang*. "I don't know what you think happened. I don't know what lies you have heard. Or—"

"I see his ghost sometimes," I interrupted, and Claude fell silent. "My father's ghost. He appears and he talks. I've seen him around you."

Claude paled, in fear or confusion, and the anger that was there a moment ago bled away. His eyes were dark, as dark as the shadows in the office. I dropped my gaze and saw the framed pictures on his desk, the one with the smaller, child version of Alex, sullen and unhappy and probably frightened by the large costumed creature behind him.

"That was taken when he was five, not long after he came to live with me," said Claude, speaking into the silence.

"Why did she leave him with you?" I asked.

"She appeared one day on my doorstep. Said she was going on tour and asked if she could leave him with me for a little while. Four months over the spring; then she'd collect him again. After the four months ended, she called. It would take a little longer. A little longer happened, then a little longer again, until she stopped calling."

"Would you have let her take him if she had come back?"

He started to answer, then stopped. "I don't know."

"You didn't even fight for him. You just let her take him." I wanted to yell and felt tears crowding my throat.

"Rosie," he said, uncomfortable. "It's not that simple. He didn't want to stay."

"That's your fault. You made him want to leave. You made him work for you, the same as my father. It made him hate you."

"No," he said, but his voice was raspy. "We were good together. We were a good team."

All those cryptic conversations between Claude and Alex made sense now. The truth that I had struggled to learn— and struggled to ignore—settled against my chest like a ton of bricks: Claude had used his son as a source to find clients for Global Securities.

"You made him want to leave. I know you did. He must have been waiting for her all this time."

Claude bowed his head. I saw my father's ghost step out from within Claude as if he had been hiding inside him. The ghost stared straight at me. Every other time I had been afraid of the ghost, with his bloody stare and his truth-filled words, but this time he gave me courage.

"You used my father. And you used Alex. And now they're both gone."

Claude's chest rose and fell, so I knew he was breathing, but he didn't move. Then he twitched and swatted at the air, swatted at the ghost.

Someone knocked on the door to the suite, calling out. It took a moment for Claude to respond to the knocking.

"Go into the copy room," he said.

I did as he asked, but once inside the copy room, I left the door open so that I could peek through the door hinge. It was the gray-haired man with the deep-set raccoon-ringed eyes who had shown up the last time.

"Come in, Harold," said Claude, backlit by the light from the window. "I was expecting you."

I could see only a sliver of Harold's profile, coming in and out of view.

"Sorry I'm late," he said.

Claude stepped back. "No worries. Sit down."

He guided Harold into his office, leaving the door open. I could no longer see, so I stepped out of the copy room, inching close enough to watch Harold rub at his gray slacks.

"I hope this doesn't come as too much of a shock, but I'll need to cash out."

There followed a long, rigid silence. "Everything all right?"

Harold's voice was like sand over gravel. "I just thought better of it—that's all." He paused. "Been talking to a few others. You know, there was that car accident. Helena Myers's girl is in the hospital. She's been talking, telling everyone you stole their money and won't give it back."

I heard papers shuffled, drawers opening and closing. "What happened to the Myerses is a tragedy—no one's denying that. They're distraught, and who can blame them? I've tried to help; I've done everything I can to help them. They need our compassion right now, so I'm being forgiving. They'll get their money. No one needs to worry about that. But their decision shouldn't have any bearing on you. I'll do as you ask, but you're my client. It's my job to stop you from making any decision you'll regret. Cashing out right now is inadvisable; you'll incur heavy fines. You haven't given your investment enough time."

"It's my money; I have a right to my money," Harold said, sounding accusative.

"Never said it wasn't your money." Claude paused; his tone shifted. "What is this really about?"

Harold took his time replying.

"I hear things. The Myerses aren't the only ones having a hard time getting their money. Mark Lieberman mentioned he's been waiting over three months. I'm a modest man. The money I have, I had to work hard for it."

"I explained to Mr. Lieberman the reason for the delay, and I explained to the Myerses that they will get their money following the normal course of business," said Claude. Then he laughed, but it was a strange, hollow laugh. "I don't know what you all think I'm doing here. This isn't a bank. You can't swing by and make a withdrawal. I require a commitment. It takes time and patience. When you need the money, the money will be there."

"You're saying I have no right to my own money?" asked Harold.

"We all have to do what we have to do," Claude said, and in the window's reflection I saw the ghost's head whispering in Claude's ear. "I think you should leave. I'm not a thief, and I resent the implication."

Claude stood.

"I've offended you," said Harold, following suit.

"Damn straight I'm offended," Claude said, putting his hand on Harold's arm and pushing him toward the door. "I'll have a check drawn for you. It'll be available in six to eight weeks, standard policy, with penalties. Remember, it's your choice."

"What if I just take half?" asked Harold.

"No, you're either in or you're out," said Claude. "It's time for you to leave. I don't go halfway. That's not how I do business. You either take your money and lose out on a once-in-a-lifetime opportunity, or you trust in me, and in this company, and make a lot of money."

"Okay, fine. Full commitment," said Harold. "But can I trust you? You're taking everything I have."

Another stretch of silence. Was the ghost pouring poison in Claude's ear again, urging him to say yes? *You have him. You did it. You're the master. Bravo.*

"Harold, I'm the only one you can trust," said Claude. Harold must have nodded, because Claude clapped him on the back and held out his hand. Harold shook it. "All right. I knew I could count on you. You won't regret this. Stay here; I have something for you."

Claude pushed the door open and left Harold alone in his office without seeing that I was there, heading for the cabinets behind the reception desk. I continued to watch Harold. He got up from his seat and walked behind Claude's desk, picking up a file from the stack of paperwork.

I must have made a noise, some indefinable whisper of shoes against the carpeted floor. Harold turned around.

"Shouldn't you be in school?" he asked, his voice turning steely all of a sudden.

I wished I could take his picture so I could study the lines of his face and how his eyes changed from weak to strong in the space of one breath. Before I could answer, Claude walked in carrying an over-the-shoulder bag. He paused when he saw me, the barest look of discomfort. "Rosie."

Harold stepped back, smiling. "Found a mouse," he said.

"My stepdaughter," said Claude, moving between us. "Say hello to Mr. Daniels."

Harold offered his hand, and his deep-set eyes glinted in the fluorescent light. "Nice to meet you, Rosie."

Claude nodded for me to return to the copy room. In the familiar scent of Xerox paper, I sat before the shredding machine, pushing the button that turned it on, but I could hear Claude as he offered Harold a Global Securities mug and a Global Securities visor to take back to his wife as a present.

THE NEXT DAY, WHEN I got home from school, I saw the VW Bug parked in the same spot from before, on the opposite side of the street underneath a tree. The sight of it caused a jolt of anxiety, but I knew now that it could only be Joey in the car, not Tina. It was there again the next day, and on Saturday it was there in the morning in the same spot. I wondered if Joey knew that Alex was gone. Maybe no one had told her? Maybe she was expecting him to emerge from the side gate?

"I'm going out," I said, touching my mother on her shoulder to make her look at me. She paused in her furious drawing, page after page of charcoal images scattered across the dining table. It took her a moment to focus. She didn't answer but squeezed my hand.

It was cool outside with that hint of dewy morning, but the sun shone warm and bright. Joey sat in the driver's side with both of her hands on the steering wheel. Her top hugged her breasts, plumped them up under her chin, big and round and lush.

When I reached the car, I knocked until Joey lowered the passenger-side window. "Are you waiting for Alex?" I asked. "Because he's not here."

She leaned across the passenger seat, peered up at me. "He said he'd go with me to see Tina."

This surprised me, since the last time I had seen Joey and Alex together they had been fighting. I couldn't believe he had agreed to visit Tina in the hospital. He never would have made it inside the building.

"He's gone," I said. "His mother took him away."

"She was here?" Joey's voice rose to a higher octave. I was fascinated by her eye makeup, which was just as elaborate as it had been the night of the Halloween party. "You mean she really came?"

Joey wasn't directing the question at me but seemed to be asking the car, or perhaps she was asking Alex, even though he wasn't there. I realized that I didn't know anything about Alex's relationship with Joey. If it had been romantic or sexual or if they were just friends the way Alex had claimed. I wasn't certain if I could trust anything Alex had ever said to me.

"He lied," Joey said, with a blank expression, blinking at the dashboard. "He told Tina he wouldn't leave—she made him swear it—but I guess he lied. Fucking asshole. I don't know why I'm surprised."

"He told you about his mom?" I should have been used to the sting of Alex's betrayal by then, but it hurt to realize that all this time, he had shared this with Joey but not with me.

"He told us everything."

Everything. Her large eyes turned toward me, and their mirror-like reflection echoed back the enormity of everything. Had he told her about Tina's parents? About working for Claude? Had he told her about us? About the way he came to my bed in the middle of the night? He might have, or maybe she would have taken one look at him and known anyway, whether he'd told her or not. He told her everything. Except that he obviously hadn't, or she would have known that his promise was a lie.

"Get in," said Joey. She tilted her head, mascara streaking out to the sides.

"Why?"

She hesitated a moment. "Come with me to see Tina."

"Don't think that would be a good idea."

"Please," she begged, quiet and desperate.

My gut reaction was to say no. She must have sensed that, because she continued to beg, and I got in the car to make her stop. We sat without speaking until she started the engine and we drove away.

"I thought he and I were friends, but I'm not sure any of us mattered to him," she said, not looking at me. Sunlight caught the halo of her hair as she spoke. "We were all just a game to him. A way for him to pass the time until he left. Me, Tina, you. He never cared."

I shook my head, even though that was what I had been feeling and thinking and worrying over. She couldn't know what it was like for Alex to live in the Cake House, with the secrets harbored in its walls, and the ever-present stranglehold of his father. Did he have a choice? Could he have said no to Claude? I didn't think so. Aaron said Alex didn't have friends, but he had been my friend. He had been Joey's friend too. In the end, it hadn't been enough.

"No," I said. "It wasn't a game." Unless the game was survival, but I didn't say that part out loud.

She looked at me with pity, blowing air through her nose in a big huff. "Have it your way," she said.

The closer we got to the hospital, the more frazzled Joey got. She drove too fast, taking corners with the tires screeching, then slamming on the brakes suddenly. After she'd parked the car in the visitors' parking lot at the hospital, I wondered if she would even get out of the car or if she would squeal out of the lot in a blind panic to get away, but she did get out and started walking forward.

When we got to the main desk on the first floor of the hospital, Joey couldn't speak, so I asked the receptionist where Tina Myers was. She looked it up in her computer and directed us to the third floor.

The shades had been opened to let in the sun, putting half of Tina's hospital room in brilliant sunlight and the other half in shadows, with a steady *beep-beep-beep* of medical monitors the only sound. A woman sat on the right side of Tina's bed. She turned, the sunlight hit her face, and I felt the impact of her tired green eyes and her familiar round face. The mall. The scene at the mall. She was the woman who had confronted Claude, who'd yelled at him, who had begged and cried and demanded that he show compassion. But he'd pretended not to know her. That same woman was Tina's mother. I hadn't put it together, not until I saw her sitting next to her daughter with the same exact eyes.

"Oh. Joey?" Mrs. Myers spoke in a blank voice. She had a lighter shade of brown hair but the same pert, upturned nose.

I had to look away, overwhelmed by the feelings of guilt and remorse that seemed to rise from the ground up to my chin, to the top of my head, so strong I was drowning in them.

Joey cleared her throat, then spoke. "Mrs. Myers, I'm so sorry."

Mrs. Myers shook her head. "Good of you to come," she said, turning back to watch her daughter.

Tina lay unmoving. Sunlight touched only her feet, the rest of her obscured in the shadows. I pulled Joey farther into the room. Someone had cut off all of Tina's hair. She had tubes in her nose and her mouth. Bruises dotted her face. One leg in a cast, suspended. An arm in a brace, every finger of her hand black and blue and swollen. Neck brace. There was more, but I stopped looking. Flowers all over the room, and cards, a pot of daisies perched by Tina's head, pink flowers, white flowers, opening in the morning sun. Tina's mother had hung up posters of Tina's favorite movie stars and musicians. She liked Madonna the same as I did, and also Tori Amos and Sonic Youth. She had posters of *The Little Mermaid* and *The Princess Bride*. She had stuffed animals in bed with her.

Tina's mother got up, took a tissue, and wiped Tina's mouth, all the while speaking to her daughter. "Joey is here. Isn't that nice? Would you like some water?" She took a large cup with a cover and a straw and held it to her daughter's mouth. I couldn't see how Tina could drink at all, but I realized it was something for her mother to do. She held the straw to Tina's chapped lips. Tina didn't move. "I'll get more water," said Tina's mother, and without a word to us, she left the room.

With Mrs. Myers's absence, I could breathe easier, but the stench of disinfectant and urine together threatened to make my eyes sting. I breathed in through my mouth, but that was no better.

"Talk to her," I said to Joey.

Joey swallowed. She stepped closer to Tina's right side. The sun hit her, and I saw how she had to squint and lean down to avoid the glare. "Hey, girl," said Joey, and touched Tina's arm.

Tina moved. She took a breath, gurgled; her eyelids rose, revealing the whites of her eyes. The monitors hiccupped.

"Oh God," Joey said, taking several steps backward before she hit a chair. It banged against the wall. Joey ran from the room.

Left alone, just Tina and me. She fell still again, and the *beep-beep-beep* of the monitors evened out. I watched the jumping line of her heartbeat: steady, easy, a slow-moving ballad. The sun had moved off Tina's legs and right into my eyes, so I moved closer, into the shadows.

Mrs. Myers returned with a refilled thermos of water, placing it on the side table by Tina's bed. I flinched as if caught doing something wrong, even though I was only standing there not doing anything. Mrs. Myers adjusted Tina's pillows, then moved a small potted plant closer. "Aren't these pretty?" she asked, and I didn't know if she was speaking to me or to Tina.

"Yes," I said.

"It's so kind of you to visit." Mrs. Myers spoke as she rearranged the flowers along the window ledge. I got the sense that she had previously moved the flowers around and would do so again. "Tina hasn't had many visitors. I thought there would be more. But I guess everyone's a little afraid."

"I guess," I said, shifting from foot to foot.

"What's your name?"

"Rosaura." Then, after a moment, I added, "Douglas," because even though Mrs. Myers would have no reason to think otherwise, I was suddenly worried that she would think my last name was Fisk, that she would know who my stepfather was and who my stepbrother was.

She tilted her head to one side, and I held my breath. If she and her husband had gone to Claude, she might have known my father. Maybe she recognized him in me. I looked down at Tina, stepping close in an effort to avoid her mother. "She's so still," I said.

"Yes," said Mrs. Myers. "She does move, though, sometimes. With music. Or when I read to her."

Mrs. Myers returned to arranging the flowers, the cards, the stuffed animals. I wondered if she did that all day. Instead, I swallowed and hummed just under my breath the French lullaby, about the little sparrow stealing grain, brave little sparrow.

"Qu'est-ce qu'elle a donc fait,
La petite hirondelle?"

The dust motes froze in mid-glide. The *beep-beep-beep* of the monitors faded into silence. It was like we fell into a vacuum, Tina, her mother, and I.

"That was pretty," said Mrs. Myers, and I stepped back, having almost forgotten that she was there.

"Thank you," I said. "My father used to sing it to me." And just like that, I remembered. I told Alex that it was my mother's song, that she used to sing it to me, but I lied.

I didn't even know that I had lied. It had always been my father who sang to me.

I tripped, crashed the chair against the wall the same way Joey had. "Sorry," I said, fixing the chair. "I'm so sorry. I have to go. Joey's waiting. I'm sorry."

I ran from the room.

Joey sat in her car, crying, her face twisted in grief: unflattering, ugly grief. I sat with her in the car and waited, with that French song ringing in my head and my heart rattling in my chest. Tears streaked down her cheeks, smeared with makeup. Twenty minutes passed before she stopped, sitting up to look at herself in the rearview mirror. She wiped at the mascara dripping from the corners of her eyes with her two thumbs, then took out her makeup from her bag, patting her face with powder, reapplying mascara.

No matter how much makeup Joey put on, I could see the same invisible scars as mine. It made me think of my mother and her diamonds and those sunglasses she used to wear.

In silence she drove me home, but before I got out of the car she asked, "See you at school?"

"Sure," I said, and then she drove off.

CHAPTER NINETEEN

I counted the days without Alex. A week passed and I began to get used to his absence. Most days, when I was home from school or on the weekends, it was just my mother and me alone in the house. Claude was gone more and more. In their room, I sat with my mother on her bed and took her sketchbook and one of her pencils. She held her breath as I first drew a circle in the center of the page. Then petals shooting out, uneven, crooked. It was about all I could draw. She watched, then picked up another pencil and started to draw along with me. A face, a pair of hands, and then a flower of her own. She drew a stem and leaves, providing a ground for it with grass growing. Then a road. With mountains. And a sun in the corner of the sky.

"I called one of my previous jobs, to see if they have anything. I thought you might like to know," she said as she drew.

I drew a smiley face inside the sun, my way of telling her what I felt and thought.

"Have you told Claude?" I asked.

"Not yet, but I will."

"Do you think he'll be okay with it?"

She turned to a fresh page and started another garden but didn't answer.

"I know Dad worked for Claude." I kept my eyes on the page.

Her pencil faltered, and the line she was drawing went crooked.

"Can you tell me why he did?" I asked.

She got up to plump the pillows, scattering the pencils and forcing me to move so she could straighten the sheets and the comforter.

"You have to understand," she said, still moving but turning her attention to the closet where Claude's and her clothing clung to the hangers and huddled against the shoe tree, attacked the tie rack. "You have to understand what it was like."

"I remember."

She turned to me, holding a pair of Claude's trousers upside down by a pant leg. "Do you?"

"Dad was always angry, yelling, or trying not to yell but still fighting. And he made you cry."

I had forgotten how he yelled at her: "What are we supposed to do now? How are we going to pay for anything? I was counting on you. You let me down. You always let me down."

"What was he like? Before, when you were married?" I asked her.

She was holding on to Claude's trousers, her fingers like claws. We stood at opposite ends of the room. She returned her attention to the trousers.

"In school your father was this strange boy, all freckles and teeth. But well liked. Popular because his parents were wealthy. His father was a lawyer, very successful, and involved with local politics. He ran for state senate but lost."

She lined the two pant legs together, the fabric held between her fingers while she clipped it to the hanger. She spoke to the clothes instead of to me.

"Why did you marry him?" I asked.

When she raised her head, her eyes were filled with little shards of memories. "It was the way he looked at me. I thought I could marry him because he loved me so much, and that would be enough. That would be all I needed. And I got pregnant."

I hadn't known that she had been pregnant with me before she married my father. "That's why you married him? Because of me?"

She smiled. "Not only because of you, but yes, you were the main reason."

"You could have had an abortion," I said. How many of her problems would have disappeared if I had never existed? She could have been free. She could have had another life, a better life.

"I wanted you. My mother had died by then, and I had no one else except Robert. I had already decided to name you after my mother. I knew you'd be a girl."

She walked to the dresser and picked up a pack of cigarettes, taking one out, but she had no match, no fire, so she just held on to the cigarette, looking at it as if it could finish the story for her. "We had no money. And his parents refused to help. He tried everything: real estate, all different kinds of sales positions and get-rich-quick programs, one scheme after another. He'd put all of himself into some venture. You had to gamble, he said, to get the rewards. He'd lose any money we had, asked me to work to make up for it, so I worked. I could never keep a job for long, though. It was difficult when you were young and we couldn't afford day care, and I didn't want to leave you with him. I didn't want to leave you at all."

"You resented him."

This startled her. "Maybe I did." She played with the cigarette, turning it around and around. "He'd get so scared sometimes. When you were about two or three, he answered an ad in the newspaper for a job. That's where he met Claude. They both worked for this company, something about oil fields in an Asian country. He became very involved. It took about four months before the person running the thing disappeared and the venture went under. We lost everything."

"What did you do?"

"He stopped eating. He either slept all the time or he raged around the apartment. We had no money for food, not even for milk. I couldn't work because I couldn't leave you with him and there was no one else. I didn't know what to do. So I called his parents. They never liked me, but I knew they'd take us in; I knew they'd want you. I put you in the car and we were going to go, but your father . . . he didn't want us to leave."

The memory of the ghost wielding his baseball bat and the way my mother's car shook each time he swung it down onto the hood slammed back into existence. Her eyes were shadowed and brilliant with the force of memory.

"I wish you had gone. I wish we had left then."

"It wasn't all terrible. I got a job, and we had a little bit of money coming in. I thought things might get better, but—" She stopped. Swallowed. Fingers to her lips, but she didn't find a cigarette there. "He kept in touch with Claude. Claude asked Robert to help him with a new company he started. Robert would pose as one of Claude's clients, and they'd work together to recruit new investments. Robert got very good at it."

"I remember hearing his name. Claude this. Claude that," I said. My mother nodded, but I wasn't certain she heard me. She was in her own world, pacing around the room.

"Claude could be very charming, and kind," she said. "With me, he never spoke as if his company was anything other than legitimate, pretending as if I didn't know. Even now, he still does it, and sometimes I'm not sure if he's aware that I know. He'd sit me down and say how he'd take care of me if anything ever happened to Robert. That he wouldn't let anything happen to us. It was easy to believe him. I wanted to believe. But it would just make Robert angry."

The room had darkened. I missed the music Alex used to play. I even missed Catherine Craig's violin.

"What happened?" I asked.

"Robert worked with Claude, but it was never on the books," she said. "This frustrated Robert. According to him, he ran that company—he was the one who knew all the moving parts; he was the one who made it work. Without him, it would fall apart. He wanted to escalate everything into a bigger enterprise. He had all these ideas of how to expand into further untapped wealth. Claude was too small-minded, but Robert could really make something big, if Claude would step aside, if he would just let Robert do it. He needed Claude's capital. It terrified me. It sounded so insane. It could all vanish in a second, and I couldn't go through that again. I begged him to get out, threatened to leave him. I said I would take you and I would run away, and—"

I knew what had happened next. I knew now why she'd thrown our things into her car, had stolen me from the steps where I was hanging out with José and Sofie, demanding that I get in the car, wearing sunglasses to hide the bruises on her face.

Even though she had no fire and couldn't light her cigarette, I thought I saw smoke drifting around her. It reminded me of the ghost, reaching out for her. "I'm glad you left him," I said, and hoped the ghost would leave her alone.

She let go of a pent-up breath, then sat down on her bed, picking up the scattered pencils. She started drawing with long sweeps, rough shapes and energetic motion. "That day, that terrible day, I wanted us to go far away. I didn't want you there anymore; I needed to get out, and at the time Claude seemed the best way to do that. But then your father showed up, and God—I thought he was going to kill us." She kept drawing, fast, her hand going around and around. "And maybe he would have. I don't know. Instead, he turned the gun on himself, and everything changed. Everything fell apart, and everything changed."

I heard the gunshot. I saw the blood spreading on the carpet of the front room. I sat next to her and put my hand over her moving arm.

"We have to get out of here," she said, still drawing. "Somehow."

"Whenever you're ready," I said.

She wasn't crying. Maybe she was beyond tears. I said nothing until the room grew dark.

———

THE NEXT NIGHT I SAW a change happen in my mother. I watched her as I did my homework on the dining table after school. She stood on the threshold before the living room, contemplating Claude, who sat in the near darkness, having pulled the phone over to the sofa with his usual briefcase and files scattered around him. But he wasn't calling anyone. Instead, he worried a paper clip with his fingers, bending it out of shape until it snapped.

She fiddled with the buttons of her blouse and called to Claude, but he ignored her. She said his name again, moving to stand in front of him. "I need to drive into Los Angeles tomorrow. For an interview," she said.

"What?" he asked, then, "No, I told you, you can work for me. There's plenty to do at the office if you don't want to be here. I need you with me."

"Claude, we discussed this." She shook her head, lips pinched. "I told you how I felt. You agreed."

He shuffled his papers. "Well, I changed my mind."

She stood in the middle of the room, stunned. Or maybe not stunned, as her initial surprise melted away to terrible understanding.

"I'm going anyway," she said.

"You'll do as I say, and that's the end of it," he said.

Her nostrils flared. Claude shook his head, ran his hand through his hair.

"I won't."

He stormed from the room, leaving my mother and me to eat dinner alone, just the two of us. A few hours later he came home and apologized, said she could do whatever she wanted. My mother nodded but then turned away.

In the morning, Claude was there as usual, waiting to drive me to school, but I brought my bike from the garden to the front of the house.

"I don't need a ride."

"Rosie, wait," he said, and force of habit made my feet stop pedaling. "What's this about?"

"I want to ride my bike to school." I didn't say that I couldn't bring myself to get into the Mercedes, not after the way he had yelled at my mother. He wasn't the same Claude I'd feared and hated from when I first came to live at the Cake House. I didn't hate him anymore, but he wasn't the Claude who helped build my darkroom either.

"All right," he said, as if he still needed to give his permission. "But be careful."

I sped down the hill. My bike felt familiar in my hands, riding rough over curbs, skidding down unpaved hills, swishing through the morning fog with only a little bit of road revealed at a time. I climbed up a hill and saw the ghost swathed in fog. I rode down a hill and saw the ghost standing at the bottom, watching. My teeth clattered in my head. On straightaways I pumped my legs very fast.

Aaron stood in front of the bulletin board. I hadn't seen him since the fight between Tom and Alex, and I wondered if he had even been in school at all or if this was his first day back. Since Alex had left, I hadn't thought of Aaron or Tom.

I must have made a noise, because he turned and saw me watching.

"There's no more room," he said, and I realized he meant the bulletin board was now so crowded with prayers he had no space for the homemade card he held in his hands. I wondered if the card was from him or from Tom but didn't ask.

"We can make room."

Together we moved around the cards, the notes written on torn lined notebook paper, and the photographs of Tina and the others from the accident. In these photographs Tina was smiling or laughing, and I wished I had brought the few photos I had taken of her. Except that she was sad in those pictures. Maybe it was better that this wall held the happier moments of her life. We stole a couple of pushpins and stuck his card on the board.

The school bell rang, but neither he nor I moved. "Let's get out of here," he said.

"Okay."

He drove fast, with all the windows down. I slid along the bench seat of the station wagon going around tight corners, bumping up against him. He put his arm around me. I felt the bones of his rib cage. He parked on a tree-lined street outside of Verdant Hill Mobile Estates.

"Is this where you live?"

"Yeah," he said with an uncertain look. "Is that okay?"

I had expected that he would drive me back to the mountain again, or some other place where we could hang out. But I didn't want him to think I was disappointed, so I took his hand. "Yeah. It's okay."

Pretty houses up on blocks, all in a row, so I could see their potted plants, the scant grass in tiny plots around each mobile home, children's toys littering the yards. Aaron walked toward one of the houses. He didn't knock but walked right in. A woman sat at the kitchen table. She had Aaron's long red hair, gone a bit gray, and his wide smile.

"He's been asking for you," she said, without acknowledging my existence.

Down a short hallway, Aaron entered a room no bigger than my darkroom. There was a pile of clothing pushed off into a corner by the door, schoolbooks tossed in a heap. Only one window, slid open, with a view of the mobile home next door. No place to sit, except on top of a stack of magazines.

Tom's eyes lit up when we walked in. His lips were cracked, almost bloody. He shivered, sweaty, lying on top of the sheets in his boxers, his left arm in a cast. Tom looked from Aaron to me and back again, then up at the ceiling.

"Good to see you guys," he said, and when I hesitated to approach, added, "Worse than it looks."

He licked his lips, hiding his free arm under the covers, but not before I saw the dimpled track marks in the crook of his elbow.

Someone knocked on the front door. I sat straight up when I heard the familiar voice of Deputy Mike.

"I'm here to take him," I heard him say.

Tom grew pale, but he didn't say anything. Aaron went out into the front room as I sat next to Tom on the bed and held his hand.

"I can't fucking believe this," we heard Aaron say. "You're his brother."

"It's because I'm his brother that I'm doing this."

"What kind of fucked-up logic is that?"

"Listen, I don't like it either. Do you think this is easy? I know this is my fault, but it's the only way I know to make it better."

Silence. Then, "How can you make it better, man? You only make things worse."

Deputy Mike took in a long breath. "If he cooperates, tells us everything he knows, he can maybe avoid a conviction, and he won't have a felony charge against him. And he has to testify with Alex Fisk as well. Meanwhile, he'll have to be institutionalized, for his own good."

"An institution?" cried Aaron.

"He'll get the help he needs there," Deputy Mike said, but they were yelling, trying to be heard over the other.

"Now you think he needs help. Man, you *suck*."

I didn't like hearing Aaron so angry. It was contrary to his essential Aaron-ness. Tom started moving, like he wanted to get up from the bed. I found a few markers and began drawing on Tom's cast and he lay back down. First a green stem, then a red-and-blue flower, then some grass. Then a second flower, this time purple and yellow.

"What does he mean, testify with Alex Fisk?" I asked.

Tom squeezed my hand, marker and all. "Alex needed help, and he came to me, the fucker. Should have told him to fuck off. I guess I know too much or something."

I took this in. The first thought I had was of Claude. "You're going to testify against Claude? When? What's going to happen?"

But Tom didn't answer my questions. He was listening to Aaron and Deputy Mike, trying to get out of the bed again. I didn't try to stop him this time, but all he could do was sit up straighter.

"He needs professional help!" Deputy Mike was yelling in the other room. "You know he does."

"I don't know that," said Aaron, but his tone changed, carrying a questioning sadness that made me squeeze Tom's hand again.

"Why don't we let him decide?"

I thought Aaron would continue to argue, but a moment

later they appeared in the doorway, and the four of us crammed into the claustrophobic space around Tom's bed. Deputy Mike looked at me first, then down at his brother.

"You don't have to go," said Aaron, speaking to Tom. "You can say no if you want."

Tom didn't answer. Deputy Mike took a step forward. He took his hat off and set it aside. I used to think Deputy Mike's eyes were gentle, like soft, loamy earth holding the strength of a mountain. And maybe they still were, glinting in the meager light. With both of his hands, he cupped Tom's face.

"*Oye, hermanito. Mírame, todo va a estar bien. Estoy aquí.*"

Tom's eyes were red, and his cheeks quivered before he turned to hide his face, gripping his brother's jacket. "Where . . . where do you want to take me?"

"I'll visit. Every week," said Deputy Mike. They were both crying.

Aaron stepped out of the room, and I followed. There was a park across from his house, and we sat on the swings. When I was younger, sometimes my father took me to playgrounds to swing on the swings. He would push and I'd go sailing up, loving the drop in my belly as I lifted off of the seat before swinging back down again. Aaron and I twisted the chains of the swings around and around, making them tighter.

Everything was changing. I didn't know what was going to happen next. It was the same feeling, deep down in the bottom of my stomach, as I had as a child swinging high up into the air. I looked over at Aaron's small house and saw Deputy Mike helping Tom walk. I wanted to run over to them and demand that Deputy Mike tell me what was going to happen, but he had other problems. I wasn't as important to him as Tom.

"As soon as he's up for it, Tom and I are leaving," said Aaron.

I didn't know if I should believe him, but Aaron seemed calm, pushing at the swing so that he swayed back and forth. I didn't want to tell him he couldn't dream.

"Where will you go?"

"Fuck if I know," said Aaron. "Anyplace that isn't here." Then, after some thought, he said, "Someplace exotic, like Portland. Isn't that were ne'er-do-wells dwell? What state is Portland in?"

I huffed a small laugh, despite the pain and uncertainty in my belly. "Can I visit you?"

"Hell, you'd better."

CHAPTER TWENTY

Aaron drove me home. The house was empty, and I sat in the living room waiting for my mother to return. The waiting felt like the tightening of the chains on the swing, tighter and tighter until you couldn't tighten any further. I remembered Tom at lunchtime days ago when I asked him what he and Alex talked about. "We talk about his dad and my brother," he had said. They would testify together. I didn't know what that would mean for me—or my mother.

My mother came home a few minutes later dressed in a new suit, and together we made dinner, every moment expecting Claude to come home, but he didn't, and so we ate without him.

"Where do you think he is?" I asked.

She looked toward the front door. "He didn't say he was going to be late. I don't know."

Around us, the house was silent, but I could hear the faint noise of traffic coming in from the outside, as well as the noise of birds and crickets and the wind that came in from the garden with the descent into nighttime. I shivered and refrained from looking behind me. It felt as if there was someone watching. Like any moment an earthquake would happen and the walls would shake.

"What if he doesn't come back? What if he's gone?"

My mother didn't answer.

In the morning, when I came downstairs, I saw a bottle of whiskey and a glass on the coffee table. A few of Claude's files were left on the couch, and the rolltop desk was pushed away from the wall. Sometime during the night, he had come home, but he was nowhere to be seen as I made a lunch to take to school.

All day as I went from class to class that feeling churned in the bottom of my stomach, as if I might sail too high off the swing and fall. I was filing into my math class behind my fellow students when Claude marched down the hallway, red-faced with boiling intensity. On instinct, I backed away, clutching my books to my chest.

Claude grabbed my arm. "Let's go. Come on," he said, without explanation.

"Wait, no," I said, trying to twist free.

"There's no time. We have to go now."

I dug my heels in as best as I could against the slick, tiled floor until the teacher appeared in the doorway.

"What is going on here? Rosaura, explain. Sir, please."

Claude ignored her, but he did let go of my arm. "Look, I'm sorry, I'm sorry. I don't mean to scare you. But it's important, all right? We have to go."

"Just who do you think you are?" the teacher asked.

"I'm her stepfather and she's coming with me."

"You can't take her out of school without a written request submitted to the—"

Claude then turned the full force of his attention toward the teacher, and she paled chalk white. "I said she's coming with me," said Claude.

The hallway filled with students. Doors opened from other classrooms. I saw Joey with her hands on her hips as if ready to fly into action and come to my rescue. She was looking at Claude, but her eyes found mine with a brilliant fierceness in her frown.

A second teacher appeared, but Claude ignored him. "Rosie," he said, holding up his hands as if to placate a wild animal, his too-long hair framed around his inflamed face. "You've liked living with me, right? I mean, I've never done anything bad to you or to your mom. I've given you everything you wanted. Isn't that right?"

I thought of those hours spent together in the darkroom, and before that when we went shopping for the equipment, the joy of that day, the happiness I felt. If nothing else, he had given me that. Without acknowledging the adults or the other students, I shook my head, feeling like a liar.

At first Claude seemed confused at my refusal; then a shift occurred, his blue eyes hardening to ice. He leaned in. "Who have you talked to? What have you done?"

"No one," I said, pushing his hands away. "*I* haven't spoken to anyone."

My teacher ordered the other students to return to their classrooms, then turned to Claude and said, "Please come with me, sir. Or I'll have to get campus security."

"Her mother's not well," he said, speaking to the male teacher. "I'm sorry for the confusion, but it's a family matter. You understand. My apologies for disrupting your class."

Claude stepped back, and I looked from him to the teacher, then back at him. "What's wrong with Mom?" I asked.

"Rosie, we have to go. We'll talk on the way," he said, and tried to reach for my arm again, but I scooted away.

"Is she okay? Did something happen?" I thought of the pills she took. I thought of her car, worried that maybe she'd crashed or had fallen down the stairs like Mrs. Wilson.

"Nothing's going on. She's . . . asking for you. We need to go home. Now."

I saw his reddened eyes and pale, splotchy skin. He looked tired, his hair uncombed and erratic, and I knew I had no choice but to go with him down the hallway. The teachers made a feeble protest, but at the same time I could sense their relief that the scene was over. Joey waved as I passed her.

Claude was silent all the way to the Mercedes. I could smell the stink of his fear, his armpits stained dark. He pushed the Mercedes faster, ramming up and down hills before screeching to a halt in the driveway.

I grabbed my bag and followed him into the house. As soon as I was inside, I called for my mother, running over to the stairs. Claude headed straight for the closet and pulled out a duffel bag and set it down on the dining table. He went to the rolltop desk and unlocked it, removing a false front from the desk and taking out stacks of bound money.

Without looking away from what he was doing, he said, "Rosie, pack some of your clothes. Just whatever you can take."

"Why? Where's Mom? Mom, where are you? Are you here?" I switched from foot to foot, afraid to move in any direction. He didn't seem worried about my mother. The money kept on coming until he had several stacks of it. It drew my eyes like magnets. I must have made a noise, because he looked at me as he crouched and took out a couple of lock boxes.

He grimaced. "Move, now. Come on. We have to leave."

But I didn't move. I couldn't have moved even if I'd wanted to. My mind raced through a mental catalog of my different possessions—my clothing, the things in the dark-room. And what about those boxes in the garage? And what about my bike? Would I have to leave it behind? Like my mother and I had done before, would we have to run away again? My chest hurt; my legs shook; I didn't want to run away again.

"What's going on? Why are you yelling?" My mother appeared, stepping down the last few stairs.

Faint with relief, I clutched at her hands.

"Rosaura, it's all right," said my mother. She touched my hair and cupped my face. I nodded and then stood by her side. Her gaze fell to the money on the table. "You better explain yourself," she said to Claude.

Claude paused in his frantic emptying of the desk. "We have to go," he said, almost pleading. "You and Rosie pack whatever you can. We're leaving now."

"I don't think so. Not until you tell us what's happened."

"There's no time for that. I'll explain everything, I swear. Once we're in the car, I'll tell you whatever you want to know. But we have to leave. Now."

My mother didn't move. She stood with one arm around the top of my chest, almost as if she held me in a chokehold. I leaned against her softness.

Claude sighed, his shoulders rounding over in frustration or defeat—I couldn't tell which. Pained, he said, "There's a possibility the police will be here any minute with a search warrant."

Her eyes dropped to the money on the dining table. "What would they find?"

He rubbed his face. "Jesus Christ," he said, and went back to the money, trying to make it fit inside the duffel. "Okay, I'm sorry," he said. "But we don't have time for this. Just get your things, and I'll explain everything later. Dahlia, I'm not kidding. Get your fucking things. You and Rosie get in the car."

"No," my mother said. She covered her face with one hand. I felt her stomach push against my back, and then the staccato of her racing heart. "So finally. We've come to this. I'm glad," she said. "How do you keep it up?"

"What? What do you mean?"

"You forget who I was married to. I've seen every kind of scam, every scheme imaginable. When Robert wanted to work for you, I knew then. I knew it all."

"But you came to me. You left him and came to me. Why would you do that if you knew, if you weren't okay with it?"

"Oh, that's convenient. Look at yourself. Look what you've done here. You suggested I leave him. You're the one who insisted we marry. Fewer questions that way, right? Think of my daughter? What would I live on? Where would I go?"

"You still could have said no. If you've known all this time about the company, what Robert and I did, what I do now, you could have said no if this wasn't what you wanted."

She gazed out to the garden as if looking out to the past, to that early part of the summer. The golden light painted over her skin. "You're right, of course. I needed to be free of him. I needed to get away and I didn't know how to do it. And I wanted to believe in you when you said you could help. Just once, I needed to believe in someone."

He took a step toward her. "You can still believe in me. It wasn't supposed to be like this. I need you to believe in me." His voice cracked. "There's still time."

She shook her head, sorrowful, as if finally, right at that moment, she'd come to understand the man she had married. "They're probably watching the house," she said, her voice shaky but calm. "You can't run, Claude. And if you do, I'm not going with you."

His face twisted in anger, in fear and shock. Something pushed and pulled between them, zinging over my head.

"Was it you? Did you talk? Did you tell about Robert and me?" he asked.

"Of course not," she said, honeyed hair swept back, her voice as rough as if she'd smoked a thousand cigarettes.

"Someone talked. Someone gave me up."

"It wasn't me," she said with false calmness.

He crossed the room, and I felt my mother tense beside me. We backed up against the wall. She had been calm a moment ago, but she was afraid now.

"I'm not sure I believe you," he said, looking at her hard.

"She already said it wasn't her." I spoke up, pushing between them. "It was Alex," I said. "And Tom Nuñez."

Alex wasn't here anymore, and Tom was safe with his brother, but I still felt sad and shamed to tell Claude the truth, as if by doing so I had betrayed them all.

"You're lying." Claude was pale, brow creased. "You're mad at Alex. You want to blame him."

"No. I'm not."

He shook his head, closed his eyes, crumbling as if in pain, and perhaps he was. It hurt me; I could only imagine how much it hurt Claude. He was saying, "No, no, no," quietly to himself.

"You can't tell me you didn't have fair warning." My mother spoke, and I marveled at the understanding in her voice. "That you didn't see the writing on the wall. You couldn't have kept it up much longer. Was it arrogance?" She continued in her calm, smoke-raspy voice. "That you couldn't believe it would ever end?"

Behind where Claude stood, the duffel bag sat on the dining room table, like a black hole sucking the light that streamed in through the sliding doors: all that money and none of it his.

Claude went back over to the money but didn't pick any of it up, answering with a dull inflection. "It was a ride," he said, with a hint of a shrug to his shoulders. "Wild and crazy. I knew it would end one day," he said. "But I thought I could get out before then."

"Robert thought the same thing," she added.

Then he flushed red and his eyes grew soft. He pleaded. "It wasn't only about the money."

She closed her eyes. "You can't stop for one minute, can you?" And her voice was almost a whisper. "You tell that to everyone you ever hurt."

He looked stricken; then his expression hardened. Claude didn't move, didn't take his eyes off hers. "You're my *wife*," he said through clenched teeth.

She shook her head and stepped back. "Yes, I guess I am."

A strong knock on the front door shook the entire house. I felt lightheaded. The knock came again, accompanied with shouts. They called Claude's name.

None of us moved. Claude breathed hard and fast. He closed his eyes. Blindly, he reached out for my mother, and in mercy, she took his hand and held on.

A bullhorn shattered the illusion of intimacy. A man's voice filled every corner of the living room. The place was surrounded. Please come out with your hands above your head.

Claude only stood there with my mother before him.

Wood splintered. The door broke open, orders were shouted, and men washed into the house through the front, the first wave crashing in. I turned toward the sliding glass doors and saw a second wave of men in the garden. My mother had her arm around me, the three of us standing close together in the center of the living room. Claude kept his eyes on her, even as an ocean of men spread out through the living room with their guns raised.

CHAPTER TWENTY-ONE

Deputy Mike held his hand up and the other men lowered their weapons. "Mr. Fisk," he said. "Could you please come with me?"

Claude didn't resist when they took first his right arm behind his back and then his left arm. He said nothing when his rights were read, silent when they clicked the handcuffs on.

Harold entered the living room, no longer the weak old man I had known in Claude's office, but taller now, strong, with his dark, heavy gaze taking in the room. He wore an FBI vest and a badge that swung from a chain around his neck.

When Claude saw Harold, something electric snapped through the air. He took a step toward Harold, hostility burning in his eyes. Deputy Mike yanked him back, blocking Claude with his body. He spoke in a whisper until Claude shifted his attention back to my mother.

Two men in FBI vests went through the contents of the

desk and the dining table, gathering paperwork and putting the money into evidence bags. I flinched when I heard things being moved in the darkroom, realizing for the first time that it was more than Claude who would lose everything. I would too, and my mother as well. My camera was in the darkroom, but I squelched the urge to run and get it, already knowing that I wouldn't be able to keep it.

I wanted to feel betrayal—at both Claude and my father, at their selfishness that kept on taking from me and my mother—but the blade of fear in Claude's eyes only made me sad.

"It's time," said Deputy Mike to Claude in a low voice. He put a hand on Claude's shoulder, another on his back, guiding him to the front door. Outside a crowd gathered. The police had set up a barrier to keep the crowd back. Two agents, one on each side, marched Claude across the lawn. He kept his head down and stumbled. I turned away when they put him into the backseat of an unmarked car. The windows were tinted, so I couldn't see if Claude watched us as the car drove out of sight, down the hill, around a corner. And he was gone.

SANTA CLARITA OFFICERS MIXED IN with the FBI men. My mother sat on a chair in the dining room while men in boots stomped through the house. I sat near her, afraid of her ashen face, her flat, distant expression.

Deputy Mike sat down at the table across from my mother. "I've been asked to speak with you, if that's all right." When she didn't answer, he looked down at his pad, tapped his pencil against the wood of the table. He reminded me of Tom, with dark rings under his eyes and an aura of unkemptness.

"Will we have to leave?" I asked, already making plans, thinking of what my mother and I would need to do.

He shook his head. "Not for a while. But," he said, lifting his gaze back to my mother, "all of Mr. Fisk's money will be frozen, pending the investigation. There were a lot of families affected by his business, a lot of people hurt. It'll take a while to untangle it all."

"Are we in trouble?" I asked, but all I really wanted to know was if my mother was in trouble.

Deputy Mike shook his head. "I don't think so, but we do have questions."

When she didn't answer, he looked down at his pad. "Did you know the nature of your husband's business?"

She shifted in her seat, gazing toward the living room.

"Your first husband, he also worked for Mr. Fisk, is that correct?"

Her cheeks turned pink. "Isn't there something about a spouse not being compelled to testify against her husband?" she asked.

"These are just questions, ma'am."

She put her hand down on the table, one finger tracing over the grain of the wood. "I think I'd better speak with an attorney before answering any questions."

Deputy Mike placed his pencil down across his notepad. "Of course. But if you're willing to listen, we're hoping you can help us. The investigation is ongoing. We've got a pretty good idea of the scope of Mr. Fisk's operation, but we're still missing some key information. The domestic bank accounts tied to Global Securities are nearly empty, as are his personal accounts. However, there may be more money, hidden somewhere."

I turned to the cash, now in labeled evidence bags on the table. It already seemed like a mountain of money.

"No," said Deputy Mike, noticing where I was looking. "More than what's there. That man"—he pointed to a short man with thinning hair searching through the contents of the rolltop desk—"is the SEC fraud examiner. He believes there might be more. Anything you can tell us would be helpful."

My mother shook her head. "Claude never shared anything with me. We never spoke about his work or where he got his money. I'm afraid I don't know."

"Please, Mrs. Fisk," said Deputy Mike. "Anything at all."

"Don't call me that," she said with a quiet, exhausted voice. "Call me Dahlia."

They both fell silent. Deputy Mike seemed reluctant to leave. I watched the SEC fraud examiner speak into a phone he held to his ear with his shoulder while he wrote on a notepad.

"How much money did he steal?" I asked.

Deputy Mike took a deep breath. "We're not sure yet. Somewhere between two and three million. It might be more—they're still figuring it out. He's been running this scam for about ten years. That's enough time to do quite a bit of damage."

I envisioned a circle of greed like a roundabout or a Ferris wheel going faster and faster until people couldn't hold on anymore and got flung off, tossed aside and left broken. No one was safe from the force of that spin; not my father, not Claude, no one.

"There is one thing," said my mother. "But I don't think it'll give you much more. You'd probably find it on your own."

"That's all right. Everything helps at this point."

She rose, and we followed her as she ascended the stairs to the third floor, into her bedroom. There were a few uniformed men inspecting the dresser drawers, checking the mattress, rifling through the clothing in the closet. The men stopped when we entered. Without a word, she went into the walk-in closet. An agent stepped aside. At the far back, she went down to her knees, almost as if to pray, and reached into the forest of coats and dresses, pushing them aside. She pulled up part of the carpet that had been cut, revealing a hidden compartment.

"I found it when I was cleaning," she said, meeting my eyes, and I remembered that long-ago day when she'd been searching for her notebook, frantic to find it one moment, then ordering me out of the room the next.

Deputy Mike opened the compartment and pulled out a stack of documents. I saw the first page, I saw the written notes, and I knew even without reading it that it was written in my father's handwriting, that my father's name and Claude's name were there.

My mother gathered her dress to her body, as if she didn't want any part of her, even her clothing, to touch anything else. When she eased out of the closet, I took her hand.

"I hope it helps," she said.

He turned his head to speak into his walkie-talkie. I heard his voice echo throughout the room, throughout the house. He ordered the carpets pulled up and the walls checked; he said, "Knock them down if you have to."

It was strange to think of Claude tucking money into

every hole in the Cake House. I visualized him sneaking around at night with bags of cash, searching for unlikely and obscure hiding places. Had that been my father's suggestion? Or perhaps the idea came from the ghost, whispering in Claude's ear. But that was who Claude was, a man who hides.

WHEN THEY LIFTED THE CARPET in the third-floor bedroom, they discovered a second hidden cubbyhole by the bed, beneath the floorboards, that held more cash. They found a safe hidden behind the new drywall in the darkroom. It took them all day to crack it open, but eventually they did. The safe held evidence of bribes and false SEC filings and computer disks. A thorough search of the house revealed more hiding places: in the second-floor bathroom under the sink, in Alex's room underneath his bed.

The closets were molested, bookshelves left ruffled and flustered, bedclothes stripped, leaving shamed, naked mattresses. Officers picked through every drawer and every cabinet, upended every vase big or small, went through each room until all of Claude's secrets were revealed. They found my mother's notebook, still wrapped in its plastic, underneath their bed. They tore the plastic off, flipped through its pages. Already so fragile, the pages came loose, scattering across my mother's mattress. I collected all the pages and put it back together again.

That night, I slept with my mother in the unfamiliar darkness of her bedroom, in the bed she had shared with Claude. They had made love in that bed. They had held each other. Next to me, she lay taut and rigid on her back, sometimes with her eyes closed, sometimes with her eyes open. Her breath was even, steady, a constant metronome in the shadows.

"Is it wrong?" she said in the darkness. "Is it wrong that I can't cry for Claude?"

I took her hand and lay on my back to stare at the ceiling with her.

"Maybe, in some ways, this is a blessing." The words were spoken under her breath, like a prayer to some god she couldn't ever believe in. "I don't have a husband anymore. I don't have a home. Nothing. Clean slate."

"Me. You have me." Her hand closed around mine. "And you're still married to him," I said. "He'll be free one day."

"Maybe," she said, already falling asleep.

I wondered if Claude and my father had been right—was it better to be rich than poor? Better to have and take than to lose, because otherwise you're left with nothing. But my father and Claude had gone about it all wrong. Maybe I could find the right way; maybe I could figure out why they failed.

THE LOCAL NEWS CARRIED THE story. I sat in my pajamas in the dark of the living room with a bowl of cereal, watching the television set.

Claude was forty-five years old. Born in a small town in Northern California called Anderson. His mother died when he was twenty-five and his father died when he was thirty. He had two younger sisters, both married: one lived in Anderson and the other had moved to Memphis for college and stayed there after graduation.

After his mother's death, he enrolled at the University of California, Los Angeles, and majored in economics. He worked for the school newspaper as a reporter and photographer. He'd graduated in the middle of his class, without distinction, without merit, but fellow classmates remembered who he was. He'd been popular; he helped his friends out of difficulties. He made it seem like it meant something to be his friend, that you were something special.

Claude's first job out of college had been with a small Los Angeles–based investment firm called Krantz Investment Securities, LLC, sometimes referred to as K.I.S., LLC. Krantz Investment Securities was still active as a valid corporation with the California secretary of state. Its address was a post office box. Paul Krantz, the legal contact for the company, couldn't be located. Krantz Investment Securities was owned by ElsieTrading. ElsieTrading also didn't appear to exist.

Krantz Investment Securities reportedly specialized in long-term wealth management, except no one could locate a single individual who had ever invested with them. No one knew if there was a real Paul Krantz or not. It had been in operation for a few years before quietly folding. Some analysts thought it a sham, that Krantz Investment Securities was the beginning of Claude's long, slow dance with the devil. What was known was that during his employment at Krantz Investment Securities, Claude reported income on his taxes anywhere between ninety thousand and two hundred thousand dollars.

A year after Krantz Investment Securities ceased to operate, Claude started Global Securities. Apparently, Global Securities began life as a legitimate business, taking investments from individuals, creating financial portfolios, trust funds, annuities, and so forth, but it didn't last long. Within a year, Claude began depositing his clients' money into special accounts, using one client's money to pay another.

If there was one thing Claude was good at, it was finding those vulnerable persons and convincing them to part with their money. He was good with soon-to-be retirees nervous about their future and wanting some security, good with restless families wanting to do something with their nest egg.

They called him a crook. They claimed he defrauded hundreds of investors, with thirty percent of Claude's victims being local to the Santa Clarita area, several families having older children attending Canyon High. They called it "affinity crimes." Claude's victims lost everything: their money, their retirement funds; they were in danger of losing their homes; their children couldn't go to college anymore. At the end of the news segment, they featured some of Claude's victims. The first photograph was of a family of three, and I nearly threw up my cereal when I recognized Tina with her parents, the three of them smiling during a happier time, followed by an image of the kid who had died in the car accident, standing with his mother, also smiling. Both of Claude's sisters invested with their brother. A couple of his old school chums invested with Global Securities.

Sweat broke out along my forehead. The montage of photographs continued, families with teenagers who went to my high school.

CHAPTER TWENTY-TWO

Deputy Mike smiled when I opened the front door. "Rosie," he said, and I tightened my grip on the door handle. Rosie was Claude's name for me. It shouldn't be used by anyone else.

"I've come to see your mother. Can you get her for me?" he asked.

My feelings for Deputy Mike had changed since that day he drove up beside me when I had chanced to run away. I no longer wanted him to rescue me. I had lost my father and I thought I had lost my mother, but I hadn't lost her. She was still here, still with me.

My mother came down the stairs, dressed in a suit and carrying her purse. "Will this take long?" she asked Deputy Mike. "I have an appointment."

"Not long," he said. He placed his hat down on the table, seeming uncertain whether he should take a seat or not. "He's asking to see you."

She placed her purse next to Deputy Mike's hat. "I'm not sure I'm ready."

"It doesn't have to be today."

An awkward silence followed, with Deputy Mike watching my mother while she fiddled with the strap of her purse.

"Do you have any questions?" he asked.

She shook her head but then rubbed at her forehead, partially dislodging the clip holding her hair back. If her posture and her composure showed nothing of her state of mind, her voice was ragged and harsh and lacking sound.

"How much has been recovered?" she asked.

"Two hundred thousand, two-fifty maybe. Not enough," said Deputy Mike.

I thought of all that cash found in the various secret places around the house. In my simplicity, in my imperfect understanding, I had thought that was all the money Claude had stolen. It had seemed like a lot to me, piles of it, and so tightly bound. Of course it was nowhere near the total he had stolen.

Deputy Mike seemed to know what I was thinking, because he said, "Even with the value of the house it won't be enough." He paused, then spoke again. "Mr. Fisk isn't speaking. He keeps asking for his son, but Alex won't talk to him. And now he's asking for you."

I thought of Alex, still out there somewhere. I wondered if he and his mother had remained in California or if they had left for her home, wherever that was. I bit my lip to stop from asking.

"The truth is, there might not be any more recovered. Certainly not all of it."

Deputy Mike kept his gaze on my mother.

She picked up her purse, and I could tell she didn't want to speak about it anymore. That she didn't want to speak with Claude at all.

"Can I think about it?" she asked.

"Of course," he said. "You have a couple weeks before he's transferred."

Deputy Mike escorted her to her car, and I watched through the curtains in the front room as they paused to speak, and he held the door open for her. He followed her blue Honda in his black-and-white cop car, down the hill.

It was strange to be alone in the house. I recalled the first time I had been left alone, the day Claude had taken my mother and Alex to a luncheon meeting without me, and now I knew why that luncheon had been important and why I hadn't been allowed to go. What had Claude asked Alex to do at that luncheon? Make friends with the rich kids? Scope out their wealthy parents?

Walking through the first floor, I trailed my hand across the bare walls. The art pieces Claude collected had been removed. Inside the darkroom, it looked as though a tornado had passed through. Men in uniforms had removed the resalable equipment, including the camera Claude had bought for Christmas. They had dismantled the drafting table and boxed up any supplies that hadn't already been opened. But I didn't let that stop me.

My photographs were scattered throughout the room. They'd gone through all of them, but except for the two photographs Claude had hidden away in the rolltop desk, they hadn't found anything of interest. I sorted them by subject: a box of Alexes, a box of Dahlias, a box of Claudes.

I turned the pages of *Photo Development: The Art of Image Manipulation* until I reached the section at the back titled "Kitchen Sink Photography." How to create without a camera, without a proper darkroom, with what you had lying around, with what was left over when everything was taken away.

IT TOOK A WEEK BEFORE Deputy Mike called to arrange the visit with Claude. During that week, I worked in the darkroom without telling my mother what I was doing.

On the chosen day, I stood in a splash of sunlight in her bedroom, brushing my mother's hair until it gleamed, like she used to do for me. She sat in front of her vanity mirror, her head jerking back each time I brushed from the scalp. Her hair flowed fine through my fingers into waves. She watched me through the mirror, an unlit cigarette in her hand. Once again, she had no fire to light it with.

"Maybe I should quit," she said, toying with it.

I twisted her hair up, a little clumsy, my fingers fumbling over the hairpins, but the twist stayed put. When I finished she leaned forward, turning her head from side to side, reaching for her face powder and makeup brushes.

"You don't think I can take care of us without Claude, do you?" she continued, spreading concealer across her cheekbones, down her nose, like an artist priming her canvas. I had a sudden memory of that day in the car when we ran away from our old life, and how much makeup she'd worn over her skin. I hadn't wanted to see the bruises underneath. She had no bruises now, none on the surface. "You've barely spoken since the arrest," she said. "You spend all of your time in that darkroom."

I went to her closet and picked through her dresses the same way I picked through what words to use. "I've been working on something," I said, choosing a blue dress that I liked because the fabric was soft and shimmery. "Do you want to see it?"

She took the dress, then nodded. I went down to the darkroom and retrieved the collage I'd finished that morning using parts of her notebook, photograms made with exposed photographic paper, and photographs developed with a cardboard box enlarger. When I returned, she had dressed and was inserting a bluebell earring into each ear. I set the collage in front of her.

"Let's get in your car, pack it up the same way you did that day we ran away, and just go," I said as she put down her makeup brush and picked up my creation. "We don't have to tell anyone. Just get in the car and go. We can get an apartment, someplace small but with lots of windows for the sun to shine through, for the moon to find us during the night. I'll go to school while you work, and sometimes you'll draw and sometimes I'll take pictures."

I could see this future reflecting back at me through her reflection in the mirror, expanding ever backward.

"Am I the woman in this story?" she asked, touching a picture of herself used in the center of the collage.

"Only if you want to be."

She set the collage down, then took my hands, turning them over to expose each palm as if she could read the lines there, the length of my life, the loves I would have, the heartbreaks.

When she stood, she asked, "How do I look?"

"Perfect." I zipped up the back, careful not to catch her skin.

She slipped her feet into high-heeled shoes, then gathered her handbag and made her way down the lonely stairs.

I navigated the streets for her, a map open on my lap and an address scribbled on a sheet of paper with Deputy Mike's handwriting. We drove the Honda, the Mercedes having been taken away along with everything else.

She put the car in park in front of the Santa Clarita Sheriff's Station. It looked exactly the same as it had that morning when Deputy Mike had brought me there. Claude was inside, held until his arraignment. With her lips pressed to a thin line, she looked at the flat, brown bricks, the tree overhanging with its spring-green leaves blooming in the breeze, folded her hands on her lap. We hadn't had time to polish her nails.

"Ready?" she asked.

Letting go of a held breath, I nodded.

The cool breeze scurried dried leaves past our feet. I trailed behind as she maneuvered through the other cars parked in the visitors' lot, singular and alone in the shade of the trees that towered over her. She walked toward the building, pausing at the front door before entering.

The "Wanted" poster of Audra Rose, with the long scar down the side of her face, still hung on the wall of the sheriff's station's wall. Maybe no one had caught her yet. Or maybe they had simply never taken down the poster. In my previous visit, I hadn't noticed the recessed fluorescent lighting that buzzed just within the range of human hearing.

It took a few minutes for Deputy Mike to be summoned. He stopped when he saw me standing next to my mother and beckoned her over.

"Are you sure about her going with you?" he asked, indicating me.

"He'll want to see her," she said. "I thought—" She swallowed. "He cares for her."

A muscle at the side of Deputy Mike's jaw twitched. He seemed to weigh the different options, uncertain which choice to make.

"He's not the same man you knew," said Deputy Mike. "Not even the same man from just a week ago."

I could tell she wasn't entirely certain about my joining her either. "I want to go with you," I begged.

"Maybe you should wait out here."

"No, I don't have to see him, but don't leave me out here." I didn't want to wait in the lobby with only Audra Rose's poster for company.

"Can she wait with you?" my mother asked Deputy Mike.

He nodded. "Rosie, wait here, and I'll come get you."

They left me in the reception area. I didn't want to sit, didn't want to go outside, so I stood with my hands drawn into fists, listening to the clicking of a keyboard from the reception desk and the murmurings of the radio dispatch.

The door that my mother and Deputy Mike went through had a window in its upper half. I could see into the larger room, where officers and plainclothes individuals crossed back and forth. At the other end of the room, I saw my mother behind a glass window, sitting at a table. She was touching her mouth in that way of hers, staring straight ahead. She wanted a cigarette. She wasn't alone. Across from her sat Claude.

I pushed the door open and crossed the room, taking a moment to search for Deputy Mike, but I couldn't find him, until I stood in front of the window. I wondered if this was one of those magic one-way windows they had in television cop shows.

A hand squeezed my shoulder, and I glanced up to see Deputy Mike.

"I was just coming to get you," he said.

"Are you listening to them?" I didn't think they should. It seemed sneaky and unfair.

Deputy Mike studied my face, searching for something, before coming to a decision. "This way," he said, and led me to a door to the left of the observation window.

The room was unlit, but a light came in from a big window that looked into the room where my mother and Claude sat. There were other men and women watching, and someone said something to Deputy Mike, but I turned my attention to the window and the sad, awkward picture it showed.

Claude's hair hung lank around his face, and he seemed thinner. Or maybe it was just the way he sat with his arms pressed close to his body and his shoulders curved inward. He wore what looked like hospital scrubs, with a short-sleeved tunic, the letters *S.C.S.S.* stenciled on with black dye, his bare arms pale, almost yellow tinged in the fluorescent light.

How long had they been sitting like that, silent and still, filling the little room with great big bubbles of unspoken conversations?

"Isn't it illegal for you guys to listen to them?" There should be lawyers present, but that wasn't why I asked. This scene, this strange, painful meeting between a husband and wife, should have been private. It was like watching the aftermath of a love scene, the bitter morning after.

"They both know they're being watched," said Deputy Mike, and I tore my eyes off of Claude to look up at him. "Mr. Fisk denied representation for the meeting; he wanted it like this. He knows that anything he tells her will be relayed to us."

I went back to observing Claude. He barely moved. He used to fill an entire room with the force of his attention. Now none of his bursting, blustering energy remained.

Finally, my mother spoke, her voice distorted through the microphone. It didn't sound like her.

"Do you need anything?" she asked.

Claude didn't answer. She put a hand down on the table between them. With the tip of her finger she started tracing a pattern on its surface. A circle. Then petals. Then a stem, a leaf.

"They said you wanted to speak with me?" she insisted. "I brought Rosaura with me today, but they didn't think it was a good idea for you to see her."

Another slight flicker behind Claude's eyes, but he didn't say anything.

"She wants to see you," said my mother.

There was a slight narrowing of Claude's eyes, and I wondered if he believed her.

She took a small, defeated breath. "Are you ever going to speak?"

"What are you planning to do?" he asked, and everyone in the observation room shifted. I gripped the cold metal frame around the window.

My mother seemed stunned for a moment. "I don't—" she started. Then, "Now you're concerned?"

"Of course I'm concerned. I care about you. And Rosie. I plan on taking care of you."

"The same way you've taken care of us all along? No, I don't think so."

"I won't be in here forever. We're still married. I'm still your husband. You look beautiful in that dress. I bought it for you, didn't I?"

My mother grew very pale. "We don't need you. I have a job now. We'll be fine."

"Don't kid yourself," he said, his voice flat.

She pinched her lips together. "I think I'd better leave."

"Hey," he said, and smiled. "I'm sorry. Don't mind me. It's just this place. It gets to you. When I get out, we'll be good. They might even give me house arrest so I won't be gone long. Take care of things for me, please? Take care of the house. Don't forget the garden. And those fishes. No one ever remembers the fishes. They'll starve if someone doesn't feed them. You keep feeding them for me, okay? You keep them."

Her brow wrinkled. She must have been thinking the same thing we all were thinking, that he was delusional.

"Tell me," Claude said before she could respond, and for the first time he moved, his chair scraping against the floor. "Did you put Alex up to it?" he asked, and once again his voice was a deadly calm. "You can tell me. I won't be angry."

The door to the interrogation room opened, and a couple of officers entered. Claude had gone stone silent again, let the officers force him to standing, turn him so they could put handcuffs on.

"I'm sorry," he said to my mother as they pulled him through the door.

I ran out of the observation room as two officers led Claude away. At the same time, Alex and his mother entered from the door leading to the reception area. There was no way for any of the policemen to block Claude's view. He saw us both but focused his attention on Alex, straining against the officers' hold. Deputy Mike barked orders and Claude was led through another set of doors. They had to drag him because he wouldn't move. He kept his eyes fixed on Alex until the last moment.

Everyone spoke at once. Deputy Mike continued to yell, angry that no one had thought to check before allowing Catherine Craig and Alex to enter. My mother asked if we could leave.

"I was promised this wouldn't happen," said Catherine, furious.

I used the commotion to creep to the edge of the room. When Alex saw me, he smiled with one corner of his mouth. I could barely breathe, afraid to get too close. He held out his hand and I took it, felt the warmth of his skin as if he touched every inch of my body.

"Hey," he said, but I couldn't hear him over the noise.

I inched a little closer. There was so much to say and ask: Where was he living? Could I call him? Was he happy now? But all I said was, "You okay?"

"What do you think?" he asked, in his typical way of answering with a question. But he smiled again, and I guessed that was all the answer I was going to get. His mother said his name and I dropped his hand as if it burned. In the next moment she led him away, and they both disappeared into a different room.

CHAPTER TWENTY-THREE

When my mother and I reached the house, she parked the car in the driveway. Someone had spray painted "LIAR" underneath the white-frosting windows in big, black letters with paint dripping from the letter *R* as if it bled from a wound. I wished for my own can of spray paint so that I could add "CHEAT" and "THIEF" to make the scene complete. Also "I WANT TO FLY AWAY" and "WHERE ARE YOU?"

Let's go, I thought, let's drive away. Let's fly.

Maybe she heard me. With her hand on the ignition, she shifted in her seat, no longer pale. And smiled.

We started packing. I got to keep my clothing and Alex's bike and the beanbag chairs. My mother went through the remaining furniture that hadn't been carted away, deciding which pieces she wanted to keep, which ones would be left behind. The first floor grew crowded with boxes.

A few days after Claude's cryptic comments at the sheriff's station, a team came out to examine the fishes in the fountain. I learned they had a name: koi. And, because of their age and coloration, they could sometimes be valued at thousands of dollars. Claude's fishes, three in total, had not been well taken care of. At least not recently, although they had managed to survive. I hadn't even realized the fishes were real, let alone that they needed caring. Collectively, the fishes were valued at a few thousand dollars, not enough to make any great difference. Along with everything else, experts had taken the fishes away to be re-homed.

I stayed by the fountain after the men left. The surface of the water dimpled with skittering bugs and water plants growing over the side. No longer concerned with slimy things or bug-eyed fishes, I dipped my arms into the cool water. Ripples spread in widening circles, and I closed my eyes, imagining what it would feel like to be underwater in the slick slime, hiding in the muck, to have my lungs filled and unable to breathe. Peaceful. Beautiful, with the world above always out of reach, always a dream, moving in the ripples.

When I opened my eyes, the reflection of my father's ghost swayed next to mine, with the blue sky dancing behind us and the roof of the house dipping in and out of view. I had wondered if the ghost would appear again, uncertain if I wanted to see him or not.

"You're here," I said.

"Yes," he answered. Instead of starting with a story as he'd done before, he waited for me to speak, knowing that I had questions to ask him. I swallowed, staring down at his rippling reflection.

"Why'd you do it?" I asked. "Why'd you kill yourself?"

It was the one question I had wanted to ask that I had never been brave enough to ask before. My mother had told me what happened leading up to his death, but only my father could answer the question of why. Why had he done it?

He turned his head so his reflection in the fountain showed his open, unhealed wound. It was all I could see.

"She ran away. She took you and left. I don't remember getting my gun, don't remember driving. Not until I got to this house and I saw her hiding behind him. I pointed my gun at his big ugly face. He was telling me to calm down and she was crying. She expected me to kill her. It was in her eyes. I said to Claude, 'I'm going to take everything from you.'"

I squeezed my eyes shut, remembering the gunshot echoing through the house. What should I say to my father's ghost? That his careful, diligently plotted revenge on Claude had been successful? That soon my mother and I would leave this house forever and never return? That I loved him?

This was the ghost's revenge, to bring about Claude's demise, bring pain and confusion to my mother. This was his plan all along, a carefully woven double cross. My father had gambled on Claude and had lost everything, and now Claude would lose everything. Not only Claude, but so many others as well. Myself, my mother, Tina and her family. The ghost hadn't cared about collateral damage.

"Are you satisfied yet?" I asked. "Are you done?"

He bent close to speak. "I know where he keeps his money, his hiding places. I've always known. The desk, under the carpet on the third floor, and the fountain."

All the air whooshed out of my lungs, and I turned toward him, toward my father, but he was climbing into the fountain. Slowly, he sank below the water.

My mother pushed the sliding doors open, and I heard

her approach. "Rosaura, I hope you're not leaving all the packing for me to do. Are you all right? What's wrong?"

"Wait," I said, and kicked off my shoes and socks and tried to roll up my jeans, climbing into the fountain. The water came up to my knees and it was cold. The bottom of the fountain squished between my toes. I crouched down to hold on to the brick wall as I shuffled around.

"What are you doing?" she asked. "Get out of there. That can't be clean."

I bent down to feel with my hands as well as my feet. The bottom of the fountain was bumpy, and I kept almost falling. "There's something in here."

"How can you see anything?" My mother leaned over the edge of the fountain with an expression of skeptical disgust, hesitating to touch the water. But then she took the plunge and immersed her arms up to her armpits. "I think I have something."

I shuffled over to her, swishing around in the dark water until I found her hands, following down to where her fingers gripped what felt like a slippery, slimy leaf. We pulled up and discovered a black garbage bag, difficult to lift, but as we did, I glanced down and saw through the murky water a floor of dollar bills.

In fact, they were one-hundred-dollar bills, vacuum-sealed in plastic, lining the fountain floor.

My mother and I stared at our hidden treasure, unable to move. My jeans were cold and clammy against my skin. The cloying, rotten smell of the unclean water hung in the air.

For some reason, I remembered one of the many *Goofus and Gallant* cartoons from the *Highlights* magazines. Goofus and Gallant each found a dollar bill lying on the ground. Gallant returned the dollar to his father in the hopes of finding whom it belonged to, but Goofus took it and bought a candy bar.

The thought came to me as I stared at the money of the many thousands of candy bars it could buy. More than I could eat. More than I wanted to eat.

My mother rubbed at the plastic, trying to clear away the muck. Claude had meant for us to find it. Maybe she thought of our future, of the new apartment we were moving to, and our lack of beds for the bedrooms and pots and pans for the kitchen.

"What should we do?" I asked.

She sighed. "What do you think?"

I smiled. I couldn't help Claude. I hadn't helped Alex or Tina. There was nothing I could do for my father. But I could do this one thing. And maybe that was my purpose, found at the bottom of the fountain.

Inside, I waited on hold while someone at the sheriff's station located Deputy Mike. Gazing out to the garden, I searched for the ghost, but he wasn't there. I wasn't sure he had ever been there.

ACKNOWLEDGMENTS

Many have helped or guided me on this journey. My deepest, sincerest gratitude to my editor at Vintage/ Anchor Books, Andrea Robinson, and my thesis advisor, Christopher Meeks, for their patience and for an incredibly enriching experience. Special thank-you to Andrea, for taking a chance on *The Cake House*. I want to thank my agent, Diana Fox, for sitting down with me one day and letting me talk about this book, and for her enthusiasm. Thank you to the many teachers in my life, too many to list here, but in particular Janet Fitch and Gina Nahai, for their constant generosity. A big hug and thank-you to my best friend, Sarah, for reading, and for so much more. Thank you to Terri Oberkamper, for her sharp grammar skills. Thank you to everyone at Vintage and Anchor Books. To my family and friends, a mere thank-you is not enough; you have my love forever. And lastly, I'd like to travel back in time and buy William Shakespeare a drink and say thank you for your writing.